Melanie,
it is good to know you.
Enjoy,
Anita
Dec 11, 2011

Anita
Attwood

AUTUMN LEAVES

© Copyright 2003 Anita Attwood. All rights reserved.

No part of this publication may be reproduced, stored in a retrieval system, or transmitted, in any form or by any means, electronic, mechanical, photocopying, recording, or otherwise, without the written prior permission of the author.

Printed in Victoria, Canada

Note for Librarians: a cataloguing record for this book that includes Dewey Classification and US Library of Congress numbers is available from the National Library of Canada. The complete cataloguing record can be obtained from the National Library's online database at:
www.nlc-bnc.ca/amicus/index-e.html
ISBN 1-4120-1376-3

TRAFFORD

This book was published *on-demand* in cooperation with Trafford Publishing.
On-demand publishing is a unique process and service of making a book available for retail sale to the public taking advantage of on-demand manufacturing and Internet marketing. **On-demand publishing** includes promotions, retail sales, manufacturing, order fulfilment, accounting and collecting royalties on behalf of the author.

Suite 6E, 2333 Government St., Victoria, B.C. V8T 4P4, CANADA
Phone   250-383-6864   Toll-free   1-888-232-4444 (Canada & US)
Fax   250-383-6804   E-mail   sales@trafford.com
Web site www.trafford.com   TRAFFORD PUBLISHING IS A DIVISION OF TRAFFORD HOLDINGS LTD.
Trafford Catalogue #03-1754   www.trafford.com/robots/03-1754.html

10   9   8   7   6   5   4   3   2

To Mom Emily who was waiting impatiently for the ending, to Mama Anna who could only listen to the words, sadly they left us before it was finished.

To my friend Evelyn, for judging it a good read.

To Natalie who displays her artistic talents on the cover.

Most of all to my husband Brian, who urged me on with unfailing belief. Your faith and love got me through it. I could never have done it without you. You are my hero.

And to all our children for their love and enthusiastic support.

Let me thank all of YOU!

CHAPTER ONE

This was all wrong! This was not a day for the sun to be shining, nor for the birds to be merrily hopping about leaving their tiny prints all over the snow-covered ground. Their merry chirping even overpowered the preacher's hushed voice. If anything, this was a day for thunder and lightning, for the fury of heaven to unleash its powers on earth. Why, why, why ...

They had come from near and far to the old castle, which was still standing proud half way up the mountain, nestled among tall pine trees. Although it had been converted into a chateau, many of the ancient walls remained, including the pointed towers, which were glistening in the afternoon sun. A thick layer of snow covered the land and the bright sunshine gave everything a silvery glow. Down below the red shingled roofs of the village peeked out from under sheets of white snowdrifts and their silver reflection bounced off the nearby lake. The rugged terrain of the Bavarian Alps stretched all around, as far as the eye could see.

Usually one would be in awe of such beauty, but not so on this day. In the rose garden of Chateau Schwarzenau, which always held a special magic, may it be winter, spring, summer or fall, the mood was somber. The darkly clad crowd, which had gathered, listened in silence to the preacher's kind words. Muffled sobs, snow-white hankies dabbing tear-filled eyes and catching running noses were mingled with the chirping of the birds. It was cold, but even so the sun did its level best to warm things up. Now the sparrows lined the barren branches, enjoying the sunshine, oblivious to the crowd below, singing their melodious song. To some it seemed that even their song had a sad sound to it.

A bright, sunny, wintry day like this should have been a happy day, but it was not. It was a dark, sinister day, a day without any ray of hope, for one person in particular. Among all those people clad in dark clothes stood a slender figure of a girl, wearing a long black coat and a wide brimmed black hat with a veil attached to cover her face. She was leaning on the arm of a tall, dark-haired, elegantly dressed man. He too had that sad expression. His lips were tightly shut and there were tears in his eyes as he glanced down at the frail girl leaning against him.

"Hold on, Autumn, let me be your strength." It was just a whisper. The girl turned her face upward and he could see the deep pain and utter helplessness reflected in her eyes, like a wounded animal. Her lips moved, she was saying something but he could barely make out the words.

"Victor, make it go away."

"I wish I could, little one, I wish I could." Although she had matured into quite a beautiful young lady, at this moment she reminded him of a little girl. His arm was around her shoulder, holding on tight. If only they could cut this ceremony short, but of course he knew they couldn't. Prince Rudolf and his Princess were too well loved by these people to give them any less than a full service funeral, befitting their royal status in life. To think that they were lying in those rosewood caskets, side by side, was totally unbelievable.

Autumn Leaves

It had happened so fast. One minute... no, it was better not to think about that now.

Victor, Prince Rudolf's only brother, had a hard time comprehending this whole event. Never in a million years did he expect such a thing to happen. When he shed his royal title, long ago, wanting to get away from it all, he thought it was forever. Now, all of a sudden, he found himself forced back into the role of assuming his royal responsibilities. If he found himself in such a state of confusion and disbelief, how could his young ward, Autumn, even begin to understand what had happened to her parents? How could he help her, when he felt he needed help himself?

Oh Lord, give me the strength and the wisdom to help this fragile child deal with her tragic loss, Victor prayed silently.

The music was playing very softly, 'Ave Maria', the song Princess Marianne had loved better than any other song.

"Mommy, Daddy!" Her cry was heart-rending. Now most everyone was sobbing openly. Nobody seemed able to bear watching the pain that was tearing this young girl apart.

Autumn's knees buckled and she would have landed on the ground, had it not been for Victor's strong arms. He scooped her up and carried her toward a row of tall evergreen hedges. Quietly the mourners stepped back, creating an eerie, darkly lined passageway for him to pass through. Gently, he put his precious burden down on a bench. Her head rested on his shoulder and her sobbing had stopped. For a while they just sat there, quietly. Watching his ward in this listless state, the color of her skin almost transparent, he felt the need to protect her rise within him so strong that he wanted to take her away at once to a place where nothing could ever hurt her again.

After a brief moment he gently reached for her hand. "Darling, do you think we can go back? Are you up to it?"

"Yes, I think I am. Will you help me, please?"

Anita Attwood

He watched her closely as she stood before her parents' caskets, eyes closed, saying good bye to the two people he knew she loved more than anything else in this world. She placed a tiny bouquet of colorful autumn leaves on her mother's casket and a single red rose on her father's. Silently she bid them farewell, gently stroking the shiny rosewood as if to touch their cheeks for a last time. A cry from above turned heads upward where an eagle circled, its magnificent wings spread wide, gliding effortlessly in the wind. Suddenly, just as the caskets were lowered into the ground, a smaller eagle joined the flight and both soared up toward the sun, disappearing from sight. A shudder went through the crowd and Victor felt a cold chill running down his back. He stepped forward and took Autumn's hand while her eyes still searched the skies. His fear that she might fold again was unfounded. She stood very still, totally lost in thought as her eyes kept looking upward. There was strength radiating from within her, which he had not seen before. From the village the church bell tolled three times.

Placing a protective arm around her shoulder, he led her to the car. His heart was heavy from worry, wondering how to ease the pain she must be feeling. Perhaps a few hours of sleep would do her good. God knows she had not done so in days; the dark circles under her eyes were proof of that. As soon as they climbed into the back seat his head fell back and he closed his eyes, while the car sped toward the chateau. Autumn's head rested on his shoulder. Victor remembered her touching gesture only moments ago at her parents' graves. The autumn leaves, the rose would be forever etched into his mind. Tears rolled down his cheeks, and he let them fall unchecked. He felt her eyes on him, but all he was able to do was to squeeze her hand. The huge lump in his throat made it impossible to say anything..

Back at the chateau things had come to a standstill. When Prince Rudolf and his lovely wife were about, there was

Autumn Leaves

always some kind of activity in the works, but now it seemed as if the 'Sleeping Beauty' syndrome had invaded the place.

Autumn isolated herself from everyone. She needed time to think, time to make some kind of sense out of all that had happened. The servants tiptoed through the halls. Victor could not gain an audience, and her best friend Laura was told to remain at a distance for a while.

At her tender age of eighteen, she felt lost, unable to cope with what lay ahead. How could God take her parents away. They had been so young and they were so good to everybody. Why them, of all people? All the crooks, thieves, robbers, you name it, why not them? Why take the good people out? It didn't make any sense. There was so much they had planned on doing, so very much. What about the time when she was ready to get married, or when her first baby would be born, what about those times? Tell me, what about those times?

"I hate you, God. You should not have taken them. Bring them back to me, I need them, I need them. Oh God - I need them. I'm sorry, God, I didn't mean to be ugly. It just hurts so bad!"

Had she spoken out loud? Exhausted, she fell across her bed and sobbed uncontrollably. Her whole world had fallen apart. How could she go on without them? They had always been there to love her, shield her, protect her, guide her, teach her, chastise her when she did wrong, counsel her in difficult situations and try to show her as much of what life was all about as possible. It never occurred to her that some day they would not be around any more. They were supposed to be here forever. What now?

Her thoughts went back to the time when they went to visit India, bringing back the biggest surprise of her life. It was the most beautiful horse she had ever seen and it was very young. She named it Maharani - or, Rani, for short. Rani was a wonderfully playful foal and very intelligent. Autumn spent a lot of time teaching the foal steps, commands and obedience.

The sugar cubes in her pockets were soon discovered by Maharani who would nudge her, not always very gently, if the reward didn't come fast enough.

"What do you think you're doing at my pockets?"

The words were spoken out loud, but she was dreaming, and a hint of a smile lingered on her face.

That's how Victor found her when he entered her room. He had knocked a few times and when there was no answer he just pushed the handle down slowly and looked in. For a moment he held his breath, thinking the worst at the silence, but soon realized that she had finally found that much needed sleep. He quietly backed out of her room and promptly bumped into old Mary. He should have guessed that she would come checking on Autumn, watching over her just like she had over him when he was young. Old Mary was more than just a nanny. Over the years she had become part of the family just like old John, the butler. When Victor turned to face her he quickly took hold of her arm to steady her. With an apologetic look on his face he said: "Sorry, I didn't hear you coming."

There were tears in her eyes when she answered, her voice shaky: " I didn't see you either. How is our missy?"

"She is sleeping, peacefully, I might add."

Now Mary was crying openly. "Thank the Lord, I do so worry about her. What are we going to do now, Mr. Victor, your Highness? She was so close to her parents. They always did things together, and they looked out for her. Now who is going to do that, Mr. Victor, I mean your Highness, who?"

Taking her by the shoulders, he gently guided her away from Autumn's door. A little way down the hall they stopped and Victor reached for his handkerchief, handing it to Mary. The old woman took it from him with trembling hands, a grateful look in her watering, faded blue eyes.

"Now there, Mary. First of all, I will always be Victor to you, so you can drop the Highness stuff. Why, Mary, you used to wipe my runny nose, among other things. But as far as the princess is concerned, you will be here, and John, and don't forget I am going to take her under my wing as well. Our little princess will soon learn that there are many loving people surrounding her and that she is not alone, I promise. For now, we have to give her time, allow her to grieve and just be there for her. You will help me, won't you? She will need all of us."

"Oh yes, Mr. Victor, I'll be here and do whatever I can for the princess. You just try to make me go away."

He hugged her close. "That's what I wanted to hear. I also want to thank you and John for playing along and not giving me away to the princess earlier on."

Victor walked through the huge sitting room out onto the balcony. He needed time to think. From here, he had the most magnificent view of the valley below and the gigantic alpine mountains, surrounding this entire splendor. There could not possibly be a more beautiful place in the whole wide world. He knew that this had been Marianne's favorite spot. Rudolf had told him this on so many occasions. He could almost picture them standing on this very spot, Rudolf and Marianne, holding hands, sharing the early morning sunrise, smiling into each other's eyes. They had been a loving couple and were not ashamed to let people around them know it.

Victor looked below. There, nestled in the valley, lay the dark blue waters of the King Lake, reflecting the snowcapped peaks of the mountains. Suddenly his breathing became a real effort, as the picture of his brother and lovely wife filled his mind. They would never stand on this spot again, enjoying this glorious sight. What lay before him could have been a page out of a fairy tale book; it didn't seem real. He closed his eyes and envisioned Marianne leaning against the balcony, her golden, shoulder length hair gently blowing in the morning breeze. To him she had always presented the appearance of some elfin-like apparition. Of course she was not. Marianne von Schwarzenau had been as real as Rudolf had and Autumn. Now they were gone, gone forever. He wished he could turn back the time, back to those earlier, happier days. God, how he missed them.

  It was a little over sixteen years ago. Autumn had already turned two when he finally met her and his beautiful sister- in- law. Six years before he had left the country and that was when he had also shed his royal title. He took the name of Victor Mulhair, plain and simple. Rudolf never understood how his younger brother could just walk out on family responsibilities, leaving him to bear it alone, but he hadn't tried to stop him nor did they part on ill terms. Rudolf told him that he had felt disappointment, yes, but he did not allow himself to hate his brother for running away. After all, their father had never shown any love for Victor, blaming him for the death of their mother while giving birth to him. Victor always thought that his father should have shouldered the blame. After all, he got his wife in the family way at her advanced age and ill health. But that thought never occurred to the old man.

  Mary, his mother's handmaiden, had been the only mother figure he had ever known, and loved. After six long years he had returned, with a wife, and had taken over the villa, which sat at the furthest corner of their vast estate. It was run down, but he didn't mind, he would fix it up and make it like new. After all, the old castle had been rebuilt and converted into a chateau, and it was magnificent. Much of the original walls were still standing, including the massive arched entrance gate. Behind that massive wall the grounds and buildings had been reconstructed in a more modern, airy style. Rudolf had the oversized balcony added as a gift to his lovely wife, so she could enjoy the magnificent view.

  That day at the racetracks marked a new beginning in their relationship. So far nobody knew of his return. He wondered if Rudolf would even be there. Of course he should

Autumn Leaves

have known that he would, because Rudolf usually placed one or two of his horses in the race. Walking around the grounds, Victor suddenly spotted his brother and guessed that the lady clinging to his arm would have to be his wife. Her elegant beauty immediately took him in. The pictures in the papers had not done her justice; she was by far much prettier. Even after all this time he felt that little pain of regret for not having attended his brother's wedding.

Perhaps this would be the perfect time to say hello and get to know his sister- in- law. He did not know that a little daughter was part of the happy couple. So, when something crashed into him from behind, followed by a loud squeal and a cold sensation running down his leg, he didn't know what to make of it. Looking down, he saw a pair of frightened deep blue eyes staring up at him, lurking out from under a shock of golden curls. Two tiny hands were clutching his pants where a sticky orange looking mass was visible and forming a puddle around his right shoe. It felt cold as ice. On the ground lay an empty cup, the word EISBALL written on it.

After the initial shock wore off, he burst out into a hearty laugh, which sent the tiny goldilocks scurrying toward Rudolf's open arms. He fell in love with this tiny doll- like whirlwind on the spot.

" I am so sorry." It was Marianne who reached down to brush the liquid from his pant leg. He stepped sideways, somewhat embarrassed.

"Please, no harm done."

"At least let me get you some water to rinse it off, otherwise it will leave an awful stain."

"Here, splash that over it." Prince Rudolf handed his cup to him, showing no sign of recognition. Noticing a slight hesitation on Victor's part he quickly added: "It's plain water, I assure you."

"I didn't doubt it. Thank you, your Highness." Victor bowed to his brother, barely able to conceal his grin.

Lifting up his right leg he tried to splash the water only on the area where the sticky mess was, but part of the water still went inside his shoe. So he kicked it off, took his handkerchief and dried his sock as much as possible before wiping the inside of his shoe. The little girl watched all of this with great fascination, peeking out from behind her daddy's pant legs.

Rudolf, unable to restrain himself any longer, stepped toward his brother and, instead of taking his hand, embraced him with such fierceness it brought all the love and longing for his sibling to light.

"Rudolf?" Marianne's questioning look went from her husband to the man he was hugging so tightly and back again.

"Sorry, darling, but this is Victor, our Victor," he added when Marianne did not show any recognition at the mention of the name. Then her face lit up.

"I am so glad to finally meet you, so very glad." She took both of his hands and shook them, smiling all the time.

"Believe me, the pleasure is all mine. But who is this young lady?"

With that he bent down and extended his hand to the little girl. To his surprise, she took it in both of her hands and shook it with all her might, trying to imitate her mom. Smiling down at her he introduced himself: "Victor Mulhair, at your service."

He mostly said it to the little girl, but his brother's frown did not escape him. Her earnest reply was a delight to all the adults within earshot.

"The pleasure is all mine, Mr. Victor Moll Air, I'm sure."

What a fast learner she was, such big words coming out of such a little girl. Everybody laughed, except one, but the spell was broken. He learned that her name was Autumn and that she was two years old, almost going on three. He also recognized that his older brother did not approve of the name he had given, but he kept silent.

When the races were over Victor was asked to come along to the chateau for a chat. Well, he knew what that meant. Rudolf had played along long enough. Victor noted right away how Autumn's eyes lit up when her daddy asked him to follow them, the attraction between them had been instant. He knew that Rudolf needed some clarification and he wouldn't mind at all spending more time with his adorable little niece and beautiful sister-in-law. However, as soon as they arrived at the chateau Rudolf asked him to step into the blue room and closed the door.

He had asked Marianne to join them as soon as she could. Victor had a glimpse of Autumn's little face as she stood there beside her mother. It was bathed in utter dismay. Nobody had asked her to come into the blue room. He felt the urge to reach out and touch her cheeks, but Rudolf was already closing the door. The two brothers stood facing each other in silence and after a few seconds suddenly embraced once again, this time with tears in their eyes.

"God, how I've missed you, little brother!"

"Same here, big brother."

"So tell me, Vic, what's going on? Why the new name? Where did you come from and where are you staying?" The questions flew toward Victor like bullets. He held up both hands as if to ward them off.

"Time out, Rolf. One question at a time. First of all, I changed my name because I didn't want a title to hang on me. By the way, I'm married and my wife doesn't know anything about me other than that I am from around here and left my homeland as a young man to find fame and fortune. I told her that I had no family and was raised in an orphanage. I'd like to keep it that way for a while, please?"

Rudolf tried to interrupt but Victor stopped him. "No, let me explain. You see, Jane, that's my wife, is a successful solicitor and very proud of it. She sort of took me under her wing until I had established myself as a worthwhile trainer of horses. I've had the privilege of working with some of the finest horses in the world, at the Queen's stables. At that time I wanted to tell Jane who I really was, but was afraid that she would love me only for my title. I had observed that she was very impressed with that sort of thing, I wanted her to love me for myself. Was that so wrong?" There was a long silence but then he went on to say: "When I was ready to confess it was too late. She had made it very clear that what she loved most about me was my honesty."

"Vic, I hear what you're saying and I can even understand it, a little bit, but why didn't you try again?"

At that moment the door opened and Marianne stepped in. She realized right away that the conversation between the two men had turned serious.

"Shall I came back later?" She looked from one to the other.

"No way, come over here and listen to Victor's tale. My little brother is quite an adventurer." Marianne gave Victor a smile and with a few light steps stood beside her husband.

"So tell me, brother-in-law, why have we not seen you before today?"

Victor rolled his eyes and let out a heavy sigh. "Forgive me, had I known that I have such a gorgeous sister-in-law and such a cute little niece I would have been here a long time ago. Well, I'm here now, me and my wife Jane. Who, by the way, is at the village inn waiting for my return."

Marianne lifted her hands, pleading with him to stay.

"Believe me, if it were up to me I would like to stay, for good. What ever happened to the villa at the far end of the park?" His question was directed at Rudolf.

"It's been empty for a while. As far as I know it should be in fairly good condition. Are you planning on taking up residence there? We have plenty of room here in the main house."

Autumn Leaves

"I think the villa would suit us just fine. If it's all right with you, I would like to take a look at it some time tomorrow. I'll tell Jane that I met you at the race track and that you offered it to me for a fair price, OK?"

"Why Vic, why not tell her who you are once and for all? You can't keep this pretense up much longer, not with Autumn calling you uncle." Rudolf placed both hands on Victor's shoulders, trying to convince him to come clean.

"Please, I need more time. Autumn calling me uncle is all right. Little children always call their grown up friends aunt or uncle, so that won't be so bad. It's you two who need keep my secret, please? ... I promise to tell you more later but now I would really like to see my little niece, just for a few minutes, OK?"

Marianne and Rudolf nodded in agreement. Victor was already at the door and opened it wide. There, on the staircase, sat the saddest little girl, her face cupped in her hands and her big, blue eyes fixed steadily in the direction of the door. With a few long steps Victor stood in front of her and scooped her up into his arms. He twirled her around, making her squeal with delight. When he put her down she pushed her little hand is his.

"Will you stay and play with me? I can show you my toys." It was hard to say no to those pleading eyes, but he really had to go.

"Some other time, Goldilocks, I'm sorry. Right now I have to go but I promise to be back real soon, perhaps tomorrow if that's all right with you?"

Her little face took on a serious look and once again her answer took him by surprise.

"I suppose it will have to be all right."

"You suppose? Young lady...." He didn't get any further. Her happy laughter filled the hall and made her parents come out of the parlor to see what was going on. They saw their little daughter hugging Victor around his legs, still laughing.

"Mommy, Daddy, he is so funny. Is it all right if he comes back to play with me?"

"Uncle Victor can come any time he wants to." It was Rudolf making the statement. Victor could not help notice the emphasis being put on the word 'uncle'.

From that day on Victor spent many hours at the Schwarzenau Chateau, watching Autumn grow from a tiny whirlwind into a lovely young girl and lady.

Strange, how all these thoughts suddenly crowded his mind. Victor didn't know how long he had been standing on the balcony; he began to feel the chill of this sunny, blustery winter morning. Then his thoughts strayed to Laura, Autumn's friend, wondering what she would be thinking at this moment. Was she truly sad for her friend or glad about her misery and pain? At this stage, it could be either way.

He shook his head and wiped his eyes, as if to clear away invisible cobwebs. It was all so senseless. The accident, taking away his brother and wife during the best years of their life. Somehow Autumn had to find a way to go on with her life and he would be there to help her find a start. But first he had to get her away from here. A change of scenery would do her good, but where could they go? Should he let her take her friend Laura? Would she want her to come? More important than that, would she even consider going? He had all these questions and no answers; they would have to come from Autumn. She startled him.

"Victor, I'm glad you're still here." He hadn't heard her coming. She stood beside him and let her eyes scan the view. "They did love it out here, remember?"

"I do, princess, I certainly do. I was just thinking about the very same thing."

"Do you miss them as much as I do?"

"Of course, not in the same way, but every bit as much. We're going to get through this, Autumn, together."

Autumn Leaves

"Will we? I don't think I can go on without them. They were all I had, there is nobody else."

Ouch, that hurt. Her words felt like a stab in his heart. She had him; did she not realize that? He was devoted to her, he loved her, perhaps more than was good for him. He would do anything for her; all she had to do was ask. How could he explain his feelings, she should know by now how deeply he cared for her. From the first moment he saw her, she had captured his heart. Now, that she was a young lady, he loved her just as much, perhaps even more. It became apparent when he saw her glancing at some good looking young men, like at his last party; there had been a strange ache in his chest. Good Lord, he acted like a parent.

"Victor, you are miles away. Tell me what you were thinking?" Her dark blue eyes looked into his, searching.

"I was thinking about you and your friend Laura and about this beautiful day. Why don't we go riding, the fresh air would do us both good. You really need some color in your cheeks, what do you say?"

She looked away. There was no answer to his question. Then she turned and walked off, shoulders slightly slumped forward, head down. A sad picture of a lonely girl. He didn't stop her, even though he wanted to. Had it even registered in her head that he was family, truly her uncle, and her father's brother? He had told her the day of the accident, but not once had she made a mention of it or even questioned him about it. It was as if the words had bounced off and gotten lost somewhere. Of course she must know that he was her uncle. Surely she had heard people addressing him by his title?

I must find a way to reach her. She is drowning right before my eyes. My promise to Rudolf was to be at her side and help her in every way. How can I do that if she won't let me? He reached up and grabbed his hair, a deep sigh rolling off his chest. Time, he had to give her time. Deep anger washed over him, anger that was mostly directed at Jane, she should be here to help him. As quickly as it arrived it went away, as resignation set in. Well, never mind Jane, she was in London and otherwise occupied.

Leaving the terrace his step was slow and just as with Autumn, his head hung low, shoulders slumped forward. At this moment it felt as if he carried the burdens of the whole world on his shoulders. It was a lonely feeling.

"Don't give up, Mr. Victor, she'll come around. You said so yourself just a while ago." Mary's pleading eyes caught his. He managed a faint smile.

"You're right, I need to remember my own words. It's just not easy, looking at that forlorn child."

"She's not a child any more. She may feel lost, but we'll help her find herself. No child of mine is going to get lost, I'll promise you that. I didn't bring her into this world for that. "

Mary's words were full of determination and her voice confirmed it. By golly, she was right. He started feeling better already. Funny, how just moments before the shoe was on the other foot. Renewed, his step became livelier and a plan of action slowly came into focus. One thing puzzled him; Mary's words 'bringing Autumn into this world.' Some day he would ask her about that. As it was, the day was too beautiful to be wasted away indoors; he needed some help in getting Autumn to come outside.

"Mary", but she had vanished down the hall. Just as well, he would find some other way to get Autumn out of the house.

Walking toward the stables, he saw Ruben sitting on the bench outside the barn door.

"Just the man I was looking for."

"What can I do for you, Mr. Victor, I mean your Highness." Ruben jumped up so fast it looked as if he was falling all over himself. My God, why did everybody have such trouble with his new identity? Well, almost everybody, he chose to ignore it.

"Tell me what shape Maharani is in. I thought it might be good if she had some exercise. It's been a while since the princess rode her."

"No need to worry about that, she gets all the exercise she needs, I see to that. But Autumn, I mean princess Autumn, might need to enjoy a day out."

"I beg your pardon?"

"Sorry, Sir, I don't mean to be so forward, it's just that before the accident the princess used to come out here almost every day and some days twice. Now I, I mean we, I mean Maharani and I... you know what I mean, Mr. Victor, she just hasn't been here at all and that's not like her. Sorry, I meant to say your...."

"It's all right, Ruben."

Ruben's confusion amused him. Besides being confused about how to address him, it was also obvious that the boy had a crush on Autumn and he could well understand that. She was a lovely young lady.

"Let's see what we can do to bring the princess down here, Ruben, shall we? By the way, Mr. Victor will be just fine, no need to make it complicated and there is no reason to mention that other stuff to anybody for the moment, if you get my drift."

Ruben's face literally beamed, he was asked to keep a secret. Of course he meant Laura, that was very clear and it pleased him. For once he felt superior and privileged over his nasty cousin.

"Mr. Victor," how easy it rolled off his tongue, "why don't you ask the princess to come and check on Maharani? Animals miss their master when neglected, and I do believe Rani seems a bit on the down side these past few days. If you pass that on to the princess she is sure to come."

"Thank you, I will. Although, I don't think Maharani is neglected or feels neglected. As you said before, you're taking care of her, don't you? Missing her master is legit enough. See you in a bit, with her highness."

Victor had already turned to leave, so he did not notice how Ruben's eyes lit up at the prospect of seeing his princess. With a feverish hurry he began to get Maharani ready, his cheeks taking on a bright red glow. This was the perfect time to show his princess how indispensable he was. Maharani would be in perfect condition for her mistress, thanks to his effort. Surely Autumn would realize that. In her grief she needed all the comforting she could get and he was willing to give her lots of it. The hunger in his eyes gave them an evil glint. This was his secret. Nobody could know about his true feelings for the princess.

Laura might think she had an inkling, but it was best that she didn't know how deep it really ran. This cousin of his had a way of messing things up and in this case, he'd just as soon she wouldn't get a chance to do so. He'd be forever grateful to her for getting him this job at the Schwarzenau stables, if only there weren't so many strings attached. He gently placed his hand on Maharani's nose, rubbing it, a troubled look on his face.

The object of Ruben's thoughts, Laura, sat brooding in her room. Too bad about Autumn's parents, but such was life. Everybody had to go through rough times, some more than others. It was about time her highness got a taste of the rougher side of life, but this was really a bit too harsh, even for Laura's standards. Actually, the Schwarzenau's had been swell folks, not at all like one might have expected them to be. The whole village was ga ga eyed over them. They really had not been bad. For Autumn to get a taste of the painful side of life was supposed to come in other ways. This time she, Laura, was totally innocent.

So why did Autumn banish her from the chateau? She had to find out what was going on up there. Ruben would know, he always knew everything, especially if it had anything to do with Autumn. Clever little fellow, that cousin of hers. One could almost think he was in love with miss high and mighty. The thought of it brought a smile to Laura's face. If that were true, it would really fit well into her plans for the future.

I must give her a call, Laura thought, already reaching for the phone.

"Chateau Schwarzenau."

"Hello John, Laura here. May I talk to Autumn?"

"Sorry, Miss Laura, her highness is not available."

"Come on, John, it's me, Laura, surely you can get her for me?"

"No, Miss Laura, she is not even here, but I will tell her that you called."

"No, just forget it. I'll call back later ... if I may." She tried to sweeten her voice hoping John hadn't noticed that she was fuming mad. Then she heard him say: "You may. Good bye."

What a stiff, of course she was there. Did he really think that she could be fooled so easy? Somehow she had to get hold of Autumn. This relationship could not come to an end, it couldn't. In no way was she ready to give up all the comforts she had enjoyed for so many years. Autumn's parents died because they were at the wrong place at the wrong time, she had nothing to do with it. To top it off, she really felt bad about it. Why wouldn't anybody believe her? Anyway, it was Prince Rudolf in person who had intertwined her life with that of his precious daughter. If he had kept his feet out of her mom's greenhouse it would never have happened. But he didn't and now she was used to the finer things in life and would do whatever it took to hang on to it. She did like Autumn, they were friends. But now and then this green-eyed monster reared its ugly head and she couldn't think straight. To be honest, at times, it was a bit frightening.

CHAPTER TWO

It was nineteen years ago when Prince Rudolf found himself leaning against the doorframe leading out onto the verandah, watching his wife in fascination. Her long flowing robe and blond hair were blowing in the early morning breeze. Arms extended, she caught a few leaves twirling about. They were brilliant in color. It was obvious that she enjoyed her little game with the autumn leaves. She was lovelier than ever swollen with their first child. Marianne knew that he was standing there, watching her; it was not the first time he had done that. Suddenly she bent over, both hands clutching her swollen stomach.

"Darling," she called out, "I think it is announcing its arrival."

Rudolf's mind did not register. "Where have you been, my love, autumn arrived weeks ago."

Marianne shot a dark look toward him and uttered through clenched teeth: " Not autumn, our baby, Rudi, our baby is coming."

He reached her side with two long steps and she leaned hard against him as another wave of pain took hold of her body.

Autumn Leaves

"Hold on, my Darling," he whispered in her ear as he swooped her up into his arms and carried her into the parlor, all the while shouting: "Mary, John, anybody, hurry..." He was still shouting even though they were already standing beside him.

"Oh my, her Highness won't make it to the hospital," Mary exclaimed, wringing her hands.

"Quick Loni, towels, linens, hot water....you know what to get..."

Rudolf just stood there, looking dumbfounded. "Mary, what are you talking about. My wife is going to the hospital!"

"Sure she will, but not to have the baby. That youngen won't wait that long. Now step aside and let me see to things." She had spoken with such authority, Rudolf automatically stepped back to make room for her. He watched as she wiped the sweat off Marianne's forehead and instructed her to take deep breaths and try to relax. He did not even realize he was breathing right along with her, as if to ease the terrible pain that convulsed her body again and again. How could he have done that to her? Guilt tried to take him over, but didn't quiet succeed. After all, they had both longed for a baby for such a long time, but it wasn't supposed to be like this.

Loni rushed in with a basin filled with hot water, followed by John who carried snow-white towels and linen sheets.

"Off with you men folk, there is women's work to be done!"

Again that commanding voice, so unlike the sweet, gentle Mary they all knew, but it did the trick, and they left. Finally Rudolf remembered: "John, call the hospital."

"The ambulance is already on its way, your Lordship."

Every agonizing scream, coming from the parlor, made him jump. His fists were curled into a tight ball and when that last blood-curdling scream echoed in the hall, Prince Rudolf's fist hit the wall. He nearly drew blood.

There, he heard a small whimper followed by a hard slap then a cry. It was a strong cry, full of protest. Why, she wouldn't have dared to slap... Nothing could stop him now; he made a wild dash for the parlor.

"Your Highness," Mary called out, thrusting a bundle towards him, misty eyed. He wouldn't dare hold something so tiny and fragile. With a knowing smile, Mary placed the infant into Marianne's waiting arms.

The ambulance arrived and in a matter of minutes mother and baby were being wheeled out. Just as they were being lifted into the waiting ambulance, a leaf tumbled down and landed on the baby's blanket, right where her little head was snuggled. Marianne stopped the orderly from brushing it away.

"Please don't. Save it for me."

The two medics exchanged knowing glances, but Rudolf had already taken the leaf and carefully placed it between the pages of his pocket calendar. Marianne gave him a grateful glance, as she drifted off to sleep. He bent down, placed a kiss on her lips and whispered; "Thank you, darling," but she had already entered dreamland. He followed in his car thinking that Mary had done an excellent job delivering his little daughter, but be that as it may, he would have to have a word with her about slapping the tiny creature so hard.

Marianne von Schwarzenau held her little daughter and gazed in amazement at the wonder she and her husband had created. She softly whispered: "Autumn, my beautiful little angel."

Autumn was Marianne's favorite time of year. She loved everything about it, the colors, the gusty winds and the tumbling leaves swirling through the air. Just like the one that had fallen on the baby's blanket. It was an omen, a sign from above and so she knew what to name her little girl. This baby was their miracle, her first and only child she would ever be able to bear. The doctor had warned them about trying to conceive a baby at this time. Her health had not been very good, something about her white blood cells not being as they should be. Even so the odds had been against them, all had gone well. Her condition had miraculously vanished, for the time being. Hopefully it was gone for good. There were tears in her eyes when her lips brushed her baby's soft satiny cheeks. Thank you God for our miracle, thank you!

At her bedside stood a vase holding branches with leaves of all the fall colors God had invented, the golden ones matching the shock of hair on the infant's head. Rudolf at once called her Goldilocks, a name that would stick with her for some time to come.

"Do you think her hair will turn a different color?" Marianne had a troubled look on her face as she put the question to her husband.

"God wouldn't allow that to happen, my Darling, knowing how much we love her just the way she is now. And you're right, that golden glimmer on her hair does look like some of the fall leaves. Our little Autumn is going to be the most beautiful child in the world, the name suits her well."

"Rudolf, what do you mean by, is going to be? She already is."

Both broke out into happy laughter at so much vanity. Rudolf bent down, his lips slightly brushing his wife's forehead. Then he gently took his little daughters hands in his and placed butterfly kisses on each tiny, chubby finger.

"I love you, princess. Daddy will always be here for you." There were tears in his eyes as he looked at his little daughter. She was sleeping peacefully lying across Marianne's breasts. He would carry this picture in his heart for all the days to come. The doctor had already told him that he could bring his new family home the next day, mother and daughter were doing remarkably well, and it was not a moment too soon. He would see to it that Marianne got a lot of rest. Getting her strength back was number one on his list. He silently prayed that his worries about her health had come to a resting-place, never to surface again. He loved her so. Finally they were the little family they had dreamed off for such a long time.

By early morning on the following day Chateau Schwarzenau was ready to welcome its newest member, the little princess, Autumn Marianne von Schwarzenau. The sun was high in the sky and autumn leaves were falling. A thousand balloons were set free over the Chateau, turning the sky into brilliant colors of green, gold, maroon, orange and white. Those were the colors of fall but white was for the innocence of the little baby girl, princess Autumn, who had been born on October twelfth in this very castle and now returned home, four days later.

On their daughter's first Christmas, Prince Rudolf and his wife decided to have a small silver coin made up, showing their little daughter's face and date of birth, to give to close friends. The coin became such a hit; it turned into a yearly event. Each Christmas thereafter the new coin would show how the little princess was growing up.

When Autumn was four years old, she was already very much at home riding on her little pony. One day she decided to go visit the village, which she was not allowed to do on her own. The walls, surrounding the chateau, were her boundary. To go beyond would be much too dangerous, with those steep slopes and winding curves leading down toward the village. Autumn, however, fancied herself quite knowledgeable and when nobody was looking, out the gate she went.

"We have to be careful, 'cause if we're not, we're going to get into trouble. So just look where you're going, OK?" The little princess was certain her pony understood every word she said. Before long they reached the first houses of the village. Autumn let herself slide off the pony and took the reins into her hand. She was leading it down the cobblestone covered main street, pointing out all the important places to see. The villagers gathered on the sidewalk, watching the little girl clad in riding gear leading her pony and making gestures with her free hand as if she was explaining something really important. Well, she was. Clip, clap, clip, clap... They were walking right in the middle of Main Street, totally oblivious of cars or horse drawn wagons. Of course most everybody knew who the tiny tyke was, commanding the whole street, and they enjoyed watching her. But when the traffic threatened to turn into chaos something had to be done.

"Now Bunny," Autumn explained to her pony, "you have to agree with me, it doesn't smell this good in our garden. That's because we don't bake bread and pastries there, we only grow flowers. Come on, Bunny..."

Autumn pulled with all her might on the bridle, but the pony had stopped and would not move. She stomped her little foot down as hard as she could and shot an angry glance at her beloved Bunny. It was of no use, Bunny would not budge. Stemming both hands on her sides, her cheeks puffed out and her lips in a pout, Autumn presented a picture any photographer would have loved to take.

"If you don't come, I'm going to tell papa and you know what he will do?" It was the most awful threat she could think of, and it worked. Bunny began to move, but only a few feet, then came to an abrupt stop again. Except that this time it was because there were two strong arms holding on to the animal and a giant was lurking at her from under two bushy eyebrows. Her little heart almost stood still. Nobody had told her that there was a monster in the village. A familiar quiver could be seen on her lips and her big frightened eyes began to fill with water. The giant took the reins out of her hand into one of his, then his other giant hand got hold of her and he led both of them toward the sidewalk. Finally he let go, grumbling something under his beard. Autumn dissolved into tears.

"There is nothing to be afraid off, little princess, it was only Sepp, he won't harm a fly on the wall." Gentle hands were drying her tears and a pretty lady, with the longest braids she had ever seen, smiled into her face.

"He wasn't going to eat me?"

"Sepp? He'd just as soon kiss you than eat you!" exclaimed the pretty lady.

"Yuck," was all Autumn could say.

"Young lady, I think it's best that we go home."

Startled, Autumn spun around and stared wide-eyed at the man standing behind her.

"Daddy?"... Although she was only four years old, she knew right from wrong, and this time she had done wrong. Her little voice had this croaking sound when she uttered his name. This was bad, this was so very bad, and she knew that for sure. Taking her hand and her pony they moved along main street, her golden curls totally covering her low bent head. That's why she did not see the smile her father extended to the onlookers. All she knew was that he must be frightfully mad. She also wondered if this was the time when children got that spanking she had heard about? Would it hurt terribly bad?

"Autumn?"

"Daddy?"

They had stopped and she felt herself being lifted up and placed on a bench lining the roadside. He was very mad at her; she could tell by the way his hands were holding her tight around her waist. She dared to glance at him from under half closed eyes and thought she could see a tiny smile on his face. Anyway, he didn't look half as mad as she figured he would be. What if she told him why she had to go to the village? After all, it was Bunny who wanted to go, wasn't it?

"Tell me, Autumn, what should I do with you now?" Wow, that sounded very stern. Maybe he was very mad after all. This was scary, but she had to give it a try.

"Maybe you want to spank me? But daddy, Bunny really wanted to see the village because she's never seen it. I just took her there so she wouldn't be so sad. 'Cause daddy,

Autumn Leaves

Bunny is my best friend and best friends take care of each other, don't they?" She knew she had won when she noticed how hard it was for her father to keep from smiling. So she laid her arms around his neck and whispered: "You're the best daddy in the whole wide world. I love you, daddy."

She was sure she had won. It always worked when she told him that she loved him. Then she heard his voice and her heart sunk, it sounded so stern: "Never do that again, do you understand? You had us scared witless, nobody knew where you had run off to until the call came."

"Did the pretty lady call you daddy?" Her whole face lit up with renewed hope.

"I don't know who called, but I'm sure it was no pretty lady. Unless your pretty lady has a very deep voice, that is." That made both of them laugh and they continued making their way home. With one swoop she landed on her pony's back and was being told to hold on tight. Then her daddy took Bunny's reigns and started leading them upward toward the Chateau, his own horse racing ahead of them.

She noticed how quiet her daddy was. Sometimes grown ups did that and then they called it 'Thinking.' That was probably what he was doing and she knew not to interrupt him.

It was a long walk from the village up to the chateau. She had insisted on walking after only a few minutes riding, and soon realized that it was a big mistake. As little as she was, her pride would not give in. It seemed to take forever, but finally the front steps of their home were in sight. She was overjoyed. Together they gave Bunny a loving pat on her hindquarters and off she trotted toward the stables. Rudolf knew that his horse had made it there some time ago.

Marianne was standing on the top of the stairs, both arms extended, ready to welcome the weary travelers. Although Autumn's little legs were ready to fall off, she managed to run up the steps into her mothers outstretched arms. How wonderful it felt to be squashed by Mommy.

It was during their way back home that Rudolf realized the need for something else in his little daughter's life, something other than what they were giving her, but what? Marianne would know, she was so good at figuring things out, especially when it came to their whirlwind daughter. In a way he was proud of her little stunt; it showed she had spunk. All too many times she appeared quiet, almost timid. Her whirlwind moments were far and in-between, but those were the moments he loved best about her.

Rudolf and Marianne came to the same conclusion. What Autumn needed was a friend, someone her own age to play with.

"I understand the new woman managing our nursery has a young daughter. Maybe I should check it out, what do you think, darling?" He put the question to his wife, hoping she would agree. To his delight she did.

"Shall I come with you, darling?"

"I don't think so, I'm going to see if I can get some flowers for my beautiful wife. That would be a perfect excuse to look around."

"But we have so many flowers all over the grounds. Won't it look silly to get more?"

"Not at all, it's so much more romantic. Besides, you've always loved getting flowers, haven't you?" Her smile said it all and the kiss reaffirmed it.

"You take my breath away, Marianne von Schwarzenau."

The next day Rudolf found himself strolling through the huge greenhouses located at the far end of the park. It had been a long time since he set foot in them and he was amazed at all the flowers, potted plants, and all those vegetables growing there. Usually his staff would just come and get what they needed to run the kitchen, so this was a real eye opener for him. Just as he was admiring the many rows of miniature

Autumn Leaves

roses, something dark pushed past him and was gone in a flash around the next corner.

"Laura, you come here this instant!" A woman's angry voice reached his ear. Slamming the flimsy wire mesh door, a tall woman strode into the greenhouse, unaware of her customer. Her dark hair was pulled back into a bun at the nape of her neck and her eyebrows were pulled together, enhancing the severity of her face. It promised nothing good would be forthcoming. No wonder the little girl was running for her life. So that's what it had been and her name was Laura. The woman almost collided with him before she was aware of his presence. She stopped, her mouth wide open, but nothing came out. Rudolf bowed slightly: "Schwarzenau, from the chateau. We haven't met, my apologies." He held out his hand but she quickly stepped back, hiding her hands under a black apron.

"Sorry, I was just digging up some bushes. Glad to meet you. What can I do for you?" Then, almost immediately: "Who did you say you are?"

"Rudolf von Schwarzenau, madam." Again he made a slight bow.

Her bewilderment was quite amusing, but he didn't dare smile. The height of this woman was very impressive and he began to feel sorry for the little girl now peeking around the corner of the rose beds. She was pretty, with her black hair and coal black eyes. She reminded him of a gypsy, but then her mother had that same black hair and dark eyes, a definite foreign look. The little girl she had called Laura now stepped into full view and marched toward them. If he had expected to see fear in her face she proved him wrong, her little face displayed a bright grin showing two rows of perfect pearly white teeth. In her right hand she held a bright orange flower which was now extended toward her mother's face. The tall woman bent to take it and to his astonishment, a tender smile softened those deep wrinkles and she placed a kiss smack on the little girl's mouth.

"Next time, answer when I call you. Go to the potting shed, lunch is on the bench. Go on child, I'll be there shortly and, Laura, thank you for my flower."

"That's alright Mama, next time I'll find you a blue one." With that Laura skipped away out of sight. Rudolf watched her as long as he could. A delightful little girl, and she couldn't be much older than Autumn.

Turning to the woman he said: "Your little daughter is very pretty. How old is she?"

"Laura just turned six, but she has the mind of a grown up. It's no wonder; she's always around me and the likes of me. Couldn't afford to send her to no kindergarten. Good helper in the greenhouse so, she knows her plants from weeds." She said it matter of fact like, without any complaint in her voice.

He noticed her looking at him quizzically: "Who did you say you are, again?"

" Rudolf von Schwarzenau. I live in the chateau with my wife and daughter. My daughter is four years old. If you don't think me too presumptuous, could I meet your little girl and talk to her?"

"Why, what has she done?" There was distrust in her voice, or was it resentment?

"Nothing, I assure you. I just would like to see her and, perhaps, if it is all right with you, invite her to meet my little girl. Autumn, that's the name of my daughter, is in need of a companion and, if the age difference is not too obvious, perhaps they could spend some time together. It's just a thought and totally subject to your approval, of course."

There was a slight pause while Laura's mother seemed to study him from head to toe. He gave her time to figure him out and turned to admire the flowers that were lined up on the shelving.

She looked at him long and hard. She had to admit he was dressed smart enough and he could be telling the truth, but how was she to know? Too many bad things were happening to little girls, especially pretty ones like her Laura. One could never be too careful. He sure had a fancy way of talking. Just then he opened his mouth and some more of those words flew at her.

"By the way, this is my nursery you are taking care off so splendidly. Thank you."

Lucky for her, Sepp walked in bringing her a box full of white pebbles she'd been waiting for. A big sigh escaped her lips that was hard to ignore. Sepp studied her for a brief moment before addressing her visitor.

"A good day to you, your lordship, and to you, Miss Selma. Here's them rocks you wanted, there's more of them, if you need more." With that he put the box on a bench nearby and turned his attention to Rudolf. "Did the little missy get home all right? I sure didn't mean to frighten her, but it's better to be safe than hurt."

"You did good, Sepp. I want to thank you. It won't happen again, I'm pretty sure of that. Next time the princess comes to the village, she will have a proper escort."

Fascinated, Selma followed the conversation open-mouthed. Well, if that didn't beat all, this guy was really who he claimed to be, and he stood in her greenhouse, well, his greenhouse. She still wasn't quite sure what he wanted, surely not flowers. Having peeked many a time through the fence, she knew that the park next door was loaded with flowers of all sorts, so flowers was not what this gent, or gentleman, was here for. Just like before, he interrupted her thoughts.

"If you could pick me out several of those peach-colored miniature roses, I would be very grateful indeed."

"Roses? Why yea, peach- colored you said, sure thing. How many are several, sir?"

"Twenty or thirty, about that much. Can you make them as full as possible? My gardener will come to pick them up later in the day, if that is all right with you? Oh, by the way, will you think about what I said, about the little ladies getting to meet each other, please? You can ring me or my wife at the chateau and we will have our chauffeur come and pick Laura up." With that he handed her a card, tipped his head and walked out.

"Sepp," Selma's yell stopped him short just as he was stepping into his pickup truck.

"Miss Selma, forget something?"

"No, just tell me about this gentleman that just left here. You've seen him before?"

"Seen him? Everybody's seen him. Miss Selma, I know you've been here only a short time, but surely, you're not trying to tell me you don't know who your bread giver is? That was Prince Rudolf, our benefactor, and if I might add in more ways than I can count on both hands."

She saw him shaking his head as if he was disappointed in her. Too bad, she liked him, but she also knew that the folks around town thought of her as a strange lady because she kept to herself. Sepp probably thought the same. Well, she didn't look like most people around here, so what? She was nice to her customers, and that was all she was going to be. There was no sense in striking up a friendship with anybody, except Sepp perhaps. She could tell that his mind was well occupied but she had to find out more.

"So, tell me about him, or don't you know either?"

"Miss Selma, the prince, his wife and their little daughter Autumn are what this valley is all about. They are our protectors, if you will. Folks here rely on them for advice, help, guidance, whatever. Not to forget the late summer picnic and ...."

"That's enough, Sepp. I get the message." Selma started to pick through the clay pots to find the fullest peach colored miniature roses. Sepp just stood there watching her. She kept on without paying any attention to him. He finally walked back to his truck, looking very disappointed.

Selma picked the most beautiful peach-colored roses she could find and when she counted thirty pots all together, she stopped looking. What a nice profit this would have made

Autumn Leaves

had it been one of the townsfolk buying it. Then she could have bought some things she had been wanting for a long time. Nothing fancy, mind you, she wasn't a fancy lady, just some things a lady should have. Up to now every spare penny had gone to Laura's needs and wants. Maybe things would be different soon; after all, the Prince wanted to get her Laura to meet his daughter. The smile on Selma's face almost made her look pretty.

"What did that fine looking man want, Moma?"

"Roses my dear, roses." Selma said it in such a way that Laura became alert.

"What's wrong with you, Moma, are you feeling all right?"

"Why, child?"

"Because you act weird."

"Not weird, Laura, I'm just thinking about what the Prince said to me. It's about you, he wants you to meet his little girl. Mind you, I really need you here to help me, but maybe you can meet her just this once."

"Why, Moma, what do I have to do?"

"Do? Nothing that I know of. He just said that he would like you to meet his little girl. Would you like that?"

"Do I get to go to the big house and can I run around in that big park and ...." Seeing her daughter's excitement did her heart good; she scooped her little girl up and twirled her around. Although Laura was not your average six-year-old, she was quite tall, but for a woman of Selma's size it was nothing to pick her up. The two laughed until they cried, something which had not happened in a long time. Yes, things were definitely looking up.

At first she'd had some thoughts about taking over the nursery, it was an odd arrangement. The household folks from the chateau could come and get anything they needed and she would work and take care of the nursery without pay. Instead she would have a roof over her head, and it was a pretty nice one at that, and she could keep half the money from the village people who came to buy things. Of course she needed to get some supplies now and then but it turned out pretty good for her and her little girl. She grew most of the things they needed and all she had to buy was some meat now and then and some spices. The chickens she kept in a large pen took care of the eggs and some times made for a fine roast. Nobody had ever bothered her from the castle, so she never gave the people living there much thought. Why should she? She liked to call the place a castle, it was much easier to say and much more befitting its looks. Well, that was her opinion anyway. Now, all of a sudden, her little Laura was going to visit the castle. If that didn't beat all.

Selma rubbed her hands together and grinned from ear to ear. Today she felt good and she had an even better feeling about the future of her precious dark-haired angel. For once, being different didn't seem to matter.

CHAPTER THREE

Rudolf and Marianne cherished their daughter. They were a family with great values and more love for each other than one normally would see. Best of all, they had a lot of fun. The good times at Chateau Schwarzenau were well known in the area, especially the late summer cook outs where everybody who wanted could join in, the villagers bringing their specialties prepared in their own kitchens. It was a marvelous feast, with dancing, eating and games for all. Usually, at the end of such a fun day, a huge amount of balloons were released into the night air, traveling in all directions, far and not so far. The next day the children often found many of the balloons hung up in trees, stuck in the crevices of the old stone wall, or simply bobbing around in the meadows, having lost a good amount of their helium. It was also a busy day for Harold, the gardener, restoring his beautiful park back to its original state. He took a lot of pride in his domain.

Little did anybody know that on the day when Rudolf and Marianne decided that their little daughter needed a playmate, it would bring about a great change in their lives, especially in Autumn's. Laura, Autumn's new friend, was two years older and exactly the opposite in looks. Laura was a leader and Autumn didn't mind following her. However, as they were getting older, Autumn's blind adoration slowly changed when things began to happen which didn't make any sense. Items would get broken or just flat disappear all together. Curiously, it always was one of her favorite things and when she tried to talk to Laura about it she got offended, vehemently proclaiming her innocence. It confused Autumn; she desperately needed somebody to help her sort things out.

In the beginning of their friendship Chateau Schwarzenau was a fairyland for the two little girls. Mostly because that's what Laura called it.

They had so much fun. They could play for hours on end and never get tired of the same thing. Every day was an adventure and soon Laura began saying things like, "I really feel like I belong here." It made Autumn feel good seeing her friend so happy. She had no idea that Laura thought whatever Autumn had was also hers, and that when she noticed Autumn getting too attached to a certain something, she would find a way to break it or make it disappear. Like the ballerina music box, that glittery oblong thing with a porcelain figurine in the middle of it. It was a ballerina, clad in pink tulle, turning in front of a crystal mirror to the tune of 'Flight of the bumblebee.' Of course the girls didn't know what kind of music it was. Autumn found it pretty while Laura called it a silly sound. Autumn would never forget that day. She ran up to Laura holding a shiny box in her hands, her little heart pounding with excitement and joy.

"Look Laura, what Daddy brought back from Vienna? Look, see what it can do!"

Then she opened the lid and a merry tune started playing and this tiny ballerina turned around and around, her reflection multiplied by a special crystal mirror, making it look as if there was a whole lineup of dancers twirling around. It was something very special and rare and she never suspected that Laura might feel jealous about it. How could she know that her friend expected to get the same things she got and considered herself part of the family? Jealousy was foreign to Autumn; she loved to share her things without any reservation. So when Laura said: "It's very pretty, here, let me set it on the dresser so we can see it better," she let her have it.

She remembered Laura taking the box from her, stumbling over something and the box hitting the wall, shattering into a thousand pieces. She was horrified. All she could do was stand there, staring at the glittering fragments on the floor, her mouth wide open for a scream but nothing came out. Laura must have realized what she had done, she began to sob.

Seeing her friend so miserable, Autumn quietly said: "Don't cry, Laura, I won't tell Daddy about it, it would hurt him too much. This was the only one of its kind in the store."

She did not see the wicked grin on her friend's face nor could she imagine that Laura had played one of her incredible tricks on her. It was Autumn's meekness that allowed Laura to manipulate her and inflict hurt after hurt.

What Laura did not realize was that on that day more than just the music box got broken. Autumn began to change. There was a new awareness in her. Hard as she tried she could not understand why Laura had tripped. There had been nothing on the floor for her to stumble over, and why did the box fly so hard against the wall, when it should have landed on the soft carpet? From that day on she would look at her best friend with different eyes, and it made her sad. Now the fine tuning of their friendship had a serious flaw, and Autumn fought hard not to let is show. The music box was never mentioned again but in the quiet hours of the night the memory of the incident would flash through her mind and sometimes a tear would roll onto her pillow. Slowly things were beginning to change.

Although many years had flown by, to Rudolf and Marianne it seemed like it was only yesterday when they'd held their little daughter for the very first time. Could it really be true that she was already in her seventeenth year? So often, when he looked at his daughter, Rudolf thought he was looking at a younger version of Marianne. They were so much alike. His chest got real tight realizing that this was his little family and that it would not remain so for very much longer.

When Victor had re-entered their life, it seemed to make the circle complete. Thinking back to that day still brought tears to his eyes; he had missed his younger brother more than he had been willing to admit. The past fifteen years had bonded them together, but even so Victor persisted in this charade of calling himself by that English name, Victor Mulhair. Rudolf thought it was pretty silly. Most of the elderly people knew who he was, and it did bother him that Autumn was kept in the dark yet even so she did call him 'Uncle'. She had no idea that he was her real uncle and this past year she had dropped the uncle anyway, too childish, she claimed. Victor had met and married the Lady Jane while staying in London. She had been a successful solicitor. But Jane gave it all up to be with her man and moved with him back to his homeland.

They took over the old horse farm and moved into the villa. Both were located near a small lake far away from the main house at the other end of the huge park. Nobody had been at that spot for a long time and Marianne had almost forgotten that it was there. Victor invited them over after all the necessary repairs had been completed. Rudolf was in awe of the place; it did not look like anything he remembered, and it made him proud of his brother's accomplishments. It was the most charming villa he had ever seen.

The totally run down horse farm had also gotten a face lift and life flourished once again. Autumn loved going to see her uncle and aunt. Victor taught her how to ride and he gave her the first pony she could call her own. It was Bunny. Now, fifteen years later, not much had changed, except that Autumn was a very lovely young lady, not a child any more and the

Autumn Leaves

owner of a beautiful horse. Jane had long ago accepted the explanation that Victor and Rudolf had been best friends in school, almost like brothers; that's why there was such a close bond. The child Autumn had captured her heart from the first moment she saw her.

Rudolf and Marianne were sitting on the verandah, Marianne's favorite place, waiting for their morning coffee. She had her face turned toward the early morning sun, eyes closed. He looked at her for a long time, thanking God for giving him such a wonderful woman to share his life with. His thoughts were on his daughter and also her long time friend, Laura. When he introduced Laura to the household, he thought it was a day of joy, Autumn would have a companion at last. Much had changed since then. There were many times when he felt regret about bringing Laura into his home; perhaps she had not been the right choice for his daughter after all. Autumn never complained, but there was something that just did not feel right. These feelings didn't rise up out of nowhere. He had been having doubts for a very long time, but never had anything to substantiate it. A bright cheery voice startled him out of his morbid thoughts.

"Can any one join in or is this a private party? Morning, Momi, morning, Daddy. You're up a bit early, don't you think?" She noticed John, standing there with the coffee tray in his hands. "Hello, John, and a good morning to you!"

"Why thank you, princess, I wish you the same."

He glanced at Marianne with pleading eyes: "Mam...."

"I'm sorry, John, yes of course you may set up here, thank you."

She stretched her arms out toward Autumn: "How fresh you look so early in the morning. Come here, child, and give me a proper hug. ... Now, that's better."

Mother and daughter laughed together, dark blue and bright blue eyes, a picture of total unison. Rudolf could not tear his eyes away from them. The smile on his face reaffirmed the pride he felt at having such a wonderful family. If only it could always stay that way. Marianne's cheery voice brought him back to reality.

"What do you think, darling, doesn't it sound like a lot of fun?"

"Yes, of course, " was the absentminded answer.

"Afterward we can milk the cows and clean the horse barn," Marianne went on.

"That sounds great," was his reply. Autumn could not contain herself, she busted out laughing. It was obvious that her dad had been miles away, not hearing a word of their conversation. His puzzled look confirmed it.

"Are you two having fun at my expense? Is that ladylike?"

He reached for his coffee cup and surveyed his women over the rim while taking a sip of that delicious smelling brew. They were up to something and it wouldn't be the first time.

"OK, out with it. What did I miss?"

"Not much, darling, Autumn was just telling 'US' about a phone call she received from Jane. Seems like there is going to be a get together at her house and......"

"Great, I'm ready for a change and so are you, my sweet, right?"

"Sorry to disappoint you, but you and I are not invited."

"What are you saying, this is our Jane you're talking about, right? We are always invited when she has something going."

"Not this time, it's for the younger generation only. A group of young athletes are invited, international I might add, and Jane would like for Autumn and Laura to attend. Like I said before, it should be fun."

"Hmmm... When did you say this was going on?"

"I didn't, but it's this coming Saturday and Autumn needs to get a few ...."

"Clothes, since she has nothing to wear." The way Rudolf mimicked Marianne's voice was so hilarious and the three of them began to laugh. Rudolf almost spilled his coffee and quickly set his cup back down.

"Is it OK, Daddy? I'd just like to get a pair of new jeans matching the boots we ordered a few weeks ago, can I?" Those pleading eyes, how could he say no.

"By the way, did your boots ever come? If not, maybe you'd better check up on it young lady."

Autumn jumped up so fast making the cups and saucers rattle. "Right away, thank you, Daddy," and she was gone.

"She didn't even drink her coffee," Marianne frowned.

"Well, that set our morning in motion. Not exactly what I had in mind..." he added with a grin and reached for her hand. "I love you, my darling wife, forever and always."

"And I love you better, my darling husband."

Their eyes locked and it was just as if they had met yesterday, the love they felt for each other burning high. He could detect an underlying sadness in her eyes, sadness he knew about only too well, sadness he himself had a hard time keeping under control. He had to be strong enough for both of them, although in quiet moments it seemed to rip him apart. There was no way he could picture himself without her, ever.

"More coffee, darling?" She waited for an answer, but it did not come. He was miles away, trying to figure out how to save the life of the woman he loved more than anything else in this world, and was hitting nothing but one brick wall after another.

"Rudi?" She only called him that when she wanted something special. It got his attention and he quickly returned back to reality . She was looking at him in a strange way. He realized that she knew he had been miles away, which he did quite often of late, but she never questioned him.

"Did you want more coffee, darling, or can John clear the table?"

Just then he noticed that John was standing right beside him. He wondered how long he had been there. With a nod of his head he gave the OK and in no time the table was cleared. Marianne had stepped over to the rail, her eyes scanning across the valley. He knew she was daydreaming, she had that far away look in her eyes. He walked over to her and put his arms around her waist. Nuzzling her ear he whispered: "A penny for your thoughts."

"Not enough money. My thoughts are their worth in gold."

"Tell me the amount and it shall be yours."

"Sorry, my Lord, you don't have enough in your lair to accommodate me."

"We shall see, my lady, we shall see." He pulled her against his chest and kissed the top of her head. "Hmm, your hair smells like spring."

"Not like autumn?"

"No, like spring, autumn doesn't have a smell, or does it?"

"I think it does, but if you say spring then that's what it is."

"Aren't we docile this morning?"

That little smile of hers was just too cute, so he kissed her again, this time a bit more thoroughly.

"Wow, you can do that any time." She sounded content and he felt her snuggle closer to him. He wished they could have remained this way for the rest of the day. How comforting it was to hold her in his arms.

"When are you and your daughter going on that big shopping spree?" Rudolf put his finger under her chin and lifted it up so that her eyes looked directly into his.

Instead of answering his question, she said: "I love your deep black eyes, I get lost in them. They are so deep it makes me dizzy." She succeeded in confusing him, but only for a moment.

Autumn Leaves

"Marianne, answer my question. When are you going?" Was that a little pout on her lips? A light feathery kiss took care of that.

"As soon as your daughter gets off the phone and gives me the signal, your highness." She bowed her head and made a deep curtsy barely able to hide her grin. His attempt at sounding stern had been a miserable failure. So far he had never been able to be stern with her, so when she put on her little pout the result was just as she hoped, he kissed her. She could kiss him from morning to night, she loved him so.

CHAPTER FOUR

Laura, cunning as she was, was well aware that Prince Rudolf did not really trust her and took special precautions not to slip up. Her mother was oblivious to her daughter's beastly behavior. All she knew was that Laura was happy and was being spoiled in the big house. Her child was able to do things she had only dreamed of. The pretty items she brought home were proof of it. All those times she had watched her daughter and the princess ride in the park convinced her that those two girls had found true friendship, worth more than any money could buy.

Everyone could see how well they got along. It had been destiny the day Prince Rudolf walked into the nursery. Thanks to Laura, her cousin Ruben had also found employment at the castle. As far as knowing anything about the goings on up on the hill, all her knowledge came from what her daughter told her. Of course she had no reason to be concerned; Laura's tales were always full of happy events. Even when Autumn stopped coming by, she did not feel alarmed. Young ladies had better things to do than to entertain old women. Anyway, Selma would never have dared to question the princess's motives. That Autumn's absence could have anything to do with Laura's behavior, never entered her mind.

So, when the phone rang this particular morning, Selma picked it up just as she normally would and was totally surprised to hear Autumn's voice. The princess sounded pleasant as always, asking to speak to Laura. Selma was itching to ask why Autumn had made herself so scarce of late, but did not dare. She asked Autumn to hold the line while she went to rouse Laura. In her mind she knew that her daughter would probably be mad to be woken up so early, but what the hell, she wasn't about to tell Autumn that Laura was still asleep. Laura shouldn't stay out so late anyway.

She yelled up the stairs: "Laura, Princess Autumn is on the phone. Pick it up, now!" Selma always addressed Autumn by her title; she had a lot of respect for that young lady. She had hoped against hope that her daughter would pick up some of Autumn's finer ways, but no such luck.

Selma was right, Laura was fuming. Who in hell would be calling this early in the morning? She didn't understand what her mother was yelling about, only that she was wanted on the phone. With a grumpy 'Hello' she picked up the receiver.

"Good God, Autumn, where is the fire?"

Autumn ignored her friend's irritation: "No fire, Laura, just some good news. We're invited to a party over at Lady Jane's home. Isn't that great?"

"Why would Lady Jane invite me to one of her parties?" She still didn't sound too happy.

" 'Cause it's a special party, only for young folks. She said there was a group of young athletes coming and guess what? They're all coming from different places."

Now Autumn had her full attention. "You mean from all over Germany?"

"No, like international. She mentioned France, Japan, America, England and I think she also said Norway. It should be fun. You are coming, aren't you?"

"If her royal highness would care to tell me when this event is to occur." Laura's voice dripped with sarcasm, but Autumn fired right back: "Knock it off, Laura, it's either yes or no. If it's yes, the party is on Saturday. So why don't you come over later on and we can go over our wardrobe."

Laura knew she had overstepped and wised up quickly. "Sure thing, see you later, girlfriend." She chided herself for being so stupid at times. Then her head fell back into the pillow. All she wanted to do was sleep. With a start she jumped back up, realizing what Autumn had just told her. This could turn into a very memorable day. A party with international flavor and not just anybody; these guys were athletes. Laura's imagination ran amok, and she grinned like a Cheshire cat. Yes, this was just great. Hello, world, here I come! Compared to her, her little friend was still wet behind her ears. This upcoming party would prove once and for all who the queen really was, she was very sure of that. These guys were looking for a good time, and she knew how to give them just that. Miss prim and proper didn't have a chance. Yea, they would have a dress rehearsal, but no way would she let on what she was going to wear.

"Did Laura agree to come to the party?" Marianne stood in the doorway leading into Autumn's room.

"Yes. She tried to act tough but I know she's looking forward to it. I asked her to come over later on so we can talk about what to wear."

"But Autumn, I thought you already knew that. Didn't you ask your father for a new pair of jeans earlier?"

"I know Mom, but I want to make sure Laura doesn't feel that I might be wanting to show off or something."

Marianne stepped forward and took her daughters hand: " Some times, Autumn, you are too sensitive for your own good. Laura knows quite well how to make herself shine, believe me darling. My only worry is that you might be

Autumn Leaves

learning the wrong things from her. She seems very advanced for her age, if you know what I mean?"

"Come on Momi, I do know that there is a difference between boys and girls and I also know how to stay out of trouble. They covered all that in sex education in school, remember?"

Autumn noticed with amusement that her mom's face turned a pretty shade of pink. How cute, her mom blushed just like a schoolgirl. Better not say anything else or the shoe would be on the other foot, after all, she got rather easily embarrassed herself. Must be inherited .

What a coincidence, the doorbell rang just as they walked down into the foyer. John appeared out of nowhere and opened the door. They saw the postman handing him a large package. John took a quick glance at the address and thrust it towards Autumn.

"For you, Princess." There was a shout: "Great, my boots are here!"

Off she was, running up the stairway. Marianne could hear a squeal coming from Autumn's room and smiled. She could just picture her daughter tearing open the parcel, pulling out the boots. A moment later footsteps could be heard and down the stairs came Autumn in a pair of the cutest white cowboy boots.

"I think I just leave them on until Saturday. Aren't they sexy?" With that Autumn made a tight pirouette on the steps to show off her new treasure.

"I don't know about sexy, but they are precious. Watch your step, Autumn, we wouldn't want you to come sliding down the stairs, now would we?" Marianne studied her daughter. "I know, you should get some white jeans to go with them?"

"Oh mom, what a great idea. You will come shopping with me, right?"

"I said I would. Let me just tell your father, but he already said that he can spare me for a while." With that she turned into the direction of her husband's study. Autumn watched her as she moved away. Her mother was the most graceful woman she had ever seen, and the most beautiful. Lately so, there was something different about her. She couldn't put her finger on it, but it was there. Watching her walk down the long hall she took in every move her mother made and noticed how her blond hair took on a golden shimmer as she passed under the chandelier. Not once did Marianne turn her head sideways to study her reflection in the many mirrors lining both sides. She never did. As if knowing that her daughter was watching, she turned around just as her hand touched the door to her husbands study. She gave Autumn a brilliant smile then stepped inside and closed the door. There was a thoughtful look in Autumn's eyes when she started to walk back upstairs. She would call Jane and confirm Laura's coming.

Meanwhile, in Rudolf's study, the conversation had lost its light tone. Rudolf studied his lovely wife with great concern. The trip to town was heavy on his mind. "Are you sure you'll be alright going to town?"

"Of course I'll be alright, Darling. We are just looking for a few things and we will take it very easy. Besides, I am not an invalid and quite capable of doing small tasks with our lovely daughter. Please let me go on living a normal life, I don't want Autumn to find out just yet, please?"

His wife's pleading broke his heart. He understood what she was saying, but at the same time he wanted to protect her under any circumstances. Rising up out of his chair he gently folded his arms around her.

"I love you, Princess Marianne von Schwarzenau, mother of my beautiful daughter. Carry on, I know that you are stronger than you look and I also know, that you would never gamble with your health. I am afraid that you are the strong one at times, just like right now."

Autumn Leaves

"Darling, you make my heart sing. When you hold me like that I just want to crawl inside you and be one with you. I could never live without you, you know that, don't you?"

Her eyes lost themselves in his, spelling the word 'desire'. Clinging together, she whispered softly: "Let's make love."

Without a word, he picked her up and carried her toward the crescent shaped lounger. There he gently lowered her onto the soft cushions. His hands brushed aside the satin material of her gown and his lips began caressing the swell of her small firm breasts. The desire to be with her, to touch her, to feel the warmth of her, consumed him like a hot flame. When he began to make love to her she matched his passion with every move and they climbed higher than ever before. Could it really be possible that their love was reaching an even higher plateau? Dear God don't let this moment end. That thought was on both their minds.

Totally spent, Marianne watched him through sleepy eyes, utterly content just laying here in his arms. Before her eyes closed she thought how well he knew her and how much she loved him, more than any words could say.

After a while he quietly rose and looked down at her, sleeping so peacefully, and his love for her was so overpowering that tears stung his eyes. There could never be another one like her; Marianne was his destiny.

Dear Lord, let her live? Please make her well? We need a miracle, one that only you can provide. She is so trusting and you know she believes in you with all her heart. I won't ask you why, but I will ask you to reconsider.

His head bowed, Rudolf let his tears fall free and was not ashamed of them. He tiptoed away, so as not to wake her, and went over to his desk. It was hard for him to concentrate on his work, his eyes kept looking over to where Marianne lay sleeping, trying to take in every inch of her beautiful face. He could never let her go.

Anita Attwood

The massive mahogany desk was covered with stacks of paperwork. It seemed that the larger the desk the more the paperwork accumulated. It did not make any sense, but it was true. Was that a knock on the door? There, he heard it again. The door opened slowly and a blond head peeked in. Rudolf automatically put a finger to his lips giving a warning to be quiet. Autumn tiptoed in, wondering why she had to be quiet.

"Daddy"...again that finger hushing her to silence. With the other hand he pointed towards the alcove where Marianne lay sleeping.

"I'll see you later, daddy, it can wait, " and out the door she vanished.

For a moment Rudolf considered going after her, but he did not want to leave his wife alone. He wanted to be there when she woke up.

Once again he tried to concentrate on his work. He was finally making some headway when a sound came from where Marianne lay sleeping, telling him that she was coming around. Two hours had almost passed.

"I think I fell asleep for a minute." She sat up and stretched herself in all directions, letting out little moans of delight. Her statement made him laugh and she looked at him quizzically.

"A minute, that's a good one. My Darling, it is nearly lunchtime. You went off to dreamland in a big way."

"And whose fault might that have been, mein Herr? I seem to remember that there were two people involved, my Darling."

Smiling, she rose, walked over to him and gave him a feather kiss on his forehead.

"I'll go and freshen up, Darling. Meet you in the dining room?"

"No, I told John to set up outside. The weather is too beautiful to stay indoors, don't you agree?"

"Oh I do."

Autumn Leaves

She left and a moment later he heard her talking to someone in the foyer. He did not recognize the voice. Curiosity got the better of him, so he stuck his head out the door to see who it was. It was Jane.

He ran towards her and almost knocked her down. "Jane, what a nice surprise," he yelled, grinning from ear to ear. It was obvious how glad he was to see her.

"I was in the neighborhood and thought 'I might as well stop by and say hello'. So here I am," she said, grinning back at him.

"Great, can you stay for lunch and did you bring Victor?"

"Sorry Rudolf, but he is fussing with his horses. You know how that is. Sometimes I think he loves his horses more than me." Even so she said it with a smile, there was a hint of annoyance present.

"Well, can you stay a while?" Marianne was asking, it sounded very much like a plea with hopes of hearing a yes.

"I wish I could, really I do, perhaps some other time. I only came by to see how you are doing."

She had turned towards Marianne, laying a hand on her shoulder, her troubled eyes searching Marianne's face..

"I'm doing just fine, please don't worry about me, one worrier is enough. I am sorry you can't stay, a chat would have been so nice. Well, maybe next time. Give Victor my love and tell him not to be a stranger." With that she turned and walked away. Jane's eyes searched Rudolf's face. His smile had vanished the minute Marianne was out of sight. He didn't have to say anything, his eyes said it all.

"What is it that everybody is so worried about?" Autumn had come down the stairs without anybody taking notice. 'How much did she hear', Rudolf wondered.

"Are we going to eat before Mom and I are going shopping? Oh, hi miss Jane. Sorry I was so rude. Is something wrong with momi? You both look so worried?"

"No Autumn, everything is just fine. Your mother had a nap in the study and she went to freshen up a bit. To your question, yes, we will eat a light lunch before you two disappear on your shopping spree." Turning to Jane: "I wish you could accompany them."

"Sorry Rudolf, I wish I could go, but I promised Victor that I would be right back. It will be all right, I'm sure. I really must be off. See you on Saturday, Autumn!"

She was gone but Autumn could not shake the feeling that things were not as they should be. Something was terribly wrong and it had to do with her mother. No use in asking her father, she was convinced he wouldn't tell her anything. She would just have to keep her eyes and ears open. Just then she noticed John motioning from the verandah for them to come.

Lunch was ready and Marianne was already seated in one of those cozy garden chairs. Even so she appeared a little bit pale, her smile was brilliant.

"Eating alone is not one of my favorite pastimes. I was hoping that you could convince Jane to stay, darling, you're not losing your touch, are you?" The words got lost on him.

"She really had to run and sends her apologies. This Saturday night party has her and Victor in a tizzy. I'm not sure we should let the girl's go by themselves." Rudolf made a deliberate serious face, glancing in Autumn's direction from under his brows. Her reaction to his words was just as he'd imagined it would be. Her chair flew back as she jumped up: "You can't mean that, daddy?" Silence. Autumn leaned forward, both hands on the table's edge, staring at her father. He seemed to pay her no mind, placing his napkin on his lap.

"Daddy?" It was a question that required an answer, but none came forth.

"Don't be cruel, darling," Marianne interjected. She had seen his grin, but she also knew that Autumn had not. It bothered her that he should make her suffer. It was a game he had begun to play with his daughter lately. She knew he meant no harm by it, but it did seem a bit cruel all the same to see Autumn hurt. Their daughter was very sensitive, almost too much, but she, Marianne, did not agree that this kind of game would help her get tougher, or would it?

While taking her seat again, Autumn's calm voice stated: "Come to think of it, it's a wonderful idea. I do think all those young, handsome athletes will love to dance with my beautiful mom, and hold her tight.. She'll be the belle of the ball. Please daddy, would you hand me the bowl with the potatoes?"

"Touché, young lady," was all he could say to that. This was not what either one expected to hear. Marianne's approving smile did not escape him. Perhaps their daughter had her feet planted more solid than they thought. She just proved what a quick mind she had. Rudolf could not help but be proud of his ladies.

CHAPTER FIVE

The night of the big event had arrived. The girls were so giggly, one could think that they had already been secretly imbibing . Autumn looked absolutely precious in her white boots, matching jeans and a pink blouse with stand up collar and silver rose- pattern embroidery. Her hair hung loose over her shoulders and her earrings were tiny sparkling pink stones, shaped like stars. Other then her watch there was no other jewelry.

Laura wore black boots and jeans, with a bright red blouse and large black earrings. Her black hair was piled high on her head and fell down in curls on her back. She looked stunning, and she knew it. Again, it was so obvious, how opposite the girls were. Laura did not mind at all telling Autumn how beautiful she looked. She, herself, did not want to be beautiful, she wanted to be gorgeous, provocative and sexy. Judging by the look on the gardener's face, she had succeeded. Both girls were very satisfied with themselves, twisting and turning in front of the mirror, giggling like little schoolgirls. The approaching footsteps put a halt to that. They straightened up and walked slowly, their hips swinging ever so slightly, down the wide staircase. John passed them, giving them a look of total approval. At the bottom of the stairs stood Victor, all dressed in a silver gray western outfit. He looked so handsome, both girls felt their hearts beat just a bit faster. Victor had always been such a fascinating man, now more than ever. Laura already fancied herself in love with him, so his look of approval was taken the wrong way, giving Laura the go ahead for some wild thoughts. The same look was extended to Autumn, not only by Victor, but also by her parents and old Mary. It was the look of admiration and joy over so much youthful beauty and charm.

"Girls, your chauffeur has arrived. You both look gorgeous, I'm beginning to feel sorry for those poor fellows over at your house, Victor." Rudolf grinned broadly at his brother. The latter made a face as if totally overwhelmed by so much responsibility, but he had to agree. Then Laura took command.

"Lead the way, young man," giving a flirtatious smile in Victor's direction. He opened the front door and Laura passed through, still keeping her eyes on him. Autumn had stopped to kiss her mother's cheek and blew a kiss to her father, before following them to the waiting car. John held the back door open for the girls to slip in, but Laura would have none of it. While Autumn took the back seat, Laura opened the front passenger door and seated herself in the passenger seat.

"Miss Laura, I don't think....." He didn't get any further.

"It's all right John, I don't mind. Thank you." Autumn gave the butler one of her pretty smiles but he shook his head, total disapproval in his eyes. John too had Laura's number, but did not know what to do with her. As long as Autumn kept covering up for her friend, there was not much to be done. It made him very sad. He knew that in the end, the princess was the one to get hurt, if not physically, then emotionally. Victor patted him on the shoulder, giving him a knowing look. It helped somewhat, knowing that Victor understood the game Laura was playing. Mr. Victor would watch over the princess, he was sure of that.

The first thing they noticed when turning into the driveway of Victor's mansion, was that all the windows were illuminated with candles, except the huge one looking into the ballroom and the front entrance. Those were ablaze with bright white lights, sparkling like crystal. Music could be heard and one could see shadows swaying in rhythm to the beat.
"I see they started without us. Come on girls, let's see if we can add some more life to this party." Victor held out his hand to help Autumn out of the car. She took it and for a split second their eyes met. Laura's lips tightened. When Victor extended his hand to help her out, she stumbled and fell against him. He had to put his arm around her to steady her.
"Thank you, Victor, " a hushed whisper and a triumphant smile, but it was lost in the night, nobody noticed, not even the one it was intended for.
Jane came toward them, looking very flattering in a peach colored jumpsuit with white high-heeled sandals.
"My, don't you girls look smashing. Let's get you both something to drink and you can mingle and join in the fun." She took one of them on each arm and they proceeded up the few steps and into the parlor. Victor followed. There, the banquet tables were lined up against the wall and from the looks of it, there was enough food to feed an army. Their butler was filling glasses with some sparkling, pink looking liquid, it tasted delicious. Laura already held her second glass and was strolling toward the ballroom. Under the archway she came to a halt and surveyed the room. Now and then a slight nod indicated her approval of what she saw. So many good-looking young people in one place, it was a feast for the eye. There were male and female athletes, all having a good time. Some of the guys were watching Laura and she would look right back at them, as if to dare them. Autumn stood a

little back, she was not sure how to go about entering the room with all those people in it. She suddenly realized that she was on her own, Laura was obviously on the prowl. Two of the guys were approaching Laura, so she just got between them, took one on each arm and marched right into the middle of the dance floor. There they stopped and Laura dropped both partners and took a third, starting to dance with him. It was a bit much, but also very funny. Nobody was mad, they all just laughed. She was a good dancer, no doubt about it. The wilder it got, the better she liked it.

Autumn felt a pair of eyes watching her. Across the room, leaning against the baby grant piano, stood a tall figure of a man, looking straight at her, not blinking at all, or so it seemed.

"Who is that guy staring at me, Victor?" He was standing beside her and followed her gaze.

"Our friend from across the pond, Ted Warnham, a great swimmer." Victor waved at Ted, motioning him to come over. He did.

"May I introduce, pr...." "Autumn, Autumn von Schwarzenau, and you?" Autumn stretched her hand towards Ted, who took it in both of his.

"Very nice, Autumn von Schw..., whatever. I am Ted and I am very pleased to meet you." Their eyes met and held. Victor knew at once that he was not needed any more, so he left to find Jane. He wondered why Autumn had interrupted his introduction. Somehow he felt in a foul mood.

"Care to dance?" It was Laura. That was all he needed. His first impulse was to send her away, but he thought better of it.

"Why not." The two of them moved over the dance floor, getting a good workout and having fun. When the music changed to a slow song, Victor excused himself longing for some cool refreshment. He had no use for Laura's advances, which he considered childish and immature. He was a married man. That he would not mind dancing with

Autumn to that same music, that was totally different, or so he told himself. Oh hell, what was wrong with him anyway.

He found Jane sitting on the steps leading upstairs. She was not sitting alone. Whoever that was sitting beside her had her in his spell. Now she was laughing and her left hand rested on his thigh. His hand covered hers, their eyes spoke volumes. Who was he?

Victor just turned and let them be, they never noticed him. Was that the reason Jane had been so distant lately? This was their house in which she flirted with this person so openly, sitting right there on their staircase, in front of God and everybody? Maybe he'd better find out who this guy was and set him straight. Without noticing he had wandered outside. The fresh night air did him good. Something had put a damper on his mood and it wasn't all Jane. Turning sharply, he went back inside and there they were, still sitting on the steps, still laughing, still holding hands.

"Sorry to interrupt ..." Jane jumped up, looking startled but made an instant recovery.

"Victor, where have you been. Come, meet Paul, my mentor from law school. I saw him in the village today and I told him to stop by. Paul, my husband Victor." She was just gushing with excitement. Paul's voice remained calm.

"I've heard so much about you. That's all Jane talks about, her handsome man. I must say that she was right. It's all right for me to say that, isn't it?"

Victor felt slightly embarrassed: "Good to meet you too, although you have the advantage, Jane never mentioned you to me."

"Now Victor, we hardly ever talked about my law practicing days. I'm quite sure that I mentioned Paul to you, you just didn't pay any attention, but then you rarely ever do."

"Oh, I pay attention to you, dear, more than you know."

Damn, this was getting on slippery ground. Victor noticed Paul's uneasiness and knew he had to stop. Why did

Autumn Leaves

he have to open his mouth. So he added, looking at Paul, "hope you have a good time tonight," and turning back to his wife, " Darling, make sure Paul gets plenty to eat and drink. I'll see that everything is all right in there."

With that he walked towards the ballroom and was soon swallowed up by those jumping, shaking bodies.

He spotted Autumn and Ted, dancing a slow dance to "Shaking it Baby". This was not good. While everybody else was having a hell of a workout, those two were swaying like tender reeds in a gentle breeze. He had better keep an eye on them, for Marianne's and Rudolf's sake. At least that's what he told himself. Finally there was a break in the music.

"Having fun?" The question was directed at Autumn, but Ted answered instead: "More than I had anticipated." His arm went around Autumn's waist in a possessive way. Victor thought, the nerve of this guy. He reached out and grabbed Autumn's hand, almost pulling her towards him. The music was playing a slow dance.

"Remember, you promised me this dance?" His voice sounded husky. They were already on the floor, leaving Ted standing there. Ted looked a bit lost, but Autumn's reassuring smile seemed to put him at ease. She saw him walking off toward the refreshments. Victor watched her eyes following Ted and his arm tightened just a fraction around her waist. He was a very good dancer and she followed his lead with such ease, as if they had been doing this for a very long time. They were a stunning couple.

The dance was over and Autumn was ready for a snack. "I'll come with you," Victor offered. Approaching the hors d'oeuvres, they saw Jane and Ted in deep conversation.

"Autumn, your ears must be ringing. This fine young man can't hear enough about you." Autumn blushed slightly. The look she gave Ted was full of questions.

"You forgot to mention that you are a princess," "and you forgot to ask me," was her quick reply. They smiled at each other. Victor was forgotten. Together they left and found a quiet table in the garden, away from that entire hullabaloo inside. The evening was filled with sounds of the night. Now and then a sharp buzz would indicate that another bug had bit the dust by flying into the special lights set up throughout the garden. Victor and Jane came out and joined them. For a while they sat quietly, each following their own thoughts. Ted reached over and took one of Autumn's hands in his. She didn't pull away and Victor gave Jane a knowing look, seeing that she had also taken notice of it.

Their serenity was suddenly broken. "There you are! I have been looking everywhere for you." It was Laura. Since she addressed the whole table, nobody knew just exactly who it was she was looking for, so nobody answered. Finally Victor broke the silence: "Aren't you having a great time in there? We just came out to get some fresh air, you are welcome to join us."

"And miss out on the dancing? No way. How about me taking this young man and trying him out?" She already had her hand on Ted's arm, pulling on his sleeve. At first it seemed as if Ted was getting annoyed, but his expression changed and he rose, letting go of Autumn's hand. His voice was filled with laughter. "Let's see what damage we can do in there. You will excuse me, princess?" They were gone.

Victor mumbled under his breath: "I could strangle her." He had seen the disappointment in Autumn's face. But she already smiled again, thinking how outrageous her friend really was. A short while later Ted was back, looking flushed.

"That friend of yours is as wild as they come. She is your friend, right?"

"That she is. Here, take my drink, you look as if you could use it." Autumn pushed her glass in front of him and he emptied it in one long gulp. Then he looked at her and pleaded: "Please, don't let her take me away again." That sounded so pitiful coming from such a strong looking man, it was quite amusing.

Autumn Leaves

The evening was a great success, for almost everybody there, except Laura. Her heart was filled with envy and jealousy.

CHAPTER SIX

Three days later, dressed in her riding outfit, Autumn was skipping down the front steps when a car came to a screeching halt right in front of her. Someone jumped out, raced toward her and pressed a huge bouquet of flowers into her arms. The bright flashy smile belonged to no other than Ted Warnham, her dance partner from the other night.

"I needed to see you and tell you how much I enjoyed the evening at the Mulhair mansion. You made it special, Autumn von Schwarzenau, you really did."

"Why thank you, Ted, I had a great time too. You didn't need to buy such a big bouquet of flowers, but I love them just the same. I would ask you in, but as you can see, I was just going to the stables to go riding."

"Let me walk with you, at least I can talk to you for a few minutes." It was a short walk. When they arrived at the stables, Ruben was already waiting for her, holding Maharani by the reins. The horse moved its head up and down upon hearing Autumn's voice. She made the introductions and when she asked if Ted would care to join her on her outing, Ruben's face clouded over. However, it brightened up the minute he heard Ted's reply.

Autumn Leaves

"Sorry princess, I really came to say good bye. I am leaving in a few hours to meet up with some friends in Salzburg. Day after tomorrow our plane goes back to the US." Taking her hand he pleaded: "May I write to you?" All Autumn could do was nod her head, her disappointment was too great, and she couldn't get the words out. Ted bent down and kissed her on the cheek, which again blessed him with a dark look from Ruben.

"See you again, I promise. Please write back to me, Autumn, will you?"

"I will." It was just a whisper. She quickly turned, pressed the flowers into Ruben's hands, mounted Maharani and rode off. Ruben had just enough time to jump back. If it hadn't been for Ted, holding on to him, he would have fallen down, which made him even more furious. Ted's eyes followed Autumn in admiration at what an excellent horsewoman she was. He never noticed the little fellows fury.

"She's a good horsewoman, isn't she?"

"The best." Ruben grumbled under his chin. Holding Autumn's flowers he turned and stomped into the stables, leaving Ted to admire the speckle of a rider disappearing in the distance.

Autumn let Rani find her own way up the small path to their favorite spot. Tears were rolling down her cheeks, she was more angry than hurt. Angry at herself for having dashed off like some little child, without saying a proper good bye to him. What would he think of her now? Laura was right, she was nothing but a spoiled girl, always wanting things to go her way. Ted couldn't help it if he had to go back home, she just wanted a little more time with him. Maybe he didn't even feel the way she did? That could explain him not coming to see her after the dance, but then, why did he come today and why the flowers? She shook her head and called herself to order. Her mind was going places that didn't even exist, how silly of her. Of course Ted cared about her, but it would have been nice if he could have met her parents, at least once, but that was clearly her fault, she could have invited him in, instead of dragging him to the stables. She was just so surprised to see him and clearly was not thinking straight. Oh well, he did say he was coming back and he also said that he would write to her. So everything was all right after all.

She noticed that Rani had come to a stop and couldn't believe her eyes, they had reached their favorite spot and she couldn't remember how they got there. "You're all right, I can always depend on you." She reached inside her pocket, "here girl, you deserve it," she bend low over Rani's neck, her hand holding two sugar cubes. "Wow, not my whole hand." Then she slid off the horse, tossed the reins across Rani's back and let herself sink into a patch of green moss. The view from this point was something she shared with no other person, it was her private place, where she could sit for hours and just let her thoughts run free. It was a spectacular view, one could see forever and ever. Mountain peak after mountain peak, some glittering like silver as the sun illuminated their snowy peaks.

Of course Rani shared this spot with her, but that was different. A long time ago somebody brought her here, it was his secret place then and he said, that she was the only person he would ever share it with. It was Peter, son of their ranger Marshall. They had been children then and he was long gone. Now it was her place and she loved it. Funny, how did Peter get into her thoughts when it was Ted she was thinking about?

The sound of church bells penetrated the quiet. Did they echo back from the mountains? It sounded like it and without conscious thought, her hands folded in prayer. The bells, the mountains, the lake, the village, this was her home, it was where she belonged, where she was happy.

"Time to go back, girl." With one fluid motion she swung herself on the back of her mare and they started their slow descent down the dangerous mountain path. Maharani was very sure-footed and Autumn knew that she could depend on her to get back safe and sound, without much guidance. Not so when the path was wet and slippery, then it took all the finesse of horse and rider to conquer this stretch of the mountain.

"Did we see you going to the stables with a young man at your side?" It was her father asking the question, as soon as she entered the hall. "Do we know him and where did he go?"

"Daddy, hello and yes thank you, I had a very nice ride. As to your onslaught of questions, number one - yes you did, number two - no you don't, number three - he went back home. Happy now?" When she saw her father's wrinkled forehead, she knew that this was not satisfactory at all. So she tried again.

" Daddy, that young man was the one from the dance at Victor's house. Remember, I told you and momi about him. He just came by to let me know that he was leaving, going back home to the States. Oh gosh, the flowers, I left them at the stables. Be right back!"

She was gone, running down the steps toward the stables. Prince Rudolf just shook his head, Autumn was certainly wound up these days. He didn't even get a chance to tell her that Laura called or that they needed to talk to her. Shaking his head he went back into the parlor. Marianne looked up at him with a questioning look: " She'll be right back," he assured her, " something about some flowers at the stables. By the way, you were right, that young man earlier was the one from the dance. How did you know that?"

"Oh Rudolf, who else could it have been? Autumn doesn't know any young men who would come visit her, and Victor certainly gave a detailed description of him, did he not?" Walking toward him she laid her hand on his chest. "Do I detect a note of jealousy here?" He swiftly kissed those smiling lips. "Not jealousy, just fatherly concern."

With his head held high he strode toward the built in bar and poured himself a stiff drink. He was not ready for men to enter into his daughters life, regardless of what his sweet wife was thinking. Somehow he did not like that smile on her face, the situation was too serious, in his opinion any way.

Marianne could just imagine what went through her husband's mind, he probably had his daughter already engaged to be married. Some times men were so silly.

Their thoughts were interrupted when Autumn waltzed into the parlor, her arms holding a huge bouquet of flowers. "Where do we put them," she asked and placed them lovingly on one of the chairs.

"Looks like they need some water in a hurry."

Marianne picked up a few of the dahlias and called for John. Without fail, he walked in with a large vase already filled with water. How did he do that?

"Will this vase be suitable?"

"Just fine John, please put it here on the table and if you could find a saucer to set it in...."

"Will this do, your Highness?" He pulled a saucer out of his coat pocket and placed it under the vase. "Will there be anything else?"

The man was a jewel, that's all there was to it. He never failed to amaze them, they could not envision their home without him. Rudolf and his wife both remembered the tears in his eyes when they brought their new little daughter home from the hospital. He has watched over her ever since and he had obviously seen her approaching, her arms loaded down with the flowers.

"Ted overdid it just a little bit, don't you think?" She was looking at her father.

"A little bit? Young lady, I think ......"

"Me to, I think they are absolutely lovely," interrupted her mother, " too bad he had to go back so quickly, we could have had a nice cookout over the weekend. Well, we'll still do that, Victor and Jane are coming over and if you want to, you can invite Laura also. We have something to tell you Darling

Autumn Leaves

and I hope you will not be too disappointed." She looked towards her husband for help.

"Disappointed, why would I be disappointed? What is it? Come on, tell me."

Her father stepped forward, put his arm around her mom's shoulder and said, with a seriousness she had not seen in a long time: "We have decided what to do on our vacation. No, hold on a moment. This time, Autumn, we are going alone, just your mother and myself. There is a reason for it, so please just hear me out, OK?"

The disappointment was written all over Autumn's face, regardless how hard she tried not to show it, but her father went on.

"Vacations have always been special to us and up to now, we had the greatest times together. Well, your mom has a wish, and since our twenty- fifth Anniversary is coming up, I thought I should grant her that wish. We are going to the mountains, skiing, and we are planning to go the latter part of November."

He had stopped talking. All eyes were on Autumn, waiting to hear what she had to say. Seconds seemed like minutes before she could utter a sound. "That's great, that's really great. You took me by surprise, for a minute I thought you were going to tell me something bad, but this is really great, for both of you, yea, really great."

She turned and ran upstairs to her room. She flung herself across the bed and let her tears fall unchecked. Why? She really didn't know. It was not because she was disappointed, a little bit, sure, but there was something else nagging on her and she could not put her finger on it.

She heard a knock on the door and her mother's voice: "I'd like to talk to you Autumn, please?"

"Sure momi, the door is open." She quickly wiped over her eyes, sat up and turned to face her mother, who was standing in the doorway with a worried look.

"It's not that we don't want you with us, Darling, we'd love to take you, only " and here she hesitated, a pink flush slowly coloring her cheeks, "well, we thought of making it something like a second honeymoon."

Oh, her mom was adorable. Autumn jumped up and hugged her as tight as she could: "I love you, momi. Of course it's all right with me. After all, I'm almost eighteen years old. A girl my age doesn't want to hang on her parents shoestrings all the time, don't you know?"

"Well, I just thought I'll let you know why the change in plans. You are really all right with this?"

"Yes, I am really all right with it. Momi, November is not here yet." After a slight pause, " I'll be down in a little bit."

Marianne started to leave, at the door she turned and said: "Autumn, your father wanted me to tell you to call Laura, she rang while you were out riding. See you downstairs, I love you."

After her mother closed the door, Autumn sat on the edge of her bed, reaching for the phone to call Laura. Something made her stop, she could not shake this feeling of uneasiness. Putting up with Laura's chatter was the last thing she wanted right now. First, Ted was leaving, now her parents planned to go on a second honeymoon. Instead of their usual vacation together, they wanted to go alone, what next? The shrill sound of the phone ringing brought her back to reality. It took a while before she reached for the receiver.

"Hello? Hello?" There was nobody on the line. Then she heard her father call from downstairs. "Coming daddy!"

"Autumn, something happened to Maharani. Ruben just called, let's go down there."

They didn't walk, they ran toward the stables and met Ruben half way. His face was twisted in agony. "It's Maharani, she went lame. I think there is something very wrong with her right hind leg. I already called the Vet," he was shouting out the words, turned and ran back inside the stable, Rudolf and Autumn right at his heels.

Autumn Leaves

"Rani," Autumn hugged the neck of her horse while it slowly sank down and lay on the straw. "What's wrong with you, girl, a little while ago you were just fine? Daddy, help her, please." Autumn buried her face in Maharani's neck, wetting it with her hot tears. The horse didn't seem to mind, it just lay there, motionless.

"Ruben, she was fine when we returned, what happened?"

"I don't know, I noticed a slight limp as you rode in, but didn't think much of it at the time."

"You're wrong, I know she was fine," her voice had taken on a high pitch. Looking at her father, her voice pleading: "Daddy, I know she was fine."

Ruben wanted to say something, but thought better of it. After all, she was just a girl and the Prince knew that he was experienced with horses. Prince Rudolf would not pay much attention to a hysterical female, daughter or otherwise. Ruben was wrong.

A car was approaching. They heard the door slam shut and heavy footsteps walking towards them. Thank God, it was Dr. Niemann, the Vet.

"What have we here?"

"It's Rani, it's her hind leg, please help her?"

"If you will let me get to her, I certainly will."

Autumn got up, but not without placing a soft kiss on Rani's neck. "You'll be fine, girl, the doctor is here." She stood beside her father as Dr. Niemann lifted the horses hind leg. They could hear a grunt coming from him and saw him shaking his head.

"It would be best if the young lady were to leave us alone for a while." His words were directed at Autumn, but she just shook her head.

"I want to know what's wrong, I'm not going any where."

"Autumn," again, that stern voice of her father, the second time today, "do as the doctor suggests, please. I'm sure you can come back when he is finished, but for now, let him help Maharani."

"All right daddy, but call me as soon as it's over." She stood on her toes, kissed her father's cheek and ran out of the stables, not once looking at Ruben.

While Autumn ran to her mother to tell her about the horse, Dr. Niemann told Rudolf that the horses leg was severely damaged. A nail had been driven deep into her foot, damaging vital nerves and tendon, it would never be fit for any racing again. The question was, how did it get there? Dr. Niemann was certain that this could not have occurred while the princess was riding, she would have known immediately when it happened. No horse can sustain such a huge nail driven into the foot without excruciating pain involved, no, it happened after the outing. For now, he kept his mouth shut. His first priority was to help the animal and for that he needed some assistance. Ruben was only to willing to help out, after all, he loved the horse almost as much as Autumn did, at least that's what everybody thought. Maharani had to be sedated for the ordeal.

It would be some time before she would be able to carry her mistress back up the mountain.

CHAPTER SEVEN

Prince Rudolf had a long conversation with Dr. Niemann. Both men agreed that Autumn would have been aware if there had been a problem with the horse. She was too careful with the animal to let something as severe as this go by unnoticed. Between the time she dismounted and the call came from Ruben, about three-quarters of an hour had elapsed. But wait, Autumn had gone back to the stables to retrieve her flowers during that time. Why had Ruben not mentioned the problem then? There were definitely some questions that needed to be answered. For now, his main concern would be for his daughter.

Anxious eyes awaited his report. That it was not good was written all over his face. Both women remained silent, allowing him to find the right words.

"Maharani will be all right, eventually. Her leg is damaged, so she won't be a champion runner or jumper any more, but then she never was."

"Daddy, will she walk again, like before?"

"We hope so, Goldilocks." She hadn't heard him call her that since she was little, somehow it made her feel sad. She felt that there was more to the story, his eyes told her so.

Should she probe deeper and find out? Maybe not just yet, later she would want to know more about it.

"Daddy, can I go back to the stables?"

"Sure. Ruben is going to look after Rani, he can tell you a little more of what instructions Doctor Niemann left about the care." He wasn't sure if Autumn had heard his last words, she was off and running before he could finish. With a deep sigh he let himself fall into the next chair, he was tired.

"What is it that you are not telling us?" There was deep concern in Marianne's voice. She did not like the way her husband sat in his chair, slouched down as if in defeat. It was not like him. She had never seen that look on him before.

"We don't know how the horse got hurt. It looks like it might have been done deliberately, but there is nothing to prove that. I don't like it, don't like it at all." Rudolf spoke more or less to himself, his words sounding monotone.

"But Darling, who would want to harm Maharani? There is only Ruben and we all know how he adores her. It must have been an accident, something laying on the floor in the stables perhaps?" She knew it sounded far-fetched, but what better explanation could there be? She did not know what Dr. Nieman had said.

It took weeks for Maharani to walk again. She had a limp, but she was up and around and Autumn was forever grateful to Ruben and Doctor Niemann. If it had not been for Ruben's unselfish love and devotion, her beloved horse would not be as well as it was. Autumn was so overjoyed, she gave Ruben a great big old hug and he hugged her back, a little bit too tight perhaps.

Rudolf's suspicions slowly waned, especially since Autumn was full of praise about their jockey, for taking such excellent care of Maharani. Anyway, he had other things to think about, like a second honeymoon, which was right around the corner.

Autumn Leaves

Autumn never told anyone about that phone call with Laura, the day her horse got hurt. At the time, she didn't think anything about it, but later on, her mind started to probe into the words.

"You must be one busy lady, I've been waiting for your call for ages. How is everything going, is everybody all right and did you have a nice ride? I'm sure Maharani carried you on wings through the mountains."

She had ended the call with a shrill laugh, amused at her own wittiness. Later, when Autumn told her that the horse was sick, Laura seemed genuinely concerned and offered her help. She even offered to sit with the horse during the night, but of course Ruben would not hear of it. He even seemed to get mad at that suggestion. How strange.

Laura had never shown much love for Maharani, so why all the concern now? If she remembered correctly, the day the horse was delivered, Laura acted almost hostile toward her. There were times when her best friend was very hard to figure out.

Then there was Victor, he got furious when he heard about the accident and was ready to start a full investigation into the matter. Good old Victor, he was always ready to protect. It took her dad some powerful persuading to calm him down.

Well, Victor was a little bit down on himself lately for allowing Jane to go back to London and try a case, specially with that friend of hers as her partner, or was it the other way around? There was no telling how long she would be gone. Some of those criminal cases could go on for weeks, even months some time. But surely she would be here for Christmas?

Victor missed the morning rides in the park with Autumn on his side. She could not bring herself to ride any other horse, out of love for Rani. Well, he could understand that. In the meantime he knew that she checked on Rani's well being every day.

A bright spot in Autumn's days were the letters from Ted. She had gotten several of them.. They were always a boost for her morale, like the one she was holding in her hand right now. He was talking about the latest swimming competition and winning another trophy to place on his mantle and how it was she who had won it for him, because he was thinking off her when his strength was almost gone and it boosted him up. But the words - I miss you - were the dearest of them all.

Laura was jealous about Ted and Autumn knew that. Nobody had offered to write to her or send flowers. Autumn thought that Laura was perhaps worried about their friendship coming to an end if there was a man in her life. That was such nonsense. So what, if her heart was beating faster when a letter from him arrived?

It was a beautiful sunny day. She was sitting on the bench in the rose garden. Maharani was nearby, grazing in the big patch of dark green lawn. The garden was located close to the fence that separated the park from the nursery, where Laura lived. It was quiet here. The sun was high and it was unseasonable warm for this time of the year. It didn't feel like winter would be knocking on the doorsteps soon, especially not in this spot, with roses blooming all around her. How did their gardener do it? It really didn't matter, it was nice and she loved it. Those miniature peach colored roses were her mom's favorite. She knew her mother sat on this bench almost every day, but not today, she was out shopping for some sexy clothes to take on her honeymoon. Not that she needed it, everything her mother had was sexy, heck, her mom was sexy naturally. She wanted to be just like her when she grew up, beautiful and sexy, and smart, we mustn't forget that.

"A penny for your thoughts."

"Victor, what are you doing here?"

"Just stopped by to see if all was going well. I see Rani is having a good time, have you been able to ride her yet?"

Autumn Leaves

"No, not yet, but very soon. Doctor Niemann said that I should try in another week, just to see how she can handle it. I miss riding and going to our favorite place, but Rani is more important than that. Have you heard anything from Jane?"

"She called yesterday. The case is not going very well, she doesn't know how long she has to stay over. I think she will try to be here for Christmas."

"Try, come on now. Surely she wouldn't leave her handsome husband all by himself, not on Christmas?"

"Thank you for the handsome, we'll see how things are then." That didn't sound very encouraging, but Autumn didn't want to pry into his affairs.

"Victor, I miss riding with you in the mornings." She saw his eyes light up at those words. He grabbed her hands and she could feel that he was about to say something very important.

"Autumn, listen, remember that gray stallion I have? How would you like to ride it while yours is recuperating?"

"You would let me? It would be wonderful, but when?"

"Tomorrow, if you like. Tell you what, why don't I pick you up, let's say around two, we go riding, so you can get used to him and then I'll bring you back? What do you say, princess?"

"I say that sounds great. I don't think I have other plans for tomorrow, but I'll check and let you know later. Thank you Victor." She threw her arms around his neck and kissed him. It was supposed to be on his cheek, but he turned his head and her lips pressed smack on his. "You can do that any time, little one." His voice took on a raspy tone and the spying eyes behind the fence saw and heard every word.

After she dropped Rani off at the stables, she leisurely walked back to the house. Just as she entered the foyer, the phone began to ring. Since nobody seemed to be answering, she picked up the receiver. "Hello?"

Anita Attwood

"Autumn, is that you? Well of course it is. Listen girlfriend, since the weather is so great, why don't we do something tomorrow afternoon. We could go to the village, there is always something going on or do you have a better idea?"

"Oh, hi Laura, I'd love to go with you to the village, but not tomorrow. Maybe the next day, that would be fine with me."

"But not with me, I have to help my mother the whole day. If you don't want to see me, why don't you just come out and say so. Or do you have something better already planed?" Autumn bit down on her lower lip, something she did at times of awkward situations, trying to think of what to say.

"Autumn, you still there?"

"Yes Laura, OK, we'll go tomorrow. I just.... never mind. Let's meet early so we won't be back too late. I'll call you after I've spoken to my parents. Bye Laura."

There was no time for a reply, Autumn had already hung up. It didn't matter, she had won this round. So our princess was trying to have it all. Well, it won't work, as long as she had anything to say about it, and she had plenty to say. Boy, Victor sure was a sly character, his wife's only been gone for a short while and he was already on the prowl. The problem was, he was looking in the wrong direction. She was more than willing to fill his lonely hours, and he could bet his last penny that she would find a way to console him. That really shouldn't be so hard. It was beyond her comprehension what a man like him saw in a wallflower like Autumn. He must be blind as a bat if he couldn't see that his precious princess had a lot of growing up to do. She, Laura, knew how to please a man, and she had known about it for quite a while. Nobody knew her secret and if her mother were to find out, it would be curtains for her friendship with the Schwarzenau family. Gosh, they were all so naive. She smiled that fiendish smile of hers, well satisfied with today's developments.

Autumn Leaves

If she thought Autumn was having a tough time trying to straighten out tomorrow's events, she was right. Autumn was totally frustrated, with herself, with Laura, with the world. Why in Gods name couldn't she put her foot down with Laura, why did she always give in, like some frightened little girl. What she really wanted to do was to go riding with Victor, not traipse through the village with Laura. Well, might as well get it over with. She picked up the phone, reluctantly. It rang, once, twice.... good, he wasn't there.

"Hello?"

"Oh, you're there."

"Autumn? Of course I'm here. So they said it's OK with tomorrow?"

"Yes, well no, I mean it's OK with them, but something came up, so I have to cancel. Maybe the day after?"

"That's too bad, little one, I was looking forward to it. Must be mighty important that you're willing to give up riding. Thanks for calling me back and again, I am really sorry you have to miss out on our outing. I'll give you a ring when I can arrange it again, day after tomorrow is not a good day for me, sorry." Then he added: "Autumn, don't worry about it, we'll just do it some other time."

He had heard that deep sigh on the other end and he was wondering what was so important, that she would give up riding, knowing how much she loved to sit on a horse and run like the wind. She obviously didn't want to talk about it.

Autumn, in the meantime, was more upset than ever. This conversation did not go like she had planned. Now Victor thought that she was making some lame excuse. He was most likely thinking that she was upset about that kiss in the park, but it was just an accident, it meant nothing, really. She didn't want to tell Victor that the change was because of Laura, because she knew that he was not very fond of her.

This was one of those times when she would really like to use some of those choice words Laura used so freely, but she was trying not to incorporate them into her vocabulary. Laura did not make things very easy, at this moment she wanted to wring her neck, if not worse.

Autumn was right, Victor thought about her excuse and came to the conclusion that no important matter had come up, other than the fact, that she probably was too embarrassed about the incident earlier. He was such a fool for not setting it right immediately, but come to think of it, it was kind of nice. His smile confirmed it.

The next day, Autumn was on her way to the village, alone. Laura had called earlier, leaving a message with John that she had to run an errand for her mother, so they would just meet in front of the bakery at around one o'clock. That was dumb, she could have gone with her and do something else while Laura took care of whatever it was she had to do. The walk to the village was pleasant and invigorating. She hardly ever got to go for a walk, it was either ride in the car or on the horse, so this was good. The few people she met on the road said a friendly "how do you do" and went on their merry way. Everybody was busy getting ready for Sunday. It was a custom around here, that on Saturdays, all chores had to be completed by three o'clock, when the church bells would begin to ring, bringing in the Sunday. Of course there were some exceptions, especially during harvest season, then the farmers even worked on Sundays when the weather threatened their crop, but mostly folks strove to fulfill this tradition.

She had reached the outskirts of the village and the smell of freshly baked bread and cakes almost made her hungry. That was one of the things she loved about this town, the mouthwatering aromas. A quick glance at her watch told her, that there would be less than two hours to look around, because the shops were closing early too. Before she knew it, she had reached the market place. Laura hadn't made it yet. She might as well sit down and enjoy the flowers and the sun. She sat on the edge of the water fountain, which was right

Autumn Leaves

smack in the middle of the market place, watching the hustle and bustle of last minute shoppers. The fountains steady flow of water had a soothing effect, it made her dreamy and her thoughts went to Ted and that there should be a letter coming from him very soon. This would also have been a perfect day to go riding, better not think about that. Laura was running late, the bell tower had just struck one thirty. I wonder what's holding her up?

What was holding her up, was Victor, or better her plans with Victor. Laura's little scheme was to get Autumn out of the way and pay a little visit to the man himself, knowing full and well that he would be there. When she drove up to his villa, she saw him out front playing with his dogs.

"What brings you here, miss Laura?"

"I'm looking for Autumn, I thought I might find her here?"

"You would have, but there was a change in plans, sorry." He continued playing with his dogs, turning his back to her. That was really not very nice. She jumped out of the car and slammed the door. The nerve of him, dismissing her just like that.

"You're still here?"

"You didn't hear my car drive off, or did you?"

"What got your temper flying this early in the day?"

"Well, Autumn and I were to meet today, then she called me to cancel and she also mentioned something about going riding with you, it got all so tangled up, I don't know what she said any more. That's why I'm here." Her look was innocent enough, except that there was nothing at all innocent about Laura, and Victor was well aware of it. His mind was working overtime, something was amiss, but what?

"Well, like I said, she's not here and I have some other things to do. Good to see you Laura and say hello to Autumn, when you see her."

"Not so fast, didn't you two plan on going riding? So why not make the same offer to me, I'm available!"

"I bet you are," he mumbled under his breath.

"What was that you said? Was it a yes?"

"Not hardly, I really don't have time to stand here and chat."

But he had not counted on Laura's persistence. She hadn't gone through all this trouble just to be blown off, no way. So, when he tried to walk away, she just grabbed him by his shirt and managed to pull part of it right out of his pants. He had no choice but to stop. Was he angry? You bet. His dark eyes were literally glowing. With a voice as cold as ice: "Young Lady, go play with someone else," he almost said someone your own age, but thought better of it.

"You are not very nice to me Victor. All I wanted was to keep you company, since you are all alone. What's wrong with that? Or am I the wrong lady?"

Victor knew of a million things he wanted to throw back at her, but he just ground his teeth and tried to ignore those wanton remarks. What in the world kept Autumn spellbound to this little witch? She was no good and probably capable of God knows what. He had long suspected her to be responsible for the many things that seem to happen to or around Autumn, but he had no proof. He had to find a way to open Autumn's eyes and see Laura for what she really was. Right now, however, he had to change his tactics with this bitch.

"OK, you win. Can you wait just a second while I run inside and get something?"

"Why sure, Mr. Victor!" That triumphant smile of hers almost made him haul out and slap her face.

Inside, he dialed the number to the Schwarzenau chateau. John answered, as usual. "John, Victor here, may I speak with the princess?"

"Sorry Sir, she had to go to the village."

"Do you know if she went there to meet someone?"

Autumn Leaves

"Sir?"

"John, I apologize, I am not being nosy, it's just that we were to go riding and..."

"That's quite all right, Mr. Victor. I just happen to know that she is meeting with miss Laura, since the former called early this morning and left that message with me."

"Thank you John, you are an angel, and please give my regards to Prince Rudolf and his wife, when you tell them about this call." John smiled, Mr. Victor knew the procedures of this household well.

Victor also had a smile on his face when he approached Laura. That little conniving bitch would not get away with this one so easy.

"So you came over here to keep me company?"

"Why yes, I did."

"Nothing better to do, well, we can certainly do something about that."

She didn't quite like the way he said that, nor did she like that smile of his.

"Come on Laura, let's go to the stables and pick a horse for you, or whatever. My stable hand is there to help us with whatever we need, or you may need. My help is very discreet, so don't worry."

What was wrong with him? She had never seen this look on his face or that tone of voice, it was almost scary. Maybe she had made a mistake? Too late now.

"Do you like the smell of fresh hay?"

That did it, she had to get away from here. She slapped her hand to her forehead: "How silly of me, I forgot I had an appointment. Victor, I have to run, I'm almost too late already."

"Not almost, you are too late."

"What do you mean by that?"

"I talked to John, your actions stink Laura. I suggest you tread lightly in the future, there are a lot of eyes watching you."

"Ha, I'm not the only one that is being watched, Victor. I saw what went on in the rose garden yesterday, very pretty, I must say. What do you think His Highness has to say about that little episode?"

Victor's hands balled into fists. His first instinct was to let her have it, but his mind stayed alert.

"You are welcome to say anything you please, provided you can tell the truth. I'll be happy to accompany you to the chateau, so we both can tell our stories. How about it Laura? We do have an awful lot to tell, don't we? Perhaps Autumn will be back from the village and she can contribute some of her tales as well."

Laura's head went up high, so high she almost tripped over her own feet as she was walking toward her little car. "You are ...." she never finished her sentence. Her car roared out of the driveway.

Victor stood as if rooted to the ground for a long time, his gaze following the cloud of dust Laura's car left behind. He felt a sense of foreboding.

Autumn Leaves

CHAPTER EIGHT

Time had a way of slipping by. Autumn could not believe that winter was already showing it's icy breath. Her relationship with Laura had cooled considerably since the village incident. To top it off, when she told her about her parents upcoming trip, Laura was so elated, that one could have thought she herself was going on a vacation. It didn't matter that Autumn would miss her parents, Laura could not relate to feelings like that. Victor had warned her to be a little bit more careful around Laura, but he did not go into any explanation. To be honest, she really missed sharing things with her best friend. She felt as if she had lost something of value. She did not like feeling suspicious about Laura, even if she did get the best of her at times. Well, actually that was happening quite a lot lately. Laura was changing.

Maharani was doing well. She had begun riding her, but since the slopes were a bit icy she was afraid to take the horse up to her favorite spot. She missed it; it had been such a long time since she last looked out over the horizon. It would be so good to just sit up there and think, something she felt a real need for. But Rani had a permanent limp, no sense in putting the horse into unnecessary danger. The outings around the park and surrounding countryside were just as much fun. Well, maybe not as much, but good enough for the time being.

Ted had stopped writing. At first it hurt quite a bit, but she had gotten over it, more or less. Relationships with such vast distances between them are bound to wither away, at least that's what she told herself. She looked out the window; all the trees were bare, except the pines of course. As much as she missed the beautiful fall colors, the frosty branches had a beauty of their own. When the sunshine illuminated them, they glistened like crystal. Her mother called it 'sparkling diamonds'.

She had known for some time that her mom needed to get away for some rest. Now, that the time had come for them to leave, the feeling of loss seemed to overwhelm her. How silly, they were only going on a well-deserved vacation. To top it off, it was their twenty- fifth anniversary, they deserved that special time all to themselves. Still, up to this point, it had always been the three of them. Guess it was OK to feel just a little bit left out. She really was happy for them, there was no doubt about that. Momi had been looking a bit pale lately. Some fresh mountain air up in snow country was probably just what the doctor ordered.

What about that frame holding a red and golden colored leaf? Her dad gave it to her on her 18th birthday and she could have sworn that his voice was shaky when he said: "Hold this in high regard. When you look at it, think of the color of the sun going down behind the mountains, bright orange red. It means a lot to your mother and me, it's were your name came from. When you were born, it tumbled from the sky and settled right on your head, an autumn leaf."

She did hold it in high regard, not even Laura knew about it. At her own request her eighteenth birthday was celebrated very quietly with only her parents and Victor present. For some unknown reason she felt the need to have them all to herself. It had been a lovely celebration. She could still see it, how graceful her parents were gliding across the parquet floor, like professionals, perfect in every way. After several dances they stopped, leaving the floor to Victor and her.

At the end of the evening she heard her father say to Victor 'Watch over her". It made her smile that her father should be so concerned, after all, she was eighteen and their vacation was only a short one. At that moment it dawned on her that they would always worry about her, regardless how old she was. Kind of nice.

She glanced down at the leaf in the frame and she could feel a special magic rise toward her. She could almost envision her mothers eyes looking at her.

It was time. They stood outside, tiny snowflakes dancing around their heads. Marianne clung to her daughter, kissing her on both cheeks, whispering an 'I love you' and climbed into the car, tears rolling down her face. Autumn tried hard not to break down. With a forced smile she shouted: "Up, up and away! Have a wonderful time and call me as soon as you get there, please?"

"Yes ma'am, anything else we can do for you?" Rudolf smiled at his beautiful daughter. As he held her close, there was just a little tug of sadness in his heart, but knowing the joy this trip would bring to his lovely wife, made all the sadness vanish. Their car pulled away, they did not see the tears streaming down their daughter's face, because their thoughts were already on the snowy slopes of the Maltese Mountain.

It was strange how empty the place seemed all over sudden. Most young people would be glad to have the run of the house for a while, so why did she not feel that way? Standing in the middle of the sitting room, Autumn felt confused about what to do next. Calling Laura was the first thing that came to her mind, but something within told her to hold off on that. Was it because she seemed to be so elated when hearing about her parents trip? Somehow her best friends reaction did not sit right with her, not then, not now. It almost made her mad. Perhaps she could go for a short ride in the park. She had to be alone for a while and think.

Maharani snorted and scratched the frozen ground with her front foot. It was her usual welcome for Autumn and it was always rewarded with a lump of sugar. Today, riding through the park seemed different somehow. Not because of the wintry scene, the snowcapped mountains, the glittering branches, no, that wasn't it at all, something was missing, and it was within herself. Out of the blue her thoughts went to her childhood friend, Peter. She had meant to ask her father about him. Perhaps he would have known something from ranger Marshall. Well, it could wait until her parents returned form their honeymoon. God, she missed them. A sudden impulse made her lean over Rani's neck and hug the horse tightly. "I love you Rani. I wouldn't know what to do if I ever lost you. As for our lost friend Peter, he is probably in Africa, taking care of wild animals. It was one of his dreams, you know."

She laughed at herself for having such outlandish thoughts, but they sure made the blues go away. The wind was blowing colder and she was sure that her nose was rosy red by now. When her fingers started getting numb, it was time to return to the stables. To sit in front of the fireplace seemed like a wonderful idea at this moment, and a short while later, she was doing just that. Laura would just have to wait a little longer.

While searching through the bookcase for a good read, she heard that familiar shuffle of footsteps. She knew at once that it had to be Mary.

"Didn't know where you'd disappeared to, missy. Here, I brought you some hot cocoa, it'll do you some good." With that she sat a steaming mug on the ledge of the fireplace.

Autumn Leaves

Before leaving, she placed her wrinkled hand on Autumn's hair and murmured: "I'll be around, if you need me."

After two days had gone by without hearing anything from Autumn, Victor decided that he had better make sure everything was all right. He had promised Rudolf, that he would look after her. Somehow he wished they had told Autumn about his true identity, it would make things a lot easier. He had only himself to blame, they were following his request, so did old Mary for that matter. Those were his thoughts as he walked up the wide steps of the chateau.

"Hello, Goldilocks, everything going all right?"

"That's what my daddy called me, a long time ago. You did too, as a matter of fact. Hi Victor, I'm glad you are here." She gave him a big hug, like she usually did, then suddenly dropped her arms and turned away, embarrassed. Something had changed, since that stupid kiss in the park, and Laura's innuendoes just made matters worse, for him anyway. His anger began to rise, but he kept it in check. The hell with her. It hurt a bit that there was a wedge between Autumn and himself, that should not be and he was going to remedy this once and for all. Her back turned to him, he realized how lonely she was. She missed her parents terribly, it was obvious. He made his voice sound as jovial as possible.

"So, how are our honeymooners doing, have you heard?"

"Oh yes, daddy called this morning. They are having a great time. The snow is just right and let me tell you something so funny, you know momi has not been on skies for some time, so when she went down the idiot hill, just for a practice run, she still landed on her behind. I can just see how embarrassed she must have been, landing on her you know what. It is so funny." Autumn just couldn't stop laughing. That was good.

"The funniest thing about it is, that momi is such a good skier!" Again she just laughed and laughed. "I wish I could have been there to see it."

Victor smiled, but somehow he could not join her in her laughter. Poor Marianne, how bad she must have felt, but how proud Rudolf must have been to see her strap on her skies.

"You are right, I wish we both could have been there. If nothing else, than to take some pictures of your mum and dad having fun on the slopes. Perhaps they took pictures anyway."

"They did, Victor, dad took a whole lot of film with him. I'm so glad you came by," and seeing his doubtful look, "really I am. What have you heard from Jane, is she almost finished?"

"I'm afraid not. Remember I told you that this thing could drag on? Well, it is. She's not too happy about it either. I'll better be getting on, I'm expecting a call from her in just a little while. I really only stopped by to see if you're all right, call me if you need anything."

"Thank you, I will. Give my love to Jane, when you talk to her, will you?"

When he left, there were no hugs this time, just a warm smile. Then the phone rang, it was Laura.

"Hello girlfriend, are you in hiding?" She sounded her usual self, the episode from the village was forgotten.

"Glad you called, I have been thinking about you. Why don't you come over for a while, if your mom doesn't need you, we can play catch up."

"Sounds great only today is a very busy day here. Perhaps tomorrow? Autumn, I'm glad you asked me to come over," she hung up. Well, that was a switch, Laura almost sounded demure, not at all her style.

Autumn had a restless night. The phone rang just as she finished up a light breakfast, it was Laura. Only twelve minutes had passed and Laura stood at the front door.

Autumn Leaves

"What did you do, fly over here?" The two friends laughed and hugged each other.

"Come into the sitting room, I think John put out some goodies." Laura followed, but remained strangely silent. Something was not right.

"Come on Laura, out with it, I can tell something is bothering you."

"I don't know how to begin, I just feel so bad about it. Remember when I was supposed to meet you in the village?"

"Laura, that's all over and done with. I am not mad at you, so let's just forget about it."

"I can't Autumn, I did a very deceitful thing and I am so ashamed of it. I was so jealous that you would rather spend time with Victor than with me, so I made up lies and ruined your whole day. Victor probably hates me, and I deserve it." Boy, she really looked down in the dumps. Just as predicted, Autumn swallowed it up line, hook and sinker. She never said what it was that she did, she didn't have too. Autumn was not one to question other peoples motives, it was enough for her to see that person admit their error.

"Come on, Laura, the day is too beautiful to wallow in self-pity, that was so long ago, I've already forgotten about it." In her mind she was wondering how Laura knew that she was supposed to go riding with Victor? Well, she didn't really say riding, but something didn't sound right. Better forget about it.

"You are a good friend, Autumn, I will not forget this. Let's do something wild, like skating on the pond."

"I think that is not such a good idea, the ice is not thick enough yet. Unless you don't mind taking an ice bath?"

"I do mind, you know how I am with cold water. Let's just go outside anyway, what do you say?"

When they stepped out the front door, the sun did not seem as bright any more. Gray clouds were moving in, making it seem colder than it already was. "Hmm, feels like snow is in the air," Autumn stated. Still, the day was full of fun and by the time they returned, shivering from head to toe, the first flurries just began to tumble down. It was turning rather gloomy outside, a definite sign of a snowstorm coming on. Laura went home before the mess got really started and Autumn settled down with a book near the fireplace.

The radio had been playing and suddenly: "This is a special weather bulletin from the National Weather Service. The heavy snowfall, that has been blanketing Zermatt and the surrounding region, has taken on dangerous proportions. Strong winds are responsible for dangerously high snowdrifts. All ski slopes are closed and roads are closed off to all travel. Those, who are still on the roads are advised to seek immediate shelter, extreme caution should be taken by all residing in those areas. We will keep you advised. Please stay tuned to this station for further updates..."

"Oh no, Victor, John ... anybody!" Autumn yelled as loud a she could. She ran towards the door and collided with Mary. Mary took the shaking girl into her arms and felt her shiver.

"Now missy Autumn, where is the fire?"

"Oh Maer, didn't you hear? There's a terrible storm where momi and daddy are and we haven't even heard from them today and they call every day, but today I haven't heard anything!" Autumn's words spilled out without taking a breath and her voice finally gave out.

"Now there, calm down and tell me again what got you so upset? Rattling on like an auctioneer, I couldn't make out a word you were saying. So, start from the beginning." But Autumn twisted out of her arms and ran towards Victor, who was just walking through the front door.

"Victor, Victor, did you hear the news? Did you hear from momi and daddy, please tell me.."

"Hold on princess, yes I have heard."

"There's a storm, a big one, right where they are and the weather station is warning everybody and they, and they,

Autumn Leaves

they don't know anything else." Once again she was looking at him for the answers, but he had little information.

He led her into the parlor and asked Mary to fetch some hot water.

"If you will let me talk, I'll tell you what I know so far. They are all right, they are at the ski lodge and perfectly safe. They are snowed in, but have all the comforts of home. The power lines are down, so they can not call us, nor can we call them. Let me call my answering service at home to see if there are any further updates." He listened intently, leaning back in a relaxed manner. When he hung up, Autumn was on him like a shot.

"Tell me, please tell me.."

"I have an update."

"What did they say?"

"It was not from them, it was from the hotel, but your parents are all right. They are still at the ski lodge, but communication has been established."

"Then we can talk to them."

"No, I didn't say that, but the hotel manager said that they send their love and they are sorry to worry you. As soon as power has been restored, they will be in touch."

"But Victor, the storm is just now getting there, how can the hotel manager give you all that information?"

"They know, because the local police got the information from the ski patrol. They made sure that every one got off the slopes before the storm hit. As I said, they'll be in touch as soon as the lines are repaired and, no Autumn, the storm started last night, it just now hit dangerous proportions, I mean, it just now got worse. What I'm trying to say, gosh you get me all jumbled up." He wiped his forehead. "What I'm trying to say is, that your parents are safe, until it lets up."

He threw a worried glance towards Mary, hoping that he had convinced Autumn enough to get a grip on herself. He was worried himself, but wouldn't dare let it show. Mary knew, she could read him like a book. He put his arm around

Autumn's small shoulders: "How about something hot to drink?"

"I'm so glad that you are here, I got so scared."

"I know Princess, I know."

They sat without saying anything, watching the flames dancing in the fireplace, each deeply absorbed in their own thoughts. He never got an answer to his question, both had forgotten about it . Suddenly Autumn shook herself as if a chill had run down her spine, it was not from being cold.

The voice from the radio startled both of them and they jumped up simultaneously.

"We interrupt this program to bring you the following flash bulletin. Zermatt radio just announced that an avalanche has been spotted. We repeat, an avalanche has been spotted. There is no further information as to the magnitude, only, that it is massive. It is believed that the ski lodge was in its direct path. As soon as information becomes available, we will bring you an update. Rescue teams have been dispatched. Please stay tuned to this station."

Autumn never heard the end of the broadcast, she lay motionless in Victor's arms, a blessed fainting spell had taken over. Mary pressed both hands against her quivering lips and moaned while Victor shook his head in total disbelief. This could not be happening, not to his brother and Marianne. They just had to be all right. Mary and Victor stared at the radio, willing it to speak, but the music kept on playing, there was no further update. Neither of them moved, they seemed to be rooted to the spot.

Autumn began to stir. For a moment she could not figure out where she was, and then it hit her. The storm, the avalanche, on the news....

"Victor!"

"I'm here princess."

"Is it true, was there an avalanche?"

"Yes, but we have not heard any update. Please try to stay calm, there is nothing we can do, but wait. Here, have a

Autumn Leaves

brandy, it will help, I promise." He handed her the glass that was already waiting for her.

"A brandy, Victor, I don't drink that stuff."

"Try it, a little sip won't hurt. Go ahead, just a little sip." Then Autumn saw Mary nodding her head and she put the glass to her lips. It smelled awful, but she lifted the glass and drank it down in one gulp. Her eyes got round like saucers and she was gasping for breath. Victor padded her on the back, grinning.

"A sip, Autumn, not the whole lot." He hit her harder and finally she stopped choking.

"There, that's better."

Autumn was shaking herself and shot a menacing glance in his direction. He didn't pay any attention to it, but he did notice the light flush creeping up her neck and into her cheeks. The soothing warmth, that suddenly engulfed her body, did feel rather good. Perhaps Victor was right after all. She settled back down into the crook of his arm, quite content.

"How long do we have to wait before we hear any more news?"

"That, I don't know, but I'm sure they will bring an update the minute they get more information. Why don't we turn on the TV, maybe we can pick up something new."

There was nothing new, hardly anything at all, to be correct. Autumn's hands were in constant motion and his heart went out to her. She was so young and so dependent on her parents, the fear in his heart for their safety was mounting. A long time ago he was involved in a rescue operation, when an avalanche had buried a whole mountain resort. It was not a pretty sight, there had been very few survivors. The crashing down snow had been packed too tight, creating an icy grave for most. Then there was always the chance of more snow crashing down. Hopefully this was not the case here. He changed the station to the weather channel. Just then the radio stopped the music.

"We interrupt our regular program to bring you the following update on the avalanche disaster here in Zermatt. Our reporters are at the Schoeneck Hotel where several of the guests are now missing and believed to be trapped in the ski lodge. Rescue teams are on the sight and reports indicate, that there is no structural damage to the lodge and no injuries have been reported. Communication has been established with those trapped inside, but rescue operations are slow due to the heavy snowfall and the ever-present danger of another avalanche. Please stay tuned to this station for further updates."

Autumn flung her arms around Victor's neck and hugged him so tight, that he was unable to breathe. As much as he loved being hugged, but dying of suffocation was not on his agenda just now.

"They're all right Victor, they're all right. Did you hear, they're all right."

"I did and I am more than just happy."

Mary and John stood in the doorway, tears streaming down their faces. Autumn went to them and placed a hand on their shoulder. "They are all right," she said it quietly. It was like a thank you for their loyalty and their caring.

"We wouldn't know what to do if anything had happened to them. Thank you Lord." With that the two walked away, leaving Autumn and Victor behind in deep thought.

"Think you'll be all right for a while?"

"Where are you going? I thought you were staying here?"

"Let me just call Jane, she must have heard the news by now and ..."

"Why not ask her to come over here? We have lot's of room and I really don't want to be alone tonight. Please Victor." He looked at her in astonishment.

"Autumn, you know Jane is in London."

Autumn Leaves

"In London?" She seemed confused, but finally got a grip on herself.

"What's wrong with me, of course I know that. I guess I am more tired than I thought I was." 'Or more worried' Victor thought, but he did not say it out loud.

He had been right, Jane had heard a news flash about the disaster.

"I was terrified Jane. The disaster from years ago flashed through my mind and it was all I could do to stay calm. Thank God it turned out all right."

"I wish I could be there with you. I'm glad you are staying at the castle, that child does not need to be all by herself. Just knowing that you are near by will help her. I love you Darling."

Wow, she had not said that in a while. It made him feel good all over.

"I love you too, and hurry back, it's lousy without you. By the way, this here is a chateau, Darling, not a castle. Sleep tight, I'll call you in the morning."

"Better make it early, we have to be in court by eight, sweet dreams." His earlier good feeling suddenly plummeted, who was "we"?

Victor and Autumn shared a light evening meal. He knew she was glad to have him near. As soon as the meal was over she kissed him good night, she looked exhausted. There had not been any more news from Zermatt. Quiet set in over the chateau. It had stopped snowing and the soft moonlight spread it's silvery glow over the estate.

While chateau Schwarzenau lay in deep slumber, two people clung to each other in their icy grave. As their lips found each other in a never ending kiss, two loving hearts stopped beating.

Anita Attwood

CHAPTER NINE

The sun was already high in the sky when Autumn opened her eyes. It promised to be a brilliant day. She suddenly remembered last night's events and flew out of bed. Strange how quiet the halls were. Usually one could hear some activity, but this morning there was nothing but silence. She slipped into her robe and opened the door. Still, not a sound came from downstairs. She quickly went to brush her teeth, splash some water on her face and brush her hair. Then she rushed downstairs into the parlor and found it empty. Then she glanced toward the doublewide sliding glass door leading out onto the terrace and saw Victor standing there gazing at the mountains. She rushed toward him, expecting him to turn around, but he did not. She whispered his name, he still did not move. So she gently tugged on his sleeve. His hand reached over and covered hers, but his face remained averted and silent. His strange behavior began to frighten her.

"Victor, please say something?"

Finally he turned and his eyes held hers. The sadness on his face nearly took her breath away. Her heart began to pound so hard, she thought it would jump out of her chest. He just kept looking at her, and then she knew. She fell against

Autumn Leaves

his chest and he held her in a tight embrace. Tears were rolling down his cheeks while he was holding her trembling body, wracked by heartrending sobs. His right hand gently stroked her hair. He kissed the top of her head and whispered: "I'm so sorry, so very sorry."

She lifted her tear stained face, her eyes pleading with him to say it wasn't true. Then her lips formed the words: "Tell me Victor they're all right? Please?"

"I wish I could, with all my heart I wish I could and bring them back to us, alive, but Darling, I can't."

Her body suddenly went limp, she had lost consciousness. He scooped her up into his arms, carried her inside and gently placed her on the sofa. He knew that the tragic news would be more than she could handle. She loved them so very much. Looking down she suddenly seemed so small. He could not tear his eyes away from her and his heart was as heavy as a cement block knowing that she had to face the awful truth about the death of her parents. When he realized the magnitude of her loss it made him shudder. At this moment he did not consider his own pain. Even so Rudolf had been his only brother and the time with his sister in law, Marianne, had been so very brief, everything within him yearned to still the pain in their only child, Autumn. Where was the justice in this world?

It was his duty to make all the necessary arrangements for a proper funeral, befitting the Prince and Princess von Schwarzenau. He also had to see to it that the Estate would continue to run in its usual manner. Prince Victor was forced to slip back into the role he thought he would never have to play again. He surely never expected to have it thrust upon him with such devastating force. If he had any doubts about his ability to function as Lord of the manor, he did not show it. Of course the staff's efficiency took a lot of the pressure off his shoulders. For that he was indeed very grateful.

Autumn, however, remained his biggest concern. She had always been slender, but now she looked downright fragile. The doctor prescribed a mild sedative to help her get through the next few days, but it was his job to keep prying eyes away from her, especially Laura. Some day he would figure out the role that young lady played in Autumn's life, but this was not the time for it.

Autumn walked through the halls as if in a trance. She neither spoke nor cried, nor did she take much nourishment. She was like a ghost, wandering from room to room, up and down the wide staircase, with no particular destination in mind. Nobody dare spoke to her, the whole castle lay in an eerie hushed silence. The day the hearse arrived, bringing her parents back home, she stood silently at the top of the stairs to welcome them. Her long white gown resembled the color of her face, her bright blue eyes had gone dark and dull, holding no tears. Those who saw her were reminded of a beautiful white alabaster statue. Her hands were holding a red rose and a branch of colorful autumn leaves.

Rudolf and Marianne would be resting in the Royal Blue Room. This decision was made by Autumn. The heavy curtains were drawn and the only light came from two candelabras, standing on either side of the coffins. Prince Rudolf and his lovely wife rested side by side, just as they had been in life. The candlelight's soft glow illuminated their faces. It looked as if they were in a peaceful slumber, their faces showing such contentment. Autumn could not tear herself away from them. She would sit for hours on end, talking to them or reading poems. Most of the time she would just silently watch over them while in the background the music of Johann Strauss, Tchaikovsky, Wagner and other Greats quietly played on. This was the music her parents had loved dearly, light classical tunes. But when the song "Ave Maria" began to play she broke down sobbing. "Momi,

Autumn Leaves

daddy," she whispered over and over. It had been her mother's favorite song.

Prince Victor was very worried about her, wondering if she could hold out until the funeral? It was only with Mary's help that he was able to gently coax her out of the room and see to it that she took at least some nourishment before getting tucked into bed. Sleep usually claimed her quickly for Mary slipped some of the doctors potion into her tea.

Then the day of the funeral approached. Close friends of the family as well as dignitaries from nearby countries came by to pay their last respect to the beloved couple. Autumn held up remarkably well during their stay. Afterwards she collapsed in a heap of misery, totally sapped of all her strength. Victor, Mary and John were desperately waiting for all of this to be over. They knew that their young princess wouldn't last much longer. They all prayed God would hear them and show mercy.

Far away, in another part of the country, a young man sat at his mahogany desk staring at the morning paper. He shook his head in disbelief for the words printed there could not possibly be true. Prince Rudolf von Schwarzenau and his wife had lost their lives in the avalanche disaster in Switzerland. How would Autumn be able to deal with such tragedy? The paper slipped out of his hands and came to rest on his desk. Images of a little girl with blond Shirley Temple curls flashed through his mind. She was always bringing some injured creature to him, believing he could cure anything. He clearly saw those bright blue eyes beseeching him, they were unforgettable. Little princess Autumn had always come to him in time of need, but that was then. Who would she turn to now, the most tragic hour in her life?

The buzzer brought him back to reality. "Dr. Marshall, we are ready for morning rounds." It took him a moment to come to grips with himself. Before stepping through the heavily padded door his last thoughts were with Autumn, wondering if he should go see her.

He was there, the day of the funeral, but he stood in the background and his heart felt like it was being crushed by a vise. His eyes beheld the slim figure totally clad in black. It was Autumn. He wanted to reach out to comfort her, but an unseen force held him rooted to the ground. She was leaning on the arm of a tall man. He could not recall having seen him before. When the last words were spoken he turned to leave, convinced she would never know that he had been there. Autumn von Schwarzenau had grown into a beautiful young woman with such an enormous burden to bear. His tears were for the girl he once knew and loved, as only innocent children could. Their lives had always been worlds apart.

At Chateau Schwarzenau the days had rolled into one. Even so more than a week had gone by since the funeral, it seemed like it had been only yesterday that the royal couple was laid to rest.

Victor leaned over the banister of the verandah where his brother and sister in law had so often lingered. He rubbed his eyes for they seemed to have gone all blurry. Everything was shrouded in a haze, nothing appeared to be real. When he made that promise to Rudolf, to watch over Autumn in case anything should ever happen to them, he was so certain that it never would have to be acted upon. Why should it? Rudolf was in excellent health and young, and there was always a chance for a cure for Marianne's illness. The papers were constantly talking about new findings and greater success for remission in breast cancer, so there really was that chance. Both men denied the fact that in Marianne's case it had spread way too far to be stopped.

How they had managed to keep the illness a secret from Autumn, was still a puzzle to him. As far a he knew, she did not even know that her mother had been wearing a wig for the better part of the last year, or that she had to undergo the agony of chemotherapy. The last month or so they had stopped all treatment, the only thing Marianne kept on hand had been painkillers. There was so much Rudolf had never explained to him. Why there was no operation, why didn't they go and seek other help, why.... Well, it didn't matter any more.

Should he tell Autumn? That question gnawed on him night and day. Usually he could talk things like that over with Jane, but she had removed herself from him, as she put it. Removed herself, what a laugh, she had left him, plain and simple. That all-important case had been nothing but an excuse to be with her lover. He had to stop thinking about her; it made his blood boil. All that bull about 'I love you' right before the death of his brother, what had that been all about? Oh, forget it, right now his first priority was Autumn. She was his only priority. Damn that case, damn Paul, and damn London and double damn Jane! She didn't even have the courtesy to come to the funeral. In his book, that was totally inexcusable. As far as he was concerned, London could keep her for as long as it wanted too. And what about that gentleman standing near the road during the funeral ceremony? He seemed to be looking in their direction the whole time. Was he watching Autumn or was it just his imagination. The guy had been too far away for him to be able to tell what he focused on. Strange, he had vanished as mysteriously as he had appeared. Wonder who he was? ...

Then his thoughts went back to Jane. He knew from the very first minute he saw her with him at their party, that this guy spelled trouble. Boy, did he ever. Come to think of it, the way things had progressed so rapidly, it was probably not the first time those two had met of late. What a line of bull Jane had fed him that night, and he had swallowed it, hook, line and sinker. How blind can one man be? Blind my eye, it was stupidity, plain and simple. But this was all behind him now, he would concentrate on Autumn. After all, that was what he had promised Rudolf if ... Did Rudolf have a premonition?

How could he ever hope to fill his brother's shoes? The answer was, never, but he sure would try. Another question, would Autumn even accept his guidance? Perhaps the best thing would be to just remain her friend, her very best friend.

Well, that sure struck a sour note, she already had one of them. The problem was that Laura probably was anything but a friend, more likely her worst enemy. That girl was pure poison and he got this gut feeling of doom whenever he saw her near Autumn. The disgusting behavior at his party and that visit on his ranch later on, he still could not get over that. Also he could not dismiss the incident with Maharani, something had been very wrong there. Even in younger years that girl was always in the middle of things when something unpleasant happened. How on earth could he convince Autumn to be on her toes when it came to Laura? He had tried to warn her before, but without solid proof there was not much he could do. It drove him crazy.

This was one of those times when he felt utterly lost. His hands were wound so tightly around the banister that his knuckles had turned white. How long had he been standing there? Long enough for the sun to move from the middle of the verandah clear to the other side. A quiet cough behind him got his attention, it was John.

"May I bring you some refreshments, your Highness?" He was already holding a tray with coffee, orange juice, some of those little sandwiches and fruit. True to form, John was always one step ahead.

"Please John, it was always Victor before, can't we continue that? To your question, yes, I would like some refreshments. If you'd like to put it on the table over there, I do thank you."

"Certainly, your Highness .... Victor. Please ring if there will be anything else." John left, a little confused it seemed, but always the perfect butler. Dressed in his charcoal gray jacket, light gray pants, white shirt and bow tie, he looked just like one of those butlers one could see in old English movies. He had such quiet dignity about himself that respect toward him came easy. How did he keep himself so immaculate, could it be that Mary was behind it? There was a certain mystery about those two. Even so their conduct was without fault, they had been working together for an eternity, so anything was possible. They had been part of the family as far back as he could remember.

Victor suddenly realized how dry his throat was. The coffee was delicious, but when he looked at all those mouthwatering hors d'oeuvres, he just didn't feel like eating alone, so he rang for John.

"Would you ask the princess to join me?"

"Sorry sir, but the princess left some time ago."

"Left? But where would she go?"

"I don't know sir, she didn't say. I did see her carrying a tree."

"A tree, John? What on earth would she do with a tree?"

"Well, it was a Christmas tree." There was a long pause. "Sir, it was just a small one, but it was fully decorated."

Victor rose and pointed at the table: "Please take this away I'm finished, thank you John." His stride was hurried as he crossed through the parlor and out the front door. He didn't notice John's sad look at the untouched food trays.

Victor was not walking, he was almost running. He knew exactly where Autumn could be found, and he was right. He crossed the park and had the rose garden in sight, when he spotted her. There, beside her parents resting place, cowered a lonely figure in the snow. In the middle of the double grave stood a small Christmas tree covered with white lights shining like miniature stars, even in the light of day. It was a simple but oh so beautiful tree. Around the bottom lay a ring of colorful leaves, representing the magic of autumn. Where she got those, God only knew.

She could feel him standing there, but she did not look up.

"I miss them," was all she said. She did not cry.

"Do you think they will like my little tree?"

"It is beautiful and so is the blanket underneath."

"You really think so?"

"Without a doubt. How did you manage.." he didn't get any further.

""You mean the lights? Well, that is my secret. I can be very inventive if I want to, didn't you know that? I'm glad we don't wait until Christmas Eve to put our tree up, like some folks do. I must tell John to light the big tree. Don't you think it's funny how one day it is so dark and gloomy and then, like today, it feels just like spring?"

Victor listened to her talking, except it sounded more like rambling. She jumped from one thing to another and her eyes glittered strangely. He knew she kept herself under control on purpose, it was not a good sign, but he didn't know what to do about it. Some day it all would come crashing down on her. He did not realize that Autumn had enormous inner strength. Up to this point she was unaware of it herself, she only knew that something within urged her to go on.

"By the way, I've also made arrangements to have our Christmas coin changed."

"Changed? Changed to what?"

She simply said, "My parents picture will be on it this Christmas." Victor did not know what to say. Autumn had changed dramatically; she suddenly was a young woman who seemed to have grown up over night. It was exactly fourteen days since the funeral.

But he was only partially right in his assumption that Autumn had matured so miraculously. Maybe she appeared very grown up, but inside she was still that frightened little girl that had been seeking refuge in his arms that dark day of the funeral. She had to will herself into getting back to a daily routine. It was hard, very hard indeed. It would have been so much easier to let oneself go, but she could not do that, during the day anyhow. The nights were a different story, they belonged to her grief and sorrow, but the days would show her a strong young woman trying to take over the run of the house just as her mother had done before her. The pain of losing her parents was hers, and hers alone to bear. There would be nobody allowed to intrude or trespass, nobody.

Autumn von Schwarzenau had indeed grown up, in that, Victor was right.

Laura was also puzzled by Autumn's strange behavior. She had not been able to really make contact since that horrible day. A short phone conversation here and there, that was all, but they had been of no significance. Sure she was concerned about her friend, but even more about the break in their relationship. This was not acceptable. She was proud to have such a prominent friend and the fact that she had unlimited access to that fine chateau, no way in hell was she going to give that up. Why, Autumn's parents had treated her as if she was one of the family, hadn't they?. Had it not been Prince Rudolf himself who had sought her out and brought her to his home?

If it had been up to her she would have been over there already but her mother insisted that she stay away and give Autumn some time to get over her loss. Maybe mom was right, it must be a terrible blow to lose both parents and without any warning. No, she wouldn't wish that on her worst enemy. Hopefully, this would not affect the gifts she usually got for Christmas, that would be a real bummer. She did feel bad for her friend, really she did. Autumn was such a softhearted creature, she probably cried every minute of the day. If she would only let her come over, she could help her a lot to get straightened out. Besides, she really did miss her. If she remembered correctly, they did have fun the last time they were together. Laura really began to worry.

So when her mother told her that Autumn had called and wanted to see her, she could literally feel a mountain fall off her chest. She lost no time getting over there and was surprised when Victor opened the door instead of John? He looked anything but friendly.

"What do you want here?"

"Hello Victor, nice to see you too. Sorry to inform you, but I am here by invitation of her Highness," and she mocked him with a curtsey. She still had no idea of his position having been kept away from the funeral.

Autumn stepped into the hall and was caught off guard, seeing Laura bow to Victor. She realized that this must be one of Laura's jokes and for the first time the hint of a smile was upon her face.

"My oh my, Laura, aren't we being formal. I'm so glad you came over." Laura smiled back at her. Her smile got even brighter when she noticed Victor's face looking downright sinister.

"Are you up to receiving any visitors," he grumbled, turning his back to Laura.

"Why yes, I asked Laura over because, well, never mind, I just wanted to see her," and in a softer tone: "Don't worry, it's really all right."

He was not so sure about that, but had no choice in the matter. So he excused himself and left. Laura's gaze followed him until he closed the door from the outside. "Not very friendly, our friend." Autumn did not respond, what could she have said, for once Laura was right. She also wondered if Laura knew about Victor's real identity, nobody really talked about it much. She herself was still trying to get used to the idea that he was related to her. She still loved him, only now there was a bit of a guilty feeling attached to it, and she could not shake it. Was it that kiss from long ago, in the rose garden? Laura's voice brought her back to reality.

Autumn Leaves

"Autumn, I am really sorry about the way I acted, specially that day before your parents left on their vacation." Laura's voice was bareley audible when she added: " If I could, I would change everything."

"I know, thank you. Come on, we have so much to talk about." She took her friends hand and led her into the parlor. They just stood there, not knowing how to go on from here. Laura looked around. "Nothing has changed."

"Why should anything change?"

"Oh, no reason, I was just talking." Another awkward silence, neither knew how to start. Autumn breathed a sigh of relief when John walked in to see if anything was needed. Both said "no" at the same time and the spell was broken.

They spent a few very pleasant hours together. Not one word was spoken that was out of line, catty or otherwise. It was the way two good friends should be with each other. It was also a wonderful healing experience for Autumn having her best friend show so much compassion and love. She almost felt bad having had all those doubts in the past, Laura was a caring person after all. When they parted there were hugs and promises to see each other again very soon.

Laura was well satisfied with the outcome of her visit. Autumn was feeling much better towards her and that was the most important thing at the moment. She did like Autumn a whole lot, she just didn't like Autumn's station in life. They should switch places, she, Laura, would fit so much better in the role of a princess. Well, one must make the best of a bad situation. Her feet had carried her down to the stables. Ruben was just coming out of the barn and she waved at him frantically. He did not notice her. His head was slunk down but jerked up immediately when she hollered at him.

"Long time no see, young man."

"True cousin, what brings you here?"

"I just left Autumn, she seems to have herself under control. I'm surprised because she's always been so wimpy, now suddenly she acts all different, sort of tough, if you know what I mean. Don't get me wrong, I'm glad she is handling things so well, I just didn't expect it. I was ready to console her."

Ruben couldn't help it, he laughed out loud. What had she said that was so funny? The audacity of him, laughing at her. Here she was letting him know just how sad she was for her best friend and he had nothing better to do but to laugh. That boy needed some help. She was very serious about her feelings, something he was obviously lacking. To think, that at one time she thought him in love with Autumn, what a bunch of bull that had been.

Ruben on the other hand was not fooled by Laura's act. Had it not been his sweet little cousin who constantly thought up new ways to make Autumn's life miserable? Here she came strolling along only two weeks after the funeral, and God only knows what mishap she was already planning again. But he was not ready to do any more harm, to anybody. The royal family had always treated him fairly and he had enough guilt feelings as it was, so enough is enough! Besides, Autumn needed protection. She was all alone now and as for him, he would do his part to make things easier for her.

"Aren't we thinking deep thoughts this afternoon?"

"Oh Laura, just leave me be. I'm in no mood for your idle chatter today."

"What's wrong with you? I only stopped by to make sure you're doing all right, you don't have to bite my head off. I know you feel bad about Autumn's parents getting killed, but so do I. As far as I'm concerned, you can laugh all you want, or make stupid faces, I really don't give a damn. What's up with you anyhow? You're not going loco on me, are you?" She was beginning to feel rather uneasy.

"Nah, I just feel bad about the whole situation". He was still shaking his head when he said: "By the way, Laura, do you remember that guy from Pr...I mean Victor's party, that American? He didn't even send a card or call her. I think he had stopped writing some time ago. That tells you how flighty those guys from over there are. She's better off with someone solid, someone who knows how to take care of a lady."

Ruben knew that he was talking too much. Damn, that's just what he didn't want to do in front of Laura. He realized by looking at her that he had messed up again. Now he had given her new ammunition against him, shit, that's all he needed.

"Tell me, my darling cousin, how do you know all that? Did your princess come and cry on your shoulder? Aren't we the protective kind, my oh my, little Ruben is carrying his heart on his sleeve. You're in love with her after all!"

At this moment, he wanted to wipe that vicious smirk off her face, permanently. He hated her more than ever before.

"Think what you like, just leave me alone and get the hell out of here. I have work to do and it does not include standing here listening to your stupid mouth."

"Wow, aren't we verbal today. Ruben darling, I am seriously worried about your state of mind." When he made a fast step in her direction, she threw up her hands: "I'm gone, don't worry, call me if you need to talk or anything else. Mother is sending her greetings. Bye couz." She left, her head held high, whistling a tune. What an infuriating woman she was.

Infuriating to most people, not to all. Harold, the gardener, was totally under her spell. To think that this gorgeous woman was his, made his head spin. Boy, did she have some moves in the sack, and her appetite was endless. What made it even more alluring was the fact that they had to keep their love trysts a secret. They were not stupid, he was not willing to risk his job and she didn't want to give up that cozy relationship she had with the high and mighty up there in that massive stone mausoleum they called a chateau. Hell, he couldn't blame her for that. Must be nice to waltz in and out of that place as one pleased. Just one little thing bothered him a lot, that thing she had made him do with those letters? Well, at first he thought of it as a little thing, now he wasn't so sure any more. It was wrong, he knew that, but he had done it any way. He would do anything she asked of him. He just could not live without her any more and he was sure that he had fallen in love with her. She was young, she was wild, she was shrewd and she was the best lover he ever had. He was sure about his feelings but what about hers? She had never told him that she loved him, he must remedy that.

Then the awful thing happened and he thought his whole world would come crashing down. How could things just go on when the two most important people had just been erased from the face of this earth? In his way of thinking, it would mean a change in everything, but it didn't happen that way. His world just went on as before.

He praised the day when those letters finally had stopped coming. It had gotten to the point where his nerves were beginning to get the better of him. Especially that last one he intercepted, right after that horrible accident. He would always remember that because it came right the day before the funeral. Boy, that was a tough one to catch, it had been send by special delivery and he had to use all of his power of persuasion to get a hold of that one. He must've been very convincing, otherwise the postman would not have relinquished that letter to him. Laura had always complimented him on how convincing he could be. He stuck his chest out a little farther, totally enamored with himself. Come to think of it, not only was he sharp as a tack, he was also pretty good looking. Well, at least not bad looking. He was tall, with a full head of dark hair, a fair build, even so his belly did hang just slightly over his belt, probably from a few too many beers, but he had bright eyes and a pleasant smile. True, he was not the smartest man in town, but he knew his gardening techniques better than anybody else did. Everybody who got a look at the Schwarzenau grounds admired them. Yes, when it came to gardening, he was the best. He was known as a loner, minding his own business, that's why nobody ever bothered him and that's why his little love nest was such a safe place.

Little did he know that things were about to take a sharp U-turn.

It was a great afternoon, much to pretty to stay indoors. So Harold decided to fix the flat on his bicycle, that thing needed an overhaul anyway. He managed to almost take it completely apart, when a whistle reached his ears. A familiar pair of legs stood right where he was kneeling, tempting him into God knows what. Although his hands were greasy, his right hand reached up and slowly crept above her knee. She did not move, just stared at him intently, daring him to go further. Finally she said: "You are messing up my skirt."

"So I am, want me to stop?" There was no answer.

Half an hour later, their naked bodies glistening with sweat, his fingers tracing a line of tiny pearls from her nipples down over her belly to that profusion of black curls, when a slap of Laura's fingers brought him to an instant halt. He had no time to react, she just blurted out: "I won't be seeing you any more."

His ears had trouble hearing. He could have sworn that she just said, that she wouldn't be seeing him any more.

"Laura?"

"You heard right, this is the last time. I, I mean we, can't take the risk any longer. Autumn needs me now more than ever and this has to stop. Don't get me wrong, it was great, but it's over." She almost said - I don't need you any more, the job is done - but of course she didn't.

Harold had obviously lost his voice, all he could do was stare at her with the most stupid look on his face. She was already dressed and out the door before he was finally able to speak, by then it was too late, she was gone. He made a fist and smashed it through the wall. His knuckles began to bleed, he didn't notice, he couldn't even think let alone feel any pain.

What in the world had just happened? One minute they were making love and the next, a kick in the ass. This didn't make any sense. What had gotten into this woman? He would find out, there was no doubt about that. He loved her, damn it, he really loved her. She was one crazy bitch, but that didn't matter, he still loved her. He would get to the bottom of this insanity, no matter what. Something was up and he would not rest until he knew what it was. You just don't dump on a guy for no reason, and Laura had better have a good one.

If Laura thought that Harold would get over this little affair, as she liked to call it, she had just made a huge mistake. This man didn't just love her, he was obsessed with her. To Laura, love was an emotion one could pick up and put down at will. It just was not that important. Hate, yes, she could immerse herself into that turmoil wholeheartedly, but not that mushy stuff they called love.

She was glad that this mess was out of the way. In due time, it would just blow away, and that was that. Never in a million years did she imagine that this could have some serious consequences. One of Laura's biggest mistakes was that she thought herself in control of all situations, specially the ones that she had engineered and was calling the shots on. To think that someone might not dance to her tune was just unheard off, least of all Harold. Those two, meaning Harold and Ruben, were like putty in her hands. Two pawns, to be pushed and shoved from one square to another. She liked playing games, especially when she was the winner. So far, she had always been the one to bring the trophy home.

Now this guy, Ted, he had looked like a real man, but he set his sights on the wrong girl, so she had no choice but to do something about that. Too bad, he could've been somebody special in her book. Well, he was gone and good riddance. Another one was Victor, she was not through with him yet. There would be other opportunities for them to get together. The poor man won't know what hit him, once the time was right and she could make her move. In the meantime,

Autumn Leaves

however, she just had to lay low for a little while longer and give Autumn time to adjust to this new lifestyle. Poor, sweet, young Autumn, things were just not fair, were they?

    Laura's thoughts came to an abrupt halt and so did her feet. She was so totally absorbed in her thinking that she didn't hear Harold approaching. Suddenly, he loomed in front of her, looking dark and sinister. For the first time ever Laura could feel her skin crawl with something very similar to fear. Good Lord, what now? He could see the fear in her eyes as she looked up at him. All of a sudden he seemed so much taller than before and there was nothing gentle about the way he scrutinized her. She felt herself break out in a sweat, unable to speak or take her eyes off his frightening, sinister looking face. She felt as if something was choking the life out of her, but he hadn't touched her. He just stood there, his dark eyes shooting daggers through her. Finally, what seemed like an eternity, he uttered one word: "Why?"

    If she could talk she would tell him, but hard as she tried, nothing came out. Then he lifted his right hand and she closed her eyes, ready to receive the blow that was coming her way. Instead, his hand very gently reached under her chin and lifted it up, so that once again they had eye contact.

    "You made a bad mistake today, you walked away from me while I was still taking to you. You see, Laura, that's worse than anything else you could have done. Now I have to tell everybody what you are, nothing but a slut. No, don't worry about me, I have nothing to lose any more, I lost it all, when you walked away from me. You, my precious, will find out how that feels, I will destroy your world unless ... now let me think?... I got it! ... Unless you will do as I say ... Yes, that is what it will have to be." He had mumbled the last few words to himself, still holding her face in his hand.

    "Harold, let's talk. Please let go of my face, you are hurting me." She spoke through clenched teeth, and he released her immediately.

"Don't want to do that, no, I don't want to hurt your face, ever."

"Thank you. Now listen to me ..."

"NO" he screamed the word at her with such fury, she automatically ducked.

"You listen to me. I make all the rules from now on. You made me fall in love with you, then you made a fool out of me, now this fool is collecting his dues. You can keep up the false facade to your friend, or anybody you please, but one thing you will do whenever I choose, and that is to give me the pleasure of your body. You are what you are, a whore, but a good one. I've paid up front for all the pleasures I want, for a very long time to come. It's either that, or good bye Laura and her nest egg up on the hill. The choice is yours, my pretty, what do ya say?"

"You're crazy, I'll never come to you again."

"I think you will. Stealing those letters was my doing, but your plot. If I go down, you'll go down. That was a criminal offense, they won't go lightly on us, and frankly my dear, I don't give a damn." He turned and walked off. He was proud of that last remark, he'd always hoped to find a way to use it some day.

Laura was in a panic. No, he wouldn't do that? Or would he? Why, it would be sheer madness. She had to stop him, she couldn't let him ruin her life just like that. She ran so fast that she tripped and almost fell, but she caught up with him just as he reached his front door.

"Stop Harold, please stop. All right, I was wrong, I did a stupid thing, but please don't do anything foolish, not now?"

"Why not now, what is the difference? I told you, it doesn't matter to me any more. Oh, I forgot, it matters to you. Well, that's just too bad, or are you willing to make a deal after all?"

She didn't look at him when she agreed. What she did not anticipate was his next move. It took her totally by surprise. He grabbed her arm, dragged her into the house and slammed the door shut. "I'm ready for the first installment."

Anita Attwood

CHAPTER TEN

Christmas was very near. Although the big tree in the parlor glittered brightly with thousands of white lights, the scent of bayberry and the smell of gingerbread mingled through the halls, nothing could wipe away the sadness that had settled over the castle, like the blanket of snow covering the slopes. The blue parlor was closed off. Inside, the big grandfather clock was silent, its hands showing five- thirty-five, the hour when the Prince and Princess von Schwarzenau had arrived at their castle for the very last time. A calendar, standing on the Victorian mahogany desk where Princess Marianne had spent many hours writing her poems, displayed the date of November 29. No warmth came from the marbled fireplace where a few charred pieces of wood lay cold on the black iron grate. Above it hung a gold framed crystal mirror, it was draped in black chiffon and showed none of its usual luster. The large portrait of Rudolf and Marianne on the wall opposite the windows was also veiled in black and the heavy blue drapes were drawn, shutting out all light. The darkness in this room, combined with the eerie quiet, gave one a feeling of being in a tomb.

Autumn Leaves

The servants often wondered if the blue parlor would ever be unlocked again. It had been Princess Marianne's favorite reading room, the one where she could listen to her music and where the royal couple had spend many quiet hours together. Perhaps it was only right that others should not disturb this room. The memories it held where sacred, not only to Autumn, but to the rest of the staff as well.

Princess Autumn had taken over the running of the chateau in a remarkable way. Prince Victor had offered to stay and see to things, she would not hear of it. He had plenty to do at his own place, tending to his horse farm. He wanted to take Maharani there, but Autumn said no, she wanted the animal near her. All his urging was futile, she would not let the horse be transferred. That he worried about the horses safety wouldn't have made sense to her anyway, since she was so sure that Maharani was in excellent hands with Ruben as her keeper, so he just gave up. She made it a habit of riding every day, weather permitting. It really would have been such an inconvenience to have Rani in Victor's stables.

Ever since that dreadful day, the winter weather had shown a much kinder face. Plenty of sunshine with very little snow, just frosty grounds and blistering winds. It gave her ample time to ride her beloved horse and not only in the park, she even ventured into the forest. Sure it was cold, as it should be with Christmas so near. The park had a special magic, especially early in the morning. The trees and bushes were glistening and sparkling like diamonds, as the early rays of the sun descended upon them. It was a winter wonderland. Here, she had peace and tranquillity, something she was in dire need of.

Maharani was a horse of distinction. It appeared as if the animal could feel its master's moods. Autumn would ride and pay little attention to her horse; her mind going over the last days she had spent with her parents. Some times she would bend low and hug Rani's neck while her tears fell on the animals coat and it would stand stock-still until Autumn had herself under control. Ruben noticed that the horse was coming back with its head hung low, but he did not say anything. Being so well attuned to horses, he knew that it was Autumn's indifference that reflected back on the animal.. Although he sensed the horses sadness, he was glad that Autumn went riding at all. He couldn't help but admire her strength and courage. A new Autumn had emerged out of this devastating tragedy.

Ruben was like so many others who did not know that the Autumn they saw during the day was quite different from the one that cried herself to sleep each night. It took all of her effort and strength to hold her head up high, specially when she knew that people could see her. The quiet rides she took with Maharani were nothing but an escape from the constant strain of having to be on her toes. Her pride would not allow her to let them see how she really felt. Well, she may have fooled some, but not Mary or Victor. Not even John believed that his princess was all that tough, he had observed her on numerous occasions, halting in front of the door leading into the blue parlor, tears rolling down her cheeks. The nights he had trouble sleeping and was roaming through the halls, he often heard the heartbreaking sobs coming from the princesses room. Not even the thickest walls could muffle her outcry. Only God could help this poor child, but he seemed to take his sweet time in that.

Two days before Christmas a letter arrived. Autumn thought at first that I may be from Ted, but it was not stamped 'Air Mail' and disappointment was written all over her face. She did not know anybody in Bad Reichenhall, Bavaria, so it could not be anything important. There was no return address on the envelope. She dropped the envelope back down on the table in the foyer; perhaps she would look at it later. Why had Ted given up on her? That question was still very much on her mind.

Autumn Leaves

Christmas Eve was here. It really helped to have Victor around. He had come over early in the day to make sure Autumn would not have any time to slip into a state of depression. The call from the mint Company came just in time announcing that the new coins were ready. Victor offered to go and pick them up, Autumn wouldn't hear of it. They cost enough money, why not have them delivered. She was not going to do anything with them anyway, at least not right away. When they arrived, a few hours later, she packed them away to be distributed some time after Christmas. She had guessed right, nobody expected a coin this year and nobody, except Victor and the mint Company, knew that there would be one. Victor did not push her on this issue, he was going to let her decide when the time for distribution was right.

"Autumn, there was a letter on the table in the hall, addressed to you, did you know about it?"

"Gosh Victor, I forgot, it came a few days ago and I just didn't open it because I don't even know who it is from. It's probably not important."

"Why don't you open it and see." He handed her the envelope; "you can always throw it away if it's junk."

"You're right." She took the letter and began to read. He noticed her eyes getting bigger and bigger and suddenly there was a shout, "I can't believe it, I can't believe it!"

She shoved the letter into Victors hands and insisted, "read it, it's from Peter."

For a moment he was confused, not remembering who Peter was or could be, but then it dawned on him, there had been only one Peter in Autumn's life but that had been ages ago. They had been children and he remembered Autumn making him swear never to tell Laura about her secret friend in the forest. That had to be the Peter she was referring too, he knew of no other. He handed the letter back to her.

"Autumn, why don't you read it first, after all, it's addressed to you. I have something to take care off, be back in a few." He left and she sank down into the easy chair, unfolding the pages, almost afraid to look at them. When her eyes read the first few lines, tears were forming, but they were mostly tears of joy. Peter remembered and he had even been at the funeral. He remembered and he cared. Sweet, gentle Peter. Reading on she found out that he did not cure sick animals any more, instead he was helping people. Dr. med. Peter Marshall, it sounded quite impressive, but the words he wrote had that old ring to them, she could almost hear his voice. To think, that she had left his letter just laying around, shame on her. Her guilt feeling however did not last long; she was much to excited to have heard from her long lost friend.

When Victor returned, he noticed Autumn sitting there, holding the letter and smiling the sweetest smile, something nobody had seen in weeks. It made his heart glad and it made him very fond of Peter, right on the spot.

"He's a doctor now, a very important doctor. Can you believe it? He doesn't cure animals any more, he heals people and he is right here in this country." The way she beamed at him, one could think that she'd gotten the biggest surprise in her life..

"Victor, he was here, I mean here at the funeral. He came just to say good bye." Now she looked thoughtful, but not sad. All at once it dawned on Victor who the stranger had been, the one standing by the road, watching them so intensely. Why did he not come and speak to them? How strange. Well, it was immaterial now, he obviously had made Autumn very happy by sending her the note. Should he tell her that he had noticed him? No, it had no value now and would probably just have an adverse effect. It was really good to see her in such a happy state, bless you Peter.

"Victor, should I write him a note or should I call him? He left his phone number, both of them, his office and home. What should I do?"

"Call him, it's Christmas, call him and wish him a happy Christmas."

Autumn Leaves

She jumped up and hugged his neck. Wow, this was great, it was just like old times, full of spontaneity and innocence. He loved this girl.

"Now, if only Jane could be here, it would be like old times..." That was a dumb thing to say, he could kick himself. Right away he noticed Autumn's face cloud over. Nothing would be like old times, the two most important people were not here, they were resting in the cold ground down in the rose garden. Then he saw the tears well up and she broke into uncontrollable sobs, right out of the blue. John had just walked in with a tray of steaming mugs, but stopped dead in his tracks at the sight of the crying princess. He could have sworn he heard her laugh, coming down the hall. Victors face spelled horror, he too was caught totally off guard. Nobody said a word so John just set the drinks on the table and excused himself with an apologetic look toward Victor. As quickly as the tears had started, they stopped.

"I am so sorry, it's Christmas," was all she said. There was no need for anything else, he understood. They sipped their hot Gluehwein, an old Christmas tradition, and it wasn't long when Autumn's cheeks began to show a rosy color. She was not used to spirits, as he well knew from an earlier occasion, so it affected her rather quickly. No harm done, she needed a relaxant at this time.

"Your Highness," John stood under the doorway, a worried look on his face.

"Yes, what is it John?"

"Miss Laura is at the door and I did not know if this would be a good time for her to come and visit."

"Why should it not be? She always comes over at Christmas," was Autumn's quick reply.

Victor saw John's embarrassment and he felt for him. He knew why John had taken the precaution of announcing Laura, he had witnessed Autumn's breakdown, but Autumn did not know that.

Victor came to the rescue. "John, it's good of you to ask, thank you." John gave him a grateful look and left to get Laura. Victor felt Autumn's questioning eyes on him, he chose not to answer.

"Merry Christmas Autumn, Victor?" Laura seemed to question Victor's presence.

"A good Christmas to you, Laura." His words did not come out very friendly, even so he tried to be cordial. She had no business being here, in his opinion. Obviously, Autumn did not share his thoughts, she welcomed the witch with open arms. Laura gave him the evil eye, without achieving the desired effect. He was not about to leave and let her have her way with Autumn. To be honest, he rather enjoyed this mind game they were playing, unbeknownst to their hostess. One thing he noticed right away, the searching glances Laura sent in all directions, especially towards the Christmas tree. Finally he realized what she was looking for, the presents. There were none.

They were sipping their second mug of Gluehwein. Autumn could not stifle her yawning any longer and asked to be excused.

"I'm sorry Laura, I seem to be overly tired tonight. Will you come by again tomorrow?"

Laura almost said, 'what for', but caught herself in time. "Sure, I can run by for a minute or two, if you want me too. I only came by to wish you a merry Christmas." She gave Autumn a hug and totally ignored Victor, which did not faze him in the least bit. She didn't get what she came for. The thought alone put a smirky grin on his face and he lifted his head and let Laura have a full view of his satisfaction. He saw her turn a shade darker, but there was nothing she could do or say to him here.

Once outside Laura thought about her other problem, Harold, he had turned into a total beast. She had hoped that the presents from Autumn would at least give her a little consolation, but where the hell were they, there was nothing

Autumn Leaves

in sight. Not a very good Christmas Eve. Seeing that idiot Victor sprawled all over the sofa didn't help either. She kicked the stone steps so hard, that her toes began to hurt. Nothing was going right for her, not a blessed thing. Things would have to change now, life could not continue this way. Damn, her foot was beginning to really hurt. How stupid of her to kick the step, but she would do it again, that much she was sure of.

Victor, in the meantime, was debating whether to stay here or go back to the villa. He opted for the chateau, it had begun to snow rather heavily. Ever since the accident, Mary was keeping his old room in readiness. Funny, but when he was a kid he thought he had the biggest room he'd ever seen, suddenly it had shrunk to where it was just acceptable. Of course it was partly because Rudolf had enlarged the bathroom quite a bit, and he had to admit, that was a very good idea. A nice long hot bath was just what the doctor ordered and with Jane out of the picture, he had no reason to go back to the villa tonight. Her Christmas card was nice and she still signed it with 'I love you', but he knew that those were empty words. He was lonely and he was getting angry again, not at Jane, more at himself. Autumn was not the only one who wanted this Christmas over and done with. He must remind her to call Peter; it would be good for her.

On Christmas morning they found the table loaded with the most appetizing fare. To every one's delight Autumn and Victor made short work of it. Neither of them realized just how hungry they had been.

There were several little packages stacked under the tree now, one for each of the Servants. Autumn had a change of heart; she had pinned the new coin, showing the picture of her parents and date of departure, on each present. When the gifts were distributed, there was not a dry eye in the house.

The rest of the day went by quietly, Laura did not come by again. It was still fairly early in the evening when the lights went out in chateau Schwarzenau, plunging it into darkness. For everyone here, Christmas was over.

Not so for others. Harold was waiting to give his present to Laura. She forgot to keep her promise to come and see him on Christmas Eve. Now it was already the second Christmas day, no Laura. So he went looking for her and found her at the stables with her cousin Ruben. Harold almost never went down there, that's why it took Ruben by surprise to see him standing in the archway.
"Anything I can do for you?"
"As a matter of fact, yes. I was looking for Laura, have you seen her? By the way, a merry Christmas to you."
"Thanks, to you too. Laura just left but will be right back. If you want to wait, be my guest, I have a few things to do." With that Ruben walked into the stables to tend to the horses. He was wondering what Harold wanted with Laura, he didn't even know that they knew each other. That's dumb, of course they had to know one another. Harold had been here longer than they had. He was laughing at himself for being so stupid. Then he heard Laura's voice, high-pitched and loud. He let the fork fall down and ran outside. Harold had Laura by her arms and was shaking her.
"Hey, what's the big deal? Let her go."
"Stay out of it Ruben, this is none of your business." Harold too was yelling.
Harold was a big man compared to Ruben, but that still didn't give him the right to jerk Laura around. Ruben ran into the stables and picked up the fork he had just dropped, but when he came back out, those two were walking arm in arm toward the chateau. The fork slipped out of his hands and he just stared after them. What in blazes was that all about? After a moment he shrugged his shoulders, retrieved the fork and went back into the stables determined to finish the job he

had set out to do. That crazy cousin of his was always up to no good.

Laura was trembling. Harold held her arm too tight, his face dark with anger, his mouth twisted into something that was supposed to be a grin. They were staggering towards his bungalow, that is, she was staggering, and he was walking, making long steps. She knew what was coming and she was afraid. Each time he had summoned her, he got a little bit rougher, this time ......

She just had to get away from him, but how? The thought of him touching her turned her stomach. She needed some excuse but it was too late now, she knew it would be very bad. Ruben could not help her, but who else was there? Nobody, that was the honest answer, nobody would come to her defense.

They had reached his front door and he was literally dragging her up the two steps. His face was set in grim determination, promising no mercy at all. She would just have to kill him.

CHAPTER ELEVEN

"Peter, is this you?"
"Halloo, this is Dr. Marshall. May I ask who is calling?"
"Peter, it's me, Autumn."
"Autumn? My God, Autumn. How are you? Did you get my letter? But of course you did, I am so glad to hear from you and I am so terribly sorry for your loss."
"Peter, I want to thank you for coming to the funeral, but why didn't you stop and say hello to me?"
"I couldn't Autumn, not at that time, sorry."
"That's all right, I do want to tell you how happy your words made me. It has been such a long time, I probably won't even recognize you any more."
"I recognized you right away, you are still a golden girl, or can't I say that any more?"
"Oh Peter, you can say anything you want to me, we are friends, aren't we?"
"Yes Autumn, we are, but I find it hard to say Merry Christmas to you. It would be so good to see you, that is, if you thought it might be all right. Why don't you take a break and come over here, it's really quite nice. A change of scenery would do you a lot of good. I can take a few days off and

show you around, it would be fun. Will you think about it or am I to presumptuous? After all, it's been a long time."

"Is that the doctor talking?" She paused. "Peter, I think it would be lovely, I just don't have an answer for you right this moment. Just talking to you made me very glad and I promise to call you again, soon. Peter?"

"Yes, Autumn?"

"Oh, nothing, just thank you." She hung up.

Two young people were deep in thought, one at chateau Schwarzenau, one in the resort town of Bad Reichenhall. Both tried to recall earlier days of their childhood and both knew, that an inner bond was connecting one to the other. Just how strong that bond was would be a test of time.

When Victor came over, he could tell right away that Autumn was in a better frame of mind, at least better than the last time he had seen her.

"Did you remember to call your long lost friend?"

"How did you guess, I just finished talking to him."

"I didn't guess, I only asked, but judging by your smile, it must have been a good conversation."

"It was and he asked me to come and visit him, what do you think of that?"

"Probably not a bad idea, are you going?" She just shrugged her shoulders wondering if her parents would approve of such a visit and quickly remembered that they were not here to voice their opinion one way or the other. Victor's eyes were upon her and he noticed a tear rolling down her cheek. It was not hard to guess where her thoughts had wandered off to. It hurt not to be able to help her more, he would gladly carry her pain. Her voice snapped him out of his thoughts.

"Victor, do you believe that they can hear me? I mean, can they somehow tell me what to do if I were to ask them?"

Anger gripped his chest, anger at the injustice of their leaving. But just as quick as it had come up, it was gone. He knew full and well that fate had dealt a bad card and there was not a soul to blame.

"Little One, I believe with all my heart that if you ask and expect an answer it will come. Somehow your heart will know what to do, but you must believe, that's all. In the meantime, if I can help you out with some of my expert advice, have at it."

She slightly punched him in the arm and grinned, "I'll take you up on that, some day."

Days had rolled into weeks and nothing remarkable happened. Winter had shown its ugliest face a few days in a row and pretty much made folks stay put near the warm fire. Autumn caught up on her reading, one of her favorite past times, but riding through the countryside was still the greatest thrill of all.

It was on such an outing that the thought of Laura's strange behavior came to mind. She hadn't seen much of her since Christmas Eve. In a way she should have seen it coming. After all, Laura was two years her senior and therefore had other interests to pursue. It had become obvious that Laura thought of her as being naive when it came to boys, and perhaps she was. Laura certainly knew a lot on that subject. Autumn wondered about that some times. As for now, when the time came and she needed to know more, she could always ask her ... mom.... She flung her head back in frustration. Would it ever go away? Every turn she made she needed them, every day. It didn't matter how often she told herself to grow up, it was not working. There was so much that needed to be sorted out.

She urged Maharani into a gallop through the meadow. Her goal was to get up the mountain, to her favorite spot. She remembered the warnings John and Ruben had given her about some bad weather moving in. So far the sky

Autumn Leaves

was clear in all directions. Some times it seemed as if men worried more than women did, that was funny. For this time of the year it was unseasonably mild, she did not even have a jacket on, only her favorite white cashmere pullover and as always, her little black riding cap, matching the color of her black riding pants and boots. She looked very smart.

This was the beginning of March, and the winds blew mighty hard over the open field. Autumn almost lost her cap, but managed to hold on to it until she reached the forest where the trees gave shelter from the gusty blows. Still, the sun was quite warm in spite of the wind. She was not a foolish girl and the warnings John and Ruben had given her did not fall on sandy ground. Now and then she checked the skyline. Satisfied that nothing threatening was rolling in; she let Rani continue with her climb. Rani knew this path so well, she needed no guidance and before long they arrived at that special place of theirs. Up here it was much cooler and for an instant she wished she had her jacket. She slid out of the saddle and stood for the longest time admiring the view of the valley below and the alpine peaks surrounding her. Why did she feel closer to her parents here? Even closer than sitting beside their grave. Was it because heaven was so near, because one could feel the touch of Gods hands?

A warm feeling surged through her body and all sadness had vanished, she was ready to hold that long overdue conversation with those she loved more than anybody else in this world. Smiling, she closed her eyes, leaned back against the rocks and let her thoughts take over. She didn't know how much time had elapsed, Maharani's hoofs scraping the grounds brought her back to reality. Sure enough, some very dark clouds were approaching rapidly, being pushed by the strong wind that been blowing all day. She didn't lose any time mounting her horse and retreating down the mountain slope.

Something didn't feel right with the saddle, but there was no time to stop and check it now. The black clouds were already right over her head and it had gotten very dark, although it was only a little after three in the afternoon.

It happened half way down. Something snapped and she lost her grip. Rani came to an immediate halt and turned her large body, thus causing Autumn to fall against the mountain slope instead of into the deep ravine on the other side. Rani had saved her life. The realization hit her the moment her head bounced off the rocks, then everything turned black.

She didn't know how long she'd been laying there; the face of her watch had shattered. She was soaked to the bone and began to shiver. Her head was aching terribly. Better a headache than having gone down that ravine, she thought. Then she tried to get up but sank back down with a loud moan, her left ankle was hurting like crazy and her head was spinning. It would be best to wait just a few minutes before trying again. This time she managed to stand, leaning hard against her horse. The question was, could she get up on Rani's back, without a saddle? Where was it any way? It must have gone over down the ravine. She counted her blessings and tried to limp alongside her horse, holding on to it's mane. It was slow going, too slow. She noticed a big boulder sitting on the wayside. She climbed on it and swung herself onto Rani's back. Her fists grabbed a handful of the horses mane. Holding on for dear life, horse and rider slowly made their steep descent, the path now being slippery from the heavy downpour. Maharani was truly an exceptional animal. She gently carried her precious cargo to the bottom of the mountain and on toward the chateau. Autumn lay motionless upon the horses back, her head throbbing and one sharp pain after another shooting through her leg. She was barely conscious and didn't notice that Rani had come to a stop. They had arrived at the front doorstep. Rani's sharp neighing could have roused the dead, and indeed did bring John to the door within seconds.

Autumn Leaves

"Oh my God!" he exclaimed, "Mr. Victor, quick, it's the Princess!"

Victor was already down the steps looking up at Autumn. At first, all he could see was the sweater, which had turned red on one side, and her limp figure slung across the horses back. He reached up and pulled her off the horse, but when he tried to stand her up she just collapsed in his arms. Thank God John was there to help him, otherwise both of them would have ended up on the gravel.

"Help me, it hurts so much," it was only a whisper before the night closed in again.

"John, bring the car around, hurry. Mary, bring me some clean towels and a blanket."

He shouted orders left and right, sweat running down his forehead. The car was already beside him and Mary moved faster than anybody had ever seen before, holding a blanket, a pillow and towels in her arms. Victor placed Autumn on the rear seat, putting her head into Mary's lap. Autumn's golden hair had turned an ugly brownish color on one side, it was saturated with blood. Mary's cheeks were wet from tears rolling down and her lips mumbled prayer after prayer on the short ride to the hospital. They just could not understand how this could have happened to their Princess and why.

John must have called ahead, for when they arrived at the hospital, the emergency crew was already standing by to receive them. She had lost a lot of blood and her face was ghostly white. Victor and Mary had little information to help the doctors. It made them both feel useless and afraid for Autumn's life. Waiting out here in the waiting room was another added burden. Victor was pacing back and forth like a caged animal, his brain working overtime trying to put the last half-hour into perspective. What about the hours before. They had searched the grounds for her, but there had been no sign of her or the horse. Ruben and the other stable hand were probably still out looking for her. He must call John and find out. Also, and that thought just hit him, where was the saddle? There was no saddle on Maharani, so what in blazes had happened out there, where ever 'out there' had been? How did Autumn get hurt? Should he send some of the servants, call the police or search for the saddle himself? He opted for taking care of it himself, but first he had to be sure that Autumn was all right. He suddenly stopped pacing. "I'm going to check on her."

He rushed down he hallway and pushed the emergency room door open. A compact middle aged nurse took hold of him and gently coaxed him back out the door.

"Now, now, we don't want to disrupt the doctors from doing their work, now do we? Your daughter is in the best of hands. Why don't you get yourself a cup of coffee and somebody will be with you as soon as they have some information."

"But you don't understand, she is not...."

"Just calm down, she is well taken care off. Call me if you need something, I'll be right over there." She was pointing towards the nurses station and, giving him a matronly smile, waddled away.

Victor buried his head in his hands and let out a big sigh. She's got to be all right, that's all there's to it. Where was that stupid saddle, how the hell did it fall off? He shot a worried glance in Mary's direction. She was sitting there with her head bent low, probably praying again.

"Mary, let me arrange for you to get back home. There is nothing either one of us can do for her here and you look worn out. I'll let you know something as soon as I hear from the doctor."

"No Victor, my place is here, near the child. But I will go and get me some coffee."

With that she got up and slowly walked down the hall, suddenly looking much older.

Autumn Leaves

"Victor, oh Victor, what's wrong with Autumn?" Laura stood before him with tears rolling down her cheeks. At once Victor felt guilty about all the bad thoughts he harbored against this girl.

"I'm still waiting to hear from the doctor."

"But how could this have happened, she is such a good horse woman, how could she just fall out of the saddle?" There was a short pause, then she began again. "Was the saddle all right? I mean, she just fell out of it, just like that?"

"We don't know. Laura, what are you getting at? Why wouldn't the saddle be all right?"

"I was just talking. Like you said, she is a very good horsewoman. Hell, I don't know what I'm saying, I'm just worried about her, that's all."

He shook his head and studied Laura's face, it had definitely turned a shade lighter. Suddenly her arms were around his neck and she whispered in his ear: "Victor Darling, it was not your fault. Whatever happened, it had to have been an accident. Please don't blame yourself."

Blame himself, where was this coming from? One hand was stroking over his hair and her head had miraculously fallen on his shoulder. Her lips began to kiss his neck. A hard slap of his hand sent her backwards, squealing.

"You son of a bitch, you'll pay for that." She was gone.

He was dumbfounded. What had just happened here? The saddle, what did she know about the saddle? Ruben, she must have talked to Ruben.

"Victor, was that Laura I saw running out the door?" Mary stood before him holding two steaming cups of coffee.

"Yes it was. She was in a hurry to get to an appointment, she only came by to check on Autumn." There was no way he could explain to Mary what had just transpired, how could he, he didn't understand it himself. He was grateful for the coffee. Once again they sat together, waiting in silence. When the doctor finally came to speak to them, it seemed like they had been there for hours.

"The Princess will be all right. She has suffered a severe head injury. Not only does she have a deep cut on her head, she also has a major concussion and needs absolute bedrest for a week or two. She will need to stay here so we can monitor her progress and to make certain that there will be no further complications."

"What kind of complications are you talking about?" Victor didn't like the sound of this. The doctor hurried to explain.

"It's just a precaution, perhaps she will be perfectly all right. Some times, with an injury such as Her Highness suffered, the forming of a blood clot is not out of the question, but we will know more in a day or so. The other injury..."

"What other injury?"

"I was going to say, the other injury to her leg is painful, but it is not broken. She has a severe sprain, which really hurts more than a break, so she will have to stay off it for a while. I am sorry, but due to the swelling, we had to cut her riding boot off, I'm afraid it's ruined."

"Now, don't you worry about no riding shoes, doctor, they can be replaced, just make sure our angel gets well." Mary voiced her opinion. She was sad and glad about the news, but mostly glad. The way her little girl had looked, she had feared the worst. She'll be just fine with a lot of tender loving care.

"Could we go see her for a minute, doctor?" Mary's eyes were pleading making the doctors heart just melt. He looked at the old woman and with a warm smile took her hand and led her down the hall with Victor right on their heels.

His head was still spinning from Laura's strange behavior. One minute she came to him crying and the next she was all over him. Then she was in such a hurry to leave she didn't even wait to hear about Autumn's condition. Should he feel guilty for slapping her? Not likely. That uneasy feeling he had every time her name came up was there again, only much stronger. Somehow he had to get to the bottom of this, whatever it was.

They entered Autumn's room. It was in semi darkness. The news from the doctor had been good, she would fully recover without any side effects, providing the next few days brought no surprises. Mary walked up to the sleeping girl, held her hand for a minute or two and told her that she loved her, then she walked back out. Standing at her bedside, Victor bent down and gave her a gentle kiss right on the lips.

"Little Princess, get well quickly, I'll miss you," he whispered softly so as not to wake her up. He did not know that she was aware of his presence. She was glad he was there, she loved him.

Two weeks later Autumn was released. Since the hospital incident, Victor hadn't heard a word from Laura. He was surprised and angry to see her standing right at the front door, just as they pulled up. She ran to Autumn and hugged her.

"I've missed you so much, girlfriend, I'm so glad that you're better. Just tell me what I can do for you and I'll do it."

Victor scanned her face and his anger turned into amusement. Laura pretended not to notice. After all, who was he any way, just a hired help to watch over Miss Precious. Autumn's voice brought her back.

"Thank you for coming, I've missed you too. Why didn't you come to visit me in the hospital? Well, never mind, come inside and we can chat over a cup of tea." Then she noticed Victor's look of disapproval. " I know I'm supposed to lay down but I also want to hear all the latest news."

Laura's words put Victor at ease. "Sorry, no can do. I promised mom that I would help her, but I'll see you tomorrow, scouts honor."

"I'll hold you to it."

"Do that. Love ya." With that, Laura left.

Victor's gaze followed her until she was out of sight, then he took hold of Autumn's arm guiding her up the steps. Mary stood at the top, dabbing her eyes with the corner of her apron. Her smile was so big that it seemed to go from ear to ear. She held her arms out in anticipation and Autumn snuggled into them. She loved this child.

While Autumn was in the hospital, Victor had taken it upon himself to pay a visit to Ruben, regarding the saddle. Ranger Marshall had found it dangling on a tree stump hanging out over the ravine. It still gave him chills thinking that Autumn could have ended up on the bottom. Close examination proved the belt had snapped but not on its own, a very clean cut had been made more than half way through. Ruben was at a total loss as to the saddle incident. He assured him, that when he placed the saddle on Rani, everything seemed to have been in perfect condition. He would never jeopardize the princess's well being, not ever, and Victor believed him. But, if it was not Ruben, then who could it have been? Laura? It was the only name that came to mind, but how did she sabotage the saddle? He would have to be especially alert to catch her in any slip-ups. Why in heavens name was she out to harm Autumn? He asked himself that question over and over. How could anybody be so cruel? The fact, that this had occurred so soon after Autumn lost her parents, made it even worse. Laura was out for blood; the hospital episode was proof of that. What was she trying to gain with all these crazy stunts? Well, they were not so crazy any more; they'd grown to a very dangerous level. He was convinced that Laura was behind this latest incident. She had to be stopped. The more he thought about it the surer he was that she had somehow found a way to tamper with the saddle. A grim determination took hold of him.

Autumn Leaves

Almost a month had gone by and Autumn improved steadily. A telegram arrived from the United States and she had to think twice before she remembered who knew her there. It was from Ted. He had not forgotten her after all. In the telegram he said that he was thinking of coming very soon. She just had to tell Victor. He would be just as glad as she was, she was sure of that. Then her thoughts turned to the kiss Victor had given her in the hospital and the words he had whispered. She would always remember his lips touching hers, so gentle, so sweet. Why did he have to be family? Her mind told her that loving Victor was wrong, but her heart was glad he was by her side. Was it because he reminded her so much of her father? Now Ted was coming back. It was all so confusing and yet she was glad to see Ted. At one time she thought she loved him. Later, when she didn't hear from him any more, she realized that it had been nothing but infatuation. How else could she have forgotten about him so quickly?

Then there was somebody else who had just stepped back into her life, Peter. She longed for somebody to sort out this horrible mess and perhaps Peter was the answer. Even when she was little he was always there to comfort her and set things right. She should just go and visit him in Bad Reichenhall; perhaps he could guide her into the right direction. They had been good friends at one time and promised to always be there for one another. She wouldn't even tell Victor where she was going, or should she? Her sigh was so big that it could be heard all the way down the hall.

"Is it that bad?" There stood Victor. She turned and looked at him, their eyes locking for a long moment, then her head came to rest against his chest and he held her tight.

"Sweet little Autumn, I'll always be here when you need me, you can count on that."

"Thank you Victor, I do need you."

He let her go and she walked through the parlor and out onto the verandah, leaning her head against the banister.

"Momi, I'm so confused, help me?" For a moment she thought she could hear her mothers silver laughter, it only lasted seconds. Her mother's golden swan chimes were moving ever so lightly, emitting a faint bell like sound, except, there was no wind.

"I heard you momi, you sound so happy, I will be happy too." She left the verandah and there was a definite spring in her step. Victor noticed it right away; he had been watching her the whole time. Good for you Autumn, take charge of your life!

Autumn Leaves

CHAPTER TWELVE

Spring was in full bloom. The colors were spectacular along the winding roads, in the meadows and most of all, in the Schwarzenau park. Harold had truly outdone himself in his array of flowers and Autumn just loved walking among them. They had by far the best gardener anybody could ever have. This was also a time for healing. She visited her parent's graveside every day and one day she noticed something new, there was a whole row of peach colored miniature roses around her mother's grave. On her fathers side was a miniature bush of dark red roses, the kind he had often given to her mom. How could the gardener have known about such intimate details? Be that as it may, it gave her such pleasure, thinking that her parents were able to enjoy their favorite flowers even now. Perhaps it was silly, but it made her heart glad. Spring was a time for new beginnings; a time to start putting the old aside and make new plans and that was just what she was going to do. She never did talk to Victor about Ted's letter, it was not important any more, she was forging new roads to travel on. One of these roads led to Victor and their lives together. Today was the day that she would confront him with that. He was her uncle, but he was also so much more than that. She needed to know where she stood with him and she wanted to know now.

Perhaps now could wait just a day or so, because on this beautiful warm spring day the one thing she wanted to do most of all was to ride with Maharani through the meadows and let the wind touch her cheeks. She was fully recovered and longed to put her arms around Rani's neck. After all, Rani was her very best friend, better than Laura proved to be. She had not seen her friend for quite some time, no phone calls, no messages, nothing. It seemed to be a pattern with Laura.

At the stables, she hugged Maharani and told her how much she had missed her. The animal seemed to know, for it nuzzled her cheeks ever so gently. Autumn knew that she could talk to her mare, even so there would never be any real answers, but Rani was a good listener. She loved her not only because she was a gift from her parents, although that was part of it.

"Did you miss me, old girl?" The mare neighed enthusiastically and rubbed her nose on Autumn's shoulder. "Well, I guess we can go for a short ride. We'll need to make this a slow one, that's what the doctor ordered, but it won't be long and we'll be riding as fast as the wind again."

Ruben stood nearby, watching her talking to the horse. In his arms he held a brand new saddle, much finer than the old one had been. Victor had asked him to pick one out for her. It was his training as a jockey that gave him that special inside. Bull, let Vic think that, he just knew what was best for his princess, that's all.

"Is that for me?"

"For nobody else, Princess."

"Oh Ruben, it's lovely." She stroked the fine leather and he imagined that she was caressing him.

"Let me put it on Maharani for you, this way I can make doubly sure that it's on right." He loved the sparkle in her eyes, glad to see some of the old Autumn returning. In his opinion she had always been the best horsewoman he had ever known. Laura was a joke on a horses back. Princess Marianne had been very good, but not as good as Autumn. His chest swelled with pride, for it was he who had taught her the finer points of riding. Could he ever tell her how he felt? A sad smile suddenly played on his lips, knowing that his dreams were just that, dreams.

"Olla, Princess, need some help getting up?"

"Thank you Ruben, yes it would be nice if you could give me a hand."

I'd like to give you more than just a hand, but out loud he said: "Sure thing."

One swift motion and she was up in the saddle, waving good bye as she rode off in the direction of the gate. He loved watching her. Anybody would have to admire the way she held herself in the saddle; horse and rider were as one.

Ruben stood transfixed. Then his thoughts suddenly turned dark and brooding, they were thoughts no stable boy should ever entertain. He just had to find a way to make her listen to him; his heart was ready to bust from longing to be with this beautiful girl. Suddenly his face showed a vicious grin and he licked his lips in anticipation. She was always sweet to him, so why not be sweet in return? The sudden screech of tires ripped him out of his stupor.

"Ruben, seen the Princess?" Victor came toward him with long strides.

"Sorry, haven' seen her in a while." He looked around making sure Autumn was out of sight. Now why did he tell Victor that lie? He wasn't really sure.

"That's strange, John said he saw her going toward the stables. Oh well, perhaps she changed her mind. Everything going all right for you?"

"Yes Sir, thank you for asking." He turned and disappeared into the barn.

Strange boy, this Ruben Hauser, he never talks much, just goes about his business. That was one thing nobody could take away from him, he was darn good with the horses. It was a shame he hadn't been in a race for a while, he was an excellent jockey and had won several races for the Schwarzenau stables. Since the accident, however, entering one of their horses into a race was probably the furthest thing from Autumn's mind. He understood why she was not ready to resume her passion for going to the races; it had always been a family thing. The Schwarzenau booth had remained empty ever since. All the same, he would have loved to accompany her to such an event. Maybe the day would not be too far off when Autumn would allow herself some of the pleasures she used to enjoy. He was really hoping something would come up and he could enter 'Red Devil', one of his horses, into a race. It was obvious that Ruben had taken a great liking to the spirited animal, ever since he brought it over from his own stables. It was done with a specific reason in mind, for the rider to bond with the horse, and it seemed to have worked out quite well.

All this was going through Victor's mind as he returned to his car.

On his drive back to the chateau he noticed Laura coming from the direction of the gardener's house. Strange to see her walking around this part of the park, was she perhaps befriended with the gardener? Victor spotted Harold walking just a few paces behind her, rather fast it seemed, as if he was trying to catch up with her. Yup, that's what it was, Harold had hold of her arm and she seemed not to pleased about it. Both of them noticed his car and separated instantly. Victor drove by, pretending not to see them. . Deep down he was wondering what that had been all about, but shrugged it off just as fast. It was, after all, their business.

The minute he arrived at the chateau, John handed him a letter. It was from Ted. That was a nice surprise, since he had not heard from him in quite a while. The content however was a bit confusing; he would have to talk to Autumn about it. Ted claimed not to have heard anything from Autumn even so he had been writing to her regularly. That was not at all in consistency with her manners, he could not remember her ever being that thoughtless. He was glad Ted was planning to come and visit, he was ready to see a different face. He also couldn't wait to see the surprise on Ted's face when he found out that there was a title attached to his benefactor's name.

Quick footsteps told him that Autumn had arrived. Good, he could confront her with the letter right away, but why was she in riding gear?

"I've been looking for you, did you go riding?"

"Of course, why else would I be wearing my boots, you silly man." She brushed by him to go upstairs, but he stopped her.

"Could I have a word with you, it'll take just a few minutes."

"Can't it wait, I really would like to change?" She didn't wait for an answer and rushed upstairs. He had no choice but to wait. Her behavior was different, something was up.

She was back down in no time, seemingly her old self again.

"You wanted to talk to me?"

"I did, I mean I do. John just handed me a letter from the United States, from Ted."

"Why?"

"Why what?"

"Why would he give you my letter?"

"It isn't your letter, it's addressed to me. What's the matter, did you get a letter from him also?"

"Yes, I meant to tell you about it, but I forgot."

"Forgot? That's not like you. Why didn't you answer any of his letters? I never imagined you to be neglectful. I thought you two were pretty good friends."

"So did I, but I never heard from him until just now. So I guess we were not such good friends after all and I am not neglectful. I understand he is planning to visit soon and that's what I wanted to ask you about. What should I tell him?"

"I can't tell you that, do whatever your heart tells you. If you would like him to come than perhaps we could throw a small get together, sort of like a swimming party. Sorry, I didn't mean a party in that sense, just a few friends getting together and if the weather keeps improving like it has, the pool will be ready in just a few weeks. We can always warm the water up a bit. What do you say, Autumn."

It was obvious that she loved his idea. "Great, let's not wait a few weeks, let's get the pool ready now. I'm so ready to do some swimming I can't wait. Would you mind organizing that for me? Please?"

He was pleased with her request but a bit confused about the letter business. She was so beautiful in her innocent charm. How patiently she stood before him waiting for his answer, there was no way he could ever refuse her anything.

"Well, all right. I'll see what can be done." She clapped her hands together and actually spun around for joy. It did his heart good to see her like that, perhaps she was coming around faster than anybody had anticipated.

"Autumn, what about the party?"

"I'll think about it. No, that's not fair, it'll be all right Victor, it would probably even be nice. I just don't know what to do with Ted when he comes." Victor had to laugh. It was the cutest thing he had heard in a long time.

"Little one, you don't have to do anything. Just be glad to see him and take it from there. You two didn't have a fight or anything?" She shook her head in denial. "How could we, remember, we haven't communicated in ages." With that she ran up the stairs.

Victor had made up his mind to find out what was going on with this letter business. He had some friends in town and one of them worked at the local post office. The village was small and a letter from the United States would be noticed by most of the postal workers, so it shouldn't be to hard to get some information.

No sooner said than done. He found out that their letter carrier's name was Hansel. Although he was not the brightest young man, he was very conscientious in his job. One could depend on him. Victor soon found out that there had been several letters from the United States for the princess. The postal worker had been looking forward to those letters, checking out those foreign stamps.

Victor's next step was to talk to Hansl. That wasn't hard either. All he had to do was to wait for the next mail delivery.

"Hansl, you brought a letter for the princess just a day ago, it came from America, have there been any others before?"

Hansl looked Victor straight in the eyes. "Well, yes Sir, several of them. I gave them all to Mr. Harold as I was instructed, but not the last one, because I was told by Mr. Harold that everything was all right now and all the mail could go to the house as always."

Victor had a hard time keeping quiet. He could tell that Hansel told the truth, there was no way he could make up a story like that. But why would Harold, the gardener, interfere with mail coming to the main house? Laura! The name flashed in his brain as bright as a halogen lamp. He was sure she had a hand in this.

"Tell me Hansl, who gave you those instructions?"

"The pretty dark haired lady, she said she was a close friend of the princess and she showed me a picture of her and the princess together."

"But didn't you know that you should have checked with her Highness about this, or with your superior at the post-office?"

"No, because she gave me some money and said it was a secret and a surprise. I like surprises for the princess, because she is always so nice to me."

"All right, thank you Hansel. But from now on, all the mail comes here, is that clear? Regardless what anybody says, you bring everything over here. I won't say anything about this to anybody, so don't worry."

Hansel did worry, he could tell from Victor's tone that he had done something wrong. Maybe the pretty dark haired lady was not so nice after all. He didn't want to see her any more, because she had made him do something wrong.

Victor whistled through his teeth. Was there no stopping that she-devil? How did Harold get involved in this? Up to now he had been a loyal employee, why risk his job over something like that? Damn Laura, damn, damn, damn. He didn't want to lose Harold. Where could they find another gardener even half as good as he was? He would have to talk this over with Autumn, she had to know, but first he would have a talk with Harold, maybe not all was lost.

That talk came sooner than expected. It was Harold who paid a visit to the main house, asking to speak to Victor. Victor decided to take him over to his villa, where they could talk undisturbed. The story Harold related to him left him visibly shaken, it was an outrage. Harold left nothing out, not even how sadistic he was to her after she betrayed him. He had nothing else to lose. He put himself completely at Victor's mercy. The two men sat together for a long time, often in utter silence, while their minds were trying to come up with a proper solution to this bizarre situation. He could not excuse Harold for the role he had played, but he understood his reasoning, this insane love for a woman who was nothing but a conniving bitch. The noose was getting tighter around Laura's neck. It was just a matter of time. Victor swore Harold to silence not a word to Laura about his discovery. He also ordered Harold to stop seeing her immediately, if he valued his position at the estate.

Next step was to make sure Ted would not mention the letters to Autumn. He wanted her to stay clear of this mess until he had figured out what to do with Laura.

Things were mighty confusing lately. Just like the other day with Ruben who must have known that Autumn was out riding. Why did he feel he had to lie about it? It didn't make any sense. To top it off, he was getting very frustrated about his lonely life; he was not born to be a hermit. Jane had vanished, or at least it appeared that way. She was taken in by her important job of defending the innocent and couldn't care less about him. Why in damnation did she not go ahead and get a divorce. It definitely would simplify things a whole lot. At least he wouldn't have these guilt feelings every time he looked at another woman, or thought about one. Here he caught himself, because the only other woman making his heart beat faster was Autumn, and she was a forbidden subject. Christ, she was a woman child and his niece. He must be losing his mind, he had to get a grip on himself, and this was one battle he had to win for all concerned. The sooner Ted got his butt over here, the sooner Autumn could get her mind on other things instead of clinging to him. Those two had seemed to hit it off at his party, so the chances were very good that it could pick up where they had left off. Then there was Peter. What was he to Autumn? They had been childhood friends, so what did that make them now? Nothing, really, they hadn't seen each other in ages. He thought he remembered that gangly boy with the black hair and dark brooding eyes. Now he was a well known doctor in a fine sanatorium in Bad Reichenhall. Probably all the rich and famous came to him to find a miracle cure for their imaginary illnesses and paying ungodly sums of money for it. Shame on you Victor, Peter is most likely a wonderful human being.

This conversation with Harold had him all stirred up. He'd be better off going fishing or something and get his mind clear. The thought of going fishing suddenly made him laugh out loud. He never went fishing; it just wasn't his thing. Why not jump on his horse and race through the valley? Now that would clear his mind for sure.

One thing was for certain, Laura had to be stopped. Autumn should be informed what her so-called best friend was capable off. Convincing Autumn would not be easy. He assured himself that once Ted got here things would brighten up. Best to phone him as soon as possible. Victor's face showed determination once his mind was made up.

Autumn was out on the verandah pondering about her state of affairs. She wanted to see Ted. So why hadn't he written to her before? She was glad that he still remembered her. The phone rang and interrupted her thoughts but just as she reached for it, it stopped ringing. Just as well. She let herself fall back in the lounging chair, enjoying the sunshine on her face. But that peaceful feeling was suddenly interrupted when John arrived, carrying the phone.

"A call for you from a man named Peter." Autumn jumped up shouting into the receiver.

"Peter?"

"No other. I hope I didn't disturb you, I just had to call."

Her heart began to beat faster at his words.

"Oh Peter, where are you? Are you coming to see me?"

"I wish I could. I was hoping to talk you into coming out here. I'm sure I could steal away for a while. What do you say? You said you would think about it, now would be a good time to say yes. Please come, you could be here tomorrow and we would have fun, I promise."

Her bright laugh gave him hope and then her words confirmed it.

"Why not, I'll make arrangements right away and I'll be seeing you some time tomorrow. Should I ring you back when I know more about the trains arrival?"

Autumn Leaves

"Better that I call you, let's say in about two hours from now?"

"Fine, I'll be waiting. Peter, I'm glad you called. See you." She hung up, smiling and feeling really happy for the first time in ages. They had so much to talk about, she needed to get away, he was right. What would Victor say?

She asked John to make the arrangements and let her know the time of departure and arrival in Bad Reichenhall. She had been there before, with her parents, and had loved it. Specially the ride in the lift up the mountainside, her father holding her in his arms so she could look out the window and watch the valley get smaller and smaller. It had all been so exciting. When they reached the top there had been snow up there, in the middle of August and they had a snowball fight.

This time the memories did not make her cry, it brought her joy. She had so many wonderful memories of her parents. They would always be part of her. Peter was also part of that world except that he was still here. She was going to see him and together they could return to times long ago and bring it all back. Oh it would be so much fun.

Victor didn't have a chance to tell her about Laura, Autumn confronted him with her news about the journey the minute he walked through the door. He didn't have the heart to spoil her fun, but he felt jealous that she should be so overjoyed to see her old friend Peter. They had been childhood companions, nothing more. It hurt that she refused his suggestion of his accompanying her on he trip. He would have liked to go as well, to see Bad Reichenhall. He was silly and he knew it. The estate needed him. Besides, there were a few details that needed his attention, mainly Laura.

CHAPTER THIRTEEN

As the train rolled into the station the speakers announced "Bad Reichenhall". She stuck her head out the window, trying to spot Peter. Of course there was no telling which one would be him, she hadn't seen him since childhood. Flowering baskets cascaded from every beam at the station and bright red geraniums spilled over the pots in each window. The vibrant colors even more brilliant in the bright sunlight. What a wonderful welcome for all those getting off the train.

He spotted her right away. Her blond hair, the color of wheat, bouncing around her shoulders as she stepped down out of the train. Her walk caused many stares, especially from the male gender, she had a body language all her own. She didn't sway like Marilyn Monroe, hers was more of a graceful promise of a swing, her head turning from left to right, smiling at everyone. He could have watched her forever, except now a worried look had taken away that beautiful smile. With a few quick steps he stood right in her path, thrusting a colorful bouquet of flowers into her arms. She stopped dead in her tracks, staring at this handsome man smiling down at her, a definite twinkle in his eyes.

"Peter!" She cried out and flung herself into his arms, oblivious of the amusement on the faces around them.

Autumn Leaves

"The flowers," was all Peter could say, totally overwhelmed by her greeting. He had often evisioned their first meeting, but not like this. This was far beyond his expectations. Their fierce embrace hopelessly crushed the flowers and both laughed like children when they discovered their misdeed. It seemed like only yesterday that they had sat together in the forest, sharing their thoughts. Time had just erased itself.

Suddenly they realized that the station was empty, everybody was gone, including the train. Peter took Autumn's small suitcase and arm in arm they walked toward his car.

"I've made reservations at the Hotel Edelweiss, it's close to the clinic and I made sure that your window has the best view available. Would you like to stop for a coffee before I get you settled?"

"Anything you say, a coffee would be nice. I'm sorry about the flowers."

"I'm not, there are more where those came from. You can crush every bouquet I give you, I wouldn't mind at all." Again they broke out laughing. What a glorious day this promised to be. She was not totally unaware of the long glances Peter gave her; it made her feel warm all over. How elegant and how handsome he was, not at all what she had expected him to look like. Then why was he not married? Or was he? Perhaps he had some lovely young lady tucked away some place? For some strange reason she did not like the idea at all. Maybe as the day went on she would find out more about his life. For right now, she would enjoy every moment of this glorious day, with Peter at her side. His voice startled her out of her thoughts.

"I have to slip into the office for a short while this afternoon, but it really shouldn't take long. Perhaps you want to rest up a little before we paint the town?"

"Good idea, but I am really not tired. While you go back to work, I may just visit a few of the shops. There used to be a place where you could watch them make glass figurines, is it still here?"

"You mean the glass blowers?"

"Right, as a little child I was here with my parents and I saw them make a swan, I will never forget it. The man gave me the swan and I still have it. He made me laugh because one time his cheeks got really fat while blowing on the stick and then I thought he was not blowing at all, but this beautiful swan was just coming to life at the end of the stick."

"Autumn, you are so funny, you remind me of the little girl I left behind." Seeing her face turn into a frown, he quickly corrected himself. "I mean when you tell me stories like that. Actually you are the most extraordinary young lady I have ever seen."

They were sitting outside in the garden of the coffeehouse. Their eyes locked and Autumn thought that she had never seen such a deep dark color, so dark, she could just drown in it. She totally lost herself as she kept looking at him and only came back to reality when she felt his kiss on her hand.

"You are so beautiful, much more than I ever dreamed anybody could be. I am glad you came, even more so now that you are here. I wish you could stay for a long time, a very long time."

"Peter, what would your friends say to that. Don't you have some lady waiting for you?" She couldn't wait any longer, she had to ask, but she wasn't sure that she wanted to hear the answer.

"Well, I might as well be honest," he made a slight pause. Autumn held her breath and her heart took a dive, "there is a young lady waiting for me."

"Oh," her voice had a high pitch and then gave out all together. Peter went on, "I want you to meet her, I'm sure you two would get along great."

Autumn Leaves

Thank goodness, she had herself under control again, even if her heart made funny jumps and her chest felt rather tight.

"I'd love to meet her. Will she go with us this evening?"

"I don't think so, I told her that I wanted to go out with a princess all by myself, but that she could meet you beforehand. She is looking forward to it."

Autumn kept her thoughts to herself. This must be a very generous young lady if she didn't mind this good-looking man escorting another woman through town. She felt sad, but didn't let it show. Perhaps she laughed just a little bit too loud and too often, but she was sure she'd put on a good show for Peter seemed pleased to see her so happy. He already knew that he had lost his heart to this beautiful woman, he knew it the day of the funeral and he also knew that he had loved her since childhood. At this moment he was more than ever convinced that this was the woman he wanted to spend the rest of his life with. The problem was, that he was not of her class, or was it a problem? Anyhow, he was sure she cared for him and perhaps what he detected a moment ago in her laugh could have been just the tiniest trace of jealousy. If that was true, he could actually have a chance of winning her heart. She had nothing to be jealous about; she was going to find that out later. For now, he was just happy to have her here and it looked as if the same was true for her.

"Will three hours give you enough time to rest or do whatever you are planning to do?"

"More than enough. Will you come and get me?"

"Of course. I'll ring you when I'm done and then we can paint the town. Thank you for coming, Autumn, I think I needed a break as much as you did. We'll have fun, just wait and see." He stood up and took her suitcase and she followed him to the car. After a short drive he pointed toward a place where his clinic was, but all she could see was what looked like a park with luscious greenery and flowers, no building of any kind. Then she spotted the hotel at the foot of the mountains. There were flowers in hanging baskets and window boxes everywhere and the walls were painted with huge murals of alpine scenery. Dark brown wooden beams and balconies stood out from the white base colored walls. All in all, it was very pretty to look at. Autumn knew that she would feel quite comfortable here.

Peter insisted on taking her suitcase up to her room. Well, it was more than just a room, he must have asked for the best suite available for it had a sitting room, bedroom and bath with Jacuzzi. The balcony opened with a view towards the mountains, a beautiful sight. He stood quietly as she looked around, and then she gave him her most brilliant smile.

"This is very beautiful, thank you."

"Only the best is good enough for you, princess. I want you to feel comfortable while staying here, but I have to run. Is there anything I can get you before I go?"

"No Peter, you've done it all. I'll be ready when you ring me." She walked toward him and gave him a kiss on the cheek. It took him by surprise and he would have liked to return the favor, but she already held the door open for him.

"Until later, my princess." He did not see the smile that was not a smile at all.

Autumn stood for a long time on the balcony gazing at the mountains. They seemed so close, she felt like reaching out to touch them. With all this beauty lying before her, why was her heart so heavy all of a sudden? Peter had been wonderful and he was such a handsome man. Was it because he had hinted that there might be somebody else in his life? But that would mean that he was not free. Why did he want her to come here in the first place? Perhaps she was being silly. Of course he wanted to see her just as much as she wanted to see him. Were they not old friends and did they not have a special bond between them? Anyway, that's what she needed, a real friend, somebody who could understand her and Peter was such a friend. Now, all she had to do, was to convince her heart that a friend was what... She could not finish that thought, she knew it was wrong. She was here to find some peace, not to look for more trouble. Fun, that's what he said they would have tonight and fun it would be.

She turned on the water and filled the Jacuzzi. It was just what her body needed to relax and it did the trick. She laid back and let the jet streams massage her body until all tension ebbed away and her mind spun nothing but romantic thoughts about an evening of dancing and candlelight, in the arms of a very handsome young man named Peter.

By the time she had gotten herself presentable, the phone rang, giving her fifteen minutes to get her thoughts together. By now she had decided that she did not want to meet the young lady in question, she just wanted Peter all to herself. Also, instead of staying three days, she would cut her visit short and return tomorrow afternoon. It was better this way. She realized that her heart was not responding to her commands and she would not allow herself to be hurt any more. A longer stay would just intensify the pain.

There was a light knock on her door, she knew it must be him. When she opened the door she thought her heart would stop. He looked so handsome it almost hurt her eyes to look at him. His tanned face appeared to be even darker against the snow-white turtleneck and his smile made her knees feel like jelly. That she might have the same effect on him never occurred to her. Once again they just stood there, looking at each other.

"Autumn, you take my breath away." That was her line, all she could do was smile. She had no idea how elegant she looked in her simple black dress, with a single strand of white pearls around her neck. Her earrings were made of a single white pearl surrounded by small diamonds that glittered with every move she made. The dress clung to her body and fanned out right below her buttocks, outlining every curve. The full skirt ended above her knees, showing off a pair of legs most women only dreamed off having. Peter felt his chest rise with pride for being able to escort this dream of a woman through his town. He would have to keep a close watch over her. Tonight she was his and he would not share her with anybody. Then he handed her a small box. It contained a white and fuchsia colored orchid, fastened on a silver wristband. He slipped it over her right hand, raised it and kissed the inside of her wrist. She could feel a warm sensation running through her body. He held her hand while his eyes searched hers. Neither knew how much time had elapsed, the chiming of the clock brought them back to reality.

Heads turned as they walked through the lobby, they made a striking couple. The valet already held the car door open and while she got seated, Peter had gotten behind the wheel. They were off to a night of fun.

"Do you mind if we make a quick stop so you can meet a certain young lady?"

Autumn had been waiting for this moment and she dreaded what she must do now. She gently placed her hand on his arm and said: "Peter, how bad would it be if we just went on to a nice place and I could meet her some other time?"

She didn't want to see the disappointment in his face, so she didn't look at him. He did not answer right away and she knew that she had hurt his feelings, but she just could not bring herself to meet the other woman.

"I'm sorry," it was just a whisper.

"Not to worry, tomorrow will be fine. Let's you and me go and start the evening right, with some good food and wine and then ..." he winked at her and left everything else to her imagination.

They were slow dancing to a very romantic tune. Autumn's head was resting on Peter's shoulder while he held her tight. Now and then his hand was caressing her back making it hard for her to breathe. She was afraid to respond; knowing that there was somebody else waiting for him. Her heart grew heavier as the hours went by. She realized that this man, her oldest and dearest friend, suddenly occupied a special place in her heart and it had very little to do with friendship. The dance was over much too soon; she could have danced all night. The song by the same title came to her mind. She looked up at Peter, their eyes locked and held for what seemed like an eternity, and then she suddenly let go and returned to their table. He could hardly keep up with her.

"Is something wrong, Autumn?" She gave him her most brilliant smile.

"What could be wrong, it's a perfect evening with a perfect gentleman." He heard her words, saw her smile, but her eyes betrayed her. She had forgotten how well he knew her; she could not fool him.

"Talk to me love, something is bothering you and don't deny it."

"I won't, but I think you already know what it is, I just can't forget about my parents. Here I am, having fun, and they are not with me any more." Tears began to form in her eyes, partly because she suddenly remembered her recent loss, but mostly because she could never tell him how she really felt and that she wanted this evening to last forever. He got up, reached for her shawl and put it around her shoulders. She was glad. To prolong this agony was more than she was willing to handle.

They drove in silence back to the hotel. When he reached for the handle to get out of the car, she stopped him.

"Let us say good night here. I want to go in by myself. Peter, I will never forget this evening, it was wonderful."

"You sound as if you are saying good bye, we still have tomorrow, don't forget."

"You're right, I almost forgot."

When he reached for her she came into his arms willingly. Their lips met and she got lost in the moment, answering his demanding touch with a fire that threatened to consume them both. Peter was unable to control the pounding in his chest nor his shaking hands. This golden child had just turned his head around with such force it was spinning. This had not been a friendly kiss. Hell, he had never been kissed like this in all his life and there had been a few hot and heavy romances in the past, but nothing like this. He noticed her chest rising and falling, the flush in her cheeks and how her slender hands were clenched into tight fists. He did not see her sweet, forlorn smile.

"May I escort you to your room, please?"

"No Peter," her hand reached up and caressed his face, "I need to be by myself. Thank you and good night."

Before he could say anything she had stepped out of the car and was walking through the revolving door and out of sight.

On the following day the phone in Autumn's room rang and rang, but she was already sitting in the train, her tear stained face pressed against the window, silently saying good bye to something that could have been so wonderful but never had a chance to be.

While Autumn's train was rushing toward her hometown, Peter stood at his office window, staring at the phone in his hand with a dumbfounded look. The question, "why" was running round and round in his head. He could not for the life of him remember doing anything wrong, just the opposite. That kiss they had shared had not come out of the blue. There was a connection between them; he felt it and he knew that she had felt it too. Why did she run? They had plans for today, one of them being a meeting between Autumn and his little daughter Barbie. He could already picture the disappointment on his little girl's face when he had to tell her that the princess would not come to meet her, again. What in the world could have been the reason for her sudden departure? Perhaps there had been an emergency at home, yes that was probably what it was. He was already dialing the number to the Schwarzenau chateau, but disconnected before the first ring. No, he wasn't going to check up on her. She would call him and explain what happened, that's just the kind of girl she was. At least he hoped that she was. He leaned back in his leather chair, his fingers tapping in rapid succession the top of his desk. Waiting would be hard.

Meanwhile, Autumn's arrival at the chateau went unnoticed. As soon as she got to her room, she changed out of her traveling clothes and into riding gear. As always, a run on Maharani's back would clear the cobwebs in her head. First she thought herself in love with Ted, then Victor dominated her thoughts and now this, Peter. She must be crazy, except that this time it felt so different.

Victor had just walked through the front door when he saw her coming down the staircase.

"Autumn, where did you come from?"

"My room, dear uncle."

Dear uncle, she had never called him that. Why was she here and why so different? Lately he had a hard time figuring her out. She seemed to be a new person every time he turned around. Judging by her clothes, she was going riding. Well, he would just have to accompany her. Somehow he had to reach her and find out what was going on and why she was back so soon.

"If you're going riding I'd like to accompany you. There are a few things we need to address and I could use the ride myself. Autumn, look at me, I really missed you Darling."

"Oh Victor, I missed you too. Forgive me, but I need to ride alone, please understand?" He did. Her beautiful blue eyes were bathed in agony.

"Will you come and talk to me when you get back?"

"I promise. Don't be mad at me, please?"

"Never. Be safe."

A nod of her head and out the door she went. What in the world was troubling her this time? He had hoped the journey to Bad Reichenhall would bring her back full of vigor, instead he found his girl obviously burdened with something pretty big. When was it going to get better for her?

At least there was one positive note; Ted was due to arrive in three weeks time. As much as he hated to admit it, but his feelings for Autumn had to be sorted out and fast. She was his family, the only one left at that. He would always love and protect her, and so it should be. Ted would be good for her. At least that's what he was trying to convince himself of. Ted had told him how much he looked forward to seeing her again and he, Victor, would be there to make sure miss Laura could not play any of her tricks this time.

After that long talk with Harold he was quite sure that things were going to be much quieter from now on. In the meantime, he would wait for Autumn's return so they could make some positive plans for the weeks to come.

While Victor was having this discussion with himself, Autumn was heading up the mountain trail to her favorite spot. There she sat, admiring the mountain peaks that nearly touched heaven, holding a silent conversation with her mum and dad. She was seeking advice and perhaps some answers to her new dilemma. Suddenly she felt a little tap on the hand that was resting on the moss and found a tiny mouse like creature snuggling against her skin. She reached over to pick it up but it scooted away.

"Well, I wasn't going to hurt you, but thanks for saying hello to me. Rani, ready to head back down?"

The horse obeyed at once and Autumn swung herself into the saddle, feeling much better. The first thing she had to do, when getting home, was to call Peter and make her apologies. Whether there was a young lady or not, she owed him that much. They did have a good time and he did tell her how much he loved seeing her again, and then there was that kiss! She would remember that kiss until the day she died.

"Victor, I'm back!" Her shout brought the whole staff out into the hallway. Victor hadn't bothered to tell anybody that she was back. Suddenly she was faced with an unexpected audience, excluding the one she had shouted for.

"Well, what an honor. Does anybody know where prince Victor is?" John was the first one to have himself under control. With a flick of his hand he dismissed the rest of the staff, then turned his attention to Autumn.

"We were not informed of your early arrival, I apologize your highness." She found his formal ways quite amusing, specially when he placed one hand on his back, the other flat against his stomach to make his impeccable bow. Smiling, she assured him:

"No harm done, John, but where is Victor?"

The moment her words came out, he appeared. She followed him into the sitting room and closed the door. She could sense his distance and it disturbed her. Why was he acting so remote? Was he not glad to see her back? She wanted to walk up to him and give him a big hug and kiss, but she did not dare move. What had changed? She had been gone less than two days?

He saw her troubled look and went to her to hold her close. She clung to him like a drowning child.

"It's all right Darling, we will build a bright future, that's what I wanted to talk to you about."

"We will?"

"Yes! We have so much to sort out and I don't know where to start. I guess the first thing I want to hear about, is your visit to Peter. Was it what you expected it to be?"

He saw her face cloud over and knew instantly that something was wrong. Would she tell him?

"My visit was wonderful, in almost every way. I can't tell you too much, except that Peter did his very best to show me around and we did have a splendid time going out dining and dancing. I had no idea what an accomplished person he had become. His clinic must be very large. I never really saw it. I only saw the park surrounding it and that was huge. Did you not tell me that he was quite well known in the medical field?"

She really did not tell him much, but he got the underlying current and it spelled a heart in trouble. If that was so, then what about Ted's visit? Instead of clearing things up, they seemed to get more jumbled by the minute. His deep sigh made her take a sharper look at him.

"What's wrong, are you having problems?"

He wanted to shout, yes I do, with you, but of course he did not do that. How could he go about easing the way for her when she was getting things more in a muddle all the time? Well, that kind of thinking wasn't fair either and he knew it.

"No, not problems, situations as I call it. By the way, the day you left I had a long talk with Ted. He is really looking forward to coming over and seeing you of course. I think he said that he would arrive in about three weeks. Does that sound all right with you?"

"Why not? My calendar seems to be clear. Ted will be a refreshing change. Will he be coming alone?"

"I thought I told you that he might bring a friend. Well, if I didn't, consider yourself told. Anyway, I'm looking forward to some good riding and hunting. Haven't done any of it for some time. Ah, don't look so crushed, my earlier invitation to our riding together was purely selfish because I missed you and wanted to talk to you. We've done that now, so brighten up, we have a lot to look forward too."

Finally, she was all smiles. Victor was right, some new faces would do them good. Who knows, it might turn out to be a good summer after all?

"By the way, did you remember to start heating the pool."

"I did and it's already feeling pretty warm. Autumn, don't you think it's just a bit to nippy outside for a swim?"

She threw her head back and laughed out loud.

"Oh Victor, does that mean women are tougher than men?"

"God forbid, woman, I'll prove it to you."

"Good, let's change and go for a swim then."

That's not what he wanted to hear, but he took her up on her challenge. She was a clever girl and he would need all his willpower not to show her that going swimming while the air was this cool was not his cup of tea. He much preferred warmer temperatures, in the water as well as outside.

At least she didn't show up in a bikini. Instead she was clad in a shiny mint green bathing suit, trimmed in black, much like the Olympic swimmers wear. It did however show off her perfect body in a most alluring way. If Ted could see her like this, he would be a goner. Once again he had to admit to himself that Autumn had turned into a beautiful woman, with all the right attributes. The man of her choosing would be lucky indeed, but it would not be him.

She stood at the edge of the deep end.

"Ready, your Highness!" She was shouting at him and hell no, he was definitely not ready.

"Ready as you are," was his reply. She dove in, a perfect dive and continued to cross the pool under water. The long hair trailing behind her reminded him of a mermaid. When she came up, he was still standing on the edge, totally dry. She pointed her finger at him, pistol fashion, and said: "Gotcha!"

"I was just admiring your swimming, that's all. Here I come," and indeed he jumped in, making the biggest splash possible, in order to hide the grimace on his face. Damn, the water was cold. Not at all as warm as he thought it would be, but he couldn't let her know that, so he proceeded to swim vigorously to the other end and back again, hoping it would warm him up. It did the trick.

Autumn was still laughing. His jump reminded her of a frog taking a leap. It was just too funny.

"Can you do that again?"

"Do what again, dear."

"That jump, it must be a specialty, I've never seen one like it."

He didn't reply, just got out of the water and dived in again, only this time it was with such perfection that there was hardly a ripple. Now it was his turn to grin, and that he did in a big way.

"Cat got your tongue, little princess?"

"Touché'." She had to admit, this was the best dive she had ever seen and she used to watch a lot of it on television. The rest of the day went by with ease and for the first time in ages she slept soundly, no bad dreams at all.

Autumn Leaves

CHAPTER FOURTEEN

Summer had set in with a vengeance. It seemed like only yesterday it had been spring and suddenly the heat was unbearable. This was unusual in this part of the country but, come to think of it, the whole weather pattern had been unusual of late. Others may be complaining, Autumn however was enjoying every minute of it, losing herself in vigorous swimming activities. Summer was her kind of season and swimming her favorite sport. She didn't even notice that Laura hadn't been around, her mind had so many other things to sort out. She enjoyed her time alone, letting her mind drift into any direction it wanted too. Thinking while floating on her air mattress seemed to work especially well. She was drifting in the middle of the pool with her arms crossed behind her head. While watching the clouds she remembered the romantic movies she used to see about "Sissy", the empress of Austria, and how this lady was dominating every man's heart. Thinking about those romantic stories became her escape from reality, her dreamland. She pictured Peter in the role of the emperor Franz Joseph and herself as the carefree, young empress, surrounded by the love of her adoring husband. Well, that's how it was in her fantasy, anyway.

History books had taught her that the reality was not quite as romantic as the movies portrayed it. Lately that fact had proven to be quite true.

Peter was way out of reach, courting that young lady of his. Their phone conversation had not gone well at all. It had left her feeling guilty as if she had done something wrong. That just wasn't so. How could a man kiss a woman, the way he had kissed her, when he was obviously bound to somebody else? Just thinking about it made her blood boil, while at the same time her heart was yearning to be in his arms. Well, she did love that kiss and she had hoped there would be more, many more.

Frustrated with herself she raised her foot and banged it down, forgetting that she was in the middle of the pool. The mattress tipped over and she found herself under water, frantically kicking her feet and gasping for breath as she surfaced. Somebody had the audacity to make fun of her dilemma. It was Laura, standing at poolside, holding her sides and bending forward with uncontrolled laughter. Autumn, really angry now, swam toward her and with one swift motion splashed her friend from head to toe. That stopped Laura's hysterical outburst instantly.

"What d' you do that for?" Her voice was not friendly, but Autumn couldn't care less.

"Nobody laughs at me and gets away with it, not even you, girlfriend." Autumn's voice showed authority, which had never been apparent before. Laura was stunned, but only for a minute or two.

"It was a joke, you looked so funny going down and even funnier coming up. No need to get offended, all right? Look what you've done, I'm soaked." Now it was Autumn who busted out laughing, earning a mean look from Laura.

"Where've you been all this time any way? I was told that you had gone on a trip. You forgot to tell me about that and now you're back and you didn't bother to let me know that either."

Autumn Leaves

Autumn could detect sadness in Laura's voice and it touched her. She expected Laura to be furious, but this was far from it. Whatever it was, it didn't sound like the Laura she knew so well.

"Sorry Laura, but I had so much on my mind, and I really needed to sort things out by myself. You can understand that, can't you?"

"Not really, but if you say so." Autumn looked at her friend closer, she had never seen Laura so subdued.

"Is everything all right with you?"

"Why shouldn't it be?"

"Just asking."

This was getting them nowhere, what in blazes was going on, they were friends, for crying out loud.

"Laura," Autumn stepped up close to her, "suppose you tell me what's really on your mind. You are not yourself and you don't look well at all."

"Gee thanks, that's all I needed to hear on top of everything else. First you go off without telling me, now you're full of insults, what's next Autumn? I thought you were my friend?" Autumn was totally bewildered. Laura's cheeks were actually getting wet and not from the water, there were real tears rolling down. What could possibly be so wrong?

"Laura, I am your friend and I am truly sorry for not telling you about going to Bad Reichenhall, but it was only for a day or two and I didn't think you would care to know about it. We hadn't spoken in quite a while and I thought you were busy with other things. If I had known that it would upset you I would have told you, you know that. Anyway, Victor knew, so he could have told you. Laura, does it really matter?"

"No, I guess not. I just missed talking to you, that's all."

"And I missed talking to you. Go on, change into a bathing costume and we'll both cool off. Go on Laura, you know where the suits are, I'll just jump back in the water."

Autumn didn't know what to make off Laura; she was definitely not herself. She had never been sensitive to anything or anybody, so why the sudden put on?

Autumn didn't realize that she had changed. The gullible little girl she once was didn't exist any more. Laura noticed it and was taken back by this new identity. She liked the old, naive Autumn a lot better.

Inside the pool cabin, she stood in front of the wardrobe, not knowing what to do. How could she possibly put on a swimsuit, knowing the damn thing wouldn't fit anyway. Those few extra pounds were easy to hide by wearing loose tops over her too tight shorts. A bathing suit would not offer her that protection. Tears of frustration welled up in her eyes once more. She would have to do something about her situation, and fast. So far Harold had no idea about her condition and neither did anybody else. Her mom thought that she had come down with some weird kind of virus and that was just fine with her. There was only one problem, this kind of virus would not go away with bed rest and lot's of fluid, it would take a lot of money and a medical person with special skills to make it go away.

Autumn was calling her; she had to do something. Think, stupid, think! Her mind would not function; it was all so useless. So she just grabbed the first outfit hanging there and wedged herself into it, all the while cursing under her breath. The darn thing wouldn't let her breathe. Holding in her stomach as much as she could, she ran towards the steps and plunged into the water. Autumn's mouth fell open and her eyes got as big as saucers.

"If I hadn't seen it with my own two eyes, I would've never believed it. Laura, you just did the impossible. What about testing the water with your big toe and what about this warm up period I had to witness all these years? What happened to it?"

"It was time for an adjustment, that's all. So come on, let's swim and have some fun, like we used to. The water is really great, I've missed it." With that she swam off towards the deep end, not waiting for any reply. Autumn followed, all the time wondering about Laura's new attitude. She wasn't sure if she could trust it, but she liked it a lot better.

After an hour or so in the pool, they both had enough and decided to get dressed. Laura asked Autumn for a towel and wrapped herself in it the minute she stepped out of the water.

"I'm hungry as a bear, think Mr. John could rustle us up a bite?"

"Knowing John, it's probably already waiting for us. I'll call the house and ask him to bring it out here. OK with you? Laura, hello Laura? Come back to earth."

"Sorry, I was just thinking ... never mind, what were you saying?"

"I was wondering if it would be all right to have a snack out here by the pool, that's all. Will you please tell me what's wrong with you, you're not yourself."

"I'm just hungry, and it's that time of the month coming up, you know how cranky I get and it makes me feel fat as a cow. I'll be all right in a few days. That swim was really great, it helped a lot, so yea, ask John to bring the stuff out here."

The girls had a great time, but something had changed. Autumn suddenly was unsure which Laura she liked better, the old unpredictable one or the new meek and somewhat quiet one. As far as she could remember, the monthlies had never bothered her before, so that sure had to be an excuse, but an excuse from what? 'Let it rest Autumn," she scolded herself. She was sitting on the verandah, when Victor's sudden appearance brought her out of her stupor.

"Had a great day, princess?"

"You can say that again. Laura was here; we had a good time. She is different somehow, I can't put my finger on it, but she is not herself." Autumn didn't see the slight grin on

Victor's face, he knew the reason for Laura's behavior, or at least he thought he did.

"Did Laura say anything to you?"

"Say what to me?"

"Well, I just thought she may have said something, since you seemed to think she is not acting right."

"I didn't say that, I just think that something is bothering her and I wish she would talk to me. We are still friends, you know?"

"If it bothers you that much, maybe I can find out what's going on."

"No Victor, I don't want you to get involved. I know how you feel about Laura, so let me just handle this by myself. At this point I don't think she needs any more sly remarks from anybody, especially you." She noticed the raise of his eyebrows. "Sorry, I don't mean that the way it sounded, but you know what I mean, so be nice and stay away from her, please?"

"Wow, your highness has had some high powered courage for lunch. I've never heard you talk like that before, good for you. By the way, Ted will be coming in the middle of September. It's a bit later than we first expected, but it should still be OK for a pool party, don't you think?" He looked at her quizzically, but all he got was a nod, her mind had already drifted off into another direction.

She was worried about her friend. Tomorrow she would find out what Laura's problem was and she wouldn't take no for an answer. All the problems from the past were forgotten. If her friend needed help, she would be there for her.

The next day Autumn waited in vain for Laura to show up. After more than an hour had passed and still no sign of Laura, she decided to take matters into her own hands. She called Laura's mom, but got no answer. So she drove over to the nursery and found it closed up for the day. That was very strange, it was not even four in the afternoon, where was everybody?

Deep in thought she drove back to the chateau and almost collided with an oncoming car. Harold pulled sharp to the right just in the nick of time, avoiding a head on collision. Shaken, both drivers stared at each other. Harold was the first to recover, got out of his car and walked over to Autumn.

"Princess, I'm sorry, but you were in the middle..."

"Say no more, I know I didn't pay attention to the road, it was not your fault. Harold, that's your name, isn't it?" Autumn's eyes were round as saucers. The fright still had her in its grip.

"Yes princess." He was no better than she was.

"Sorry, but I was looking for my friend Laura, she's not around, sorry to have been a problem!" Autumn began to roll the window up; ready to drive off, when Harold put his hand inside stopping it from going up any further.

"May I have a word with you, your highness?" It was the way his voice sounded that made her turn the engine off and roll the window down again. He stood before her nervously twisting his cap in his hands. After a minute he finally blurted out: "It's Laura, I've been looking for her myself, she needs help and I told her to blow it..."

"Harold, what are you saying?"

"She's sick, and I told her to go away."

"But you have nothing to do with that, it's her mother that should be concerned, not you?"

"Oh princess, you don't understand, it's me she turned too for help and I refused." His head sank low and she could see his lips twitching. What in blazes was going on, she didn't understand any of this.

"Harold, get a grip on yourself and tell me what is going on, now!"

"Yes, your highness, Laura is in deep trouble, she is going to get hurt, and hurt bad..."

"For goodness sake, Harold, will you stop talking in riddles?"

"She went to town to look for a doctor, only she is not looking for a doctor, she is looking for a would be doctor..."

"Hold it right there, what do you mean by "would be doctor" and why would she need a doctor in the first place?"

"Don't you know, miss Autumn? Don't you know?" Harold was totally dumbfounded. He stared at Autumn in total disbelief. Laura had told him that her best friend knew about it, her best friend was Autumn, was it not? Autumn had given her money, money for an abortion. Now here she was, trying to make him think that she didn't know a thing. He looked into her eyes, he believed her. Suddenly it dawned on him. Laura had lied, like so many times before, only this time it was going to bite her in the butt, big time. If Autumn had not given her any money, and he hadn't, then how was she going to have the...

"Got to go princess, sorry." He jumped into his car and was gone. All that was left was a cloud of dust.

Autumn slowly rolled her window up and set off driving towards the chateau. Her head was spinning. She was wondering what in the world was going on with Laura. Why would Harold take such an interest in her well being and for that matter, why would Laura be in trouble in the first place? It was all so mysterious. She felt she just had to get to the bottom of this. Perhaps Victor would know. Then she remembered asking him to stay out of Laura's business, so she couldn't ask him. On the other hand, there wasn't anybody else she could ask, except for Ruben, but he really was no choice at all. She liked Ruben, he was so good with the horses, but she never felt very comfortable around him. She didn't know why, perhaps it was the way he stared at her or the way he was so overly attentive. Anyway, that didn't matter at the moment. Right now her main concern was not Ruben it was Laura.

Autumn Leaves

Running up the front steps she almost collided with Victor.

"Where's the fire?"

"It's Laura, oh, never mind..." she dashed through the front door, but Victor was right on her heels.

"Come on Autumn, what's going on?"

"That's what I want to know. Harold stopped me, no, I mean we ran into each other, well...almost. I mean... oh Victor, I think Laura is in deep trouble and I don't know what to do about it." In her anguish she was shouting at him, which prompted Victor to put his arms around her.

"Little One, start from the beginning. I can't make out a thing you're saying." He didn't dare make fun of her, this was obviously serious.

"Harold told me that she went to see a doctor, only that he wasn't a doctor and I don't know why Harold knows this and why Laura needs to see a doctor who isn't a doctor." Her eyes stared into his, full of fear and bewilderment.

Victor was stunned. Was Autumn incoherent because of some trauma, or was there really a problem with Laura? As far as he knew, she didn't know anything about Laura's involvement with Harold or the letters, but this obviously had something to do with Harold.

"Autumn, what about Harold, how do you know about him and...."

"I told you, we almost had a head on collision. He was looking for Laura and so was I and he told me about the doctor. Aren't you listening to me?" Now she sounded totally frustrated.

"I'm listening, I just didn't understand, that's all. I'll look up Harold and find out what's going on, OK princess?"

"Thank you Victor, I knew I could count on you." Her arms went around his neck and her head rested on his chest. She was so relieved to have him at her side. He gently freed himself from her embrace, although he would have loved to crush her to him, but he knew better.

"Give me a little time and I'll let you know what I can find out." With that he rushed out the door, breathing hard. God he wanted this girl, woman, she was not a girl any more, even if she didn't seem to know it.

Harold was nowhere to be found. Even Ruben had no idea where he was, and why should he. When he asked about Laura's whereabouts he got the same answer, Ruben didn't know anything. Just by chance he checked at the nursery, but of course it was closed for the day, it was Wednesday. It was never open on Wednesday's; therefore it stayed open on Saturdays, that was a long-standing arrangement. Well, he had to find out something; there was no way that he would he go back to Autumn without some kind of news. Murphy's law, when you needed someone, they were nowhere to be found, but when you didn't, they were everywhere. He just about gave up when he saw Harold's car turn the corner. Judging by the grim look on his face, the news was not very good.
"Harold, I've been looking for you." He eyed Victor from head to toe. He didn't say anything, just stood there, staring at him. Then finally he blurted out: "She's gone!"
"You mean Laura? Gone where? Speak up man."
"Just gone. Took a train to somewhere, don't know where. She's gonna have my baby, but I didn't believe her and threw her out, now she's gone." Harold raised his eyes; they had a dull look to them. He had said all he was gonna say, then he walked on toward his front door and into his house. The door closed quietly behind him.
Victor had no idea how long he had been standing there, his mind was reeling with the news. A baby, could that really be? A baby, lord how awful, a baby...
While Victor was trying to digest Harold's revelation, Autumn held the phone to her ear, her hand slightly shaking. The voice on the other end filled her heart with longing.

"I had to call you. The explanation about your departure just doesn't compute. I've tried to accept it, I buried myself into my work, but Autumn, something doesn't make sense. If you don't want to see me any more then tell me. I can't stop thinking about you."

"Peter, I can't talk about it now, maybe later. You'll always be dear to me, remember that. Thank you for calling, I'll be in touch later. Good bye Darling."

"Don't..." hang up, is what he wanted to say, but the line had gone dead. Two young people had once again missed the chance to reach each other.

Autumn buried her face in her hands and sobbed quietly. She loved him, but she would never interfere in his life, which seemed to be mapped out for him. Or was it? He had never said so. It was what she understood it to be. Was she wrong? Was she reading things that weren't there? Why didn't she let him explain, why didn't she answer his questions, what was she afraid off? Peter, Peter, Peter...

She called herself to order; knowing that her first priority today was Laura. Victor should have been back by now, so what kept him? She would have to find out on her own what the problem was and the answer would have to come from Harold. Before she had even made one step, the phone rang again. She knew it was Peter calling her back and eagerly reached for the receiver.

"Hallo princess!" It wasn't Peter. This voice had a foreign accent.

"Ted, Ted Warnham, where are you?"

"At the other end of the line, golden girl." A hearty laugh followed, making her smile instantly. He had that effect on her. He could always cheer her up.

"Are you in Austria?"

"Not yet, but I will be in about two weeks from now. Am I still welcome?"

"Of course you are, why wouldn't you be. Oh Ted, it will be so good to see you again."

"You're sure about that?"

"What a funny question. Victor already told me about your coming, but he wasn't sure when you would arrive. Two weeks from now is perfect, it's still warm enough to go swimming. It will be fun."

"Do you know what makes me really glad? Don't answer, I'll tell you, it's the sound of your voice and especially the laughter I can hear in it. We'll talk when I get there. I have a whole lot to tell you. Keep me in your thoughts, you sure are in mine. I'll let you know the day and time of my arrival. Love yea princess."

Ted's wonderful sense of humor would be just what she needed. Perhaps he could help her get over Peter, although deep inside she had her doubts. Her feelings for Peter were different. She had never felt like this about anybody before. Getting over Ted had not been that hard and even her feelings for Victor couldn't compare, Peter was another matter. Maybe she had never been in love before; perhaps this was the real thing? Well, if this was it, they could have it, this was just too painful and she had endured enough pain to last her a lifetime. All these romance novels, they always had a happy ending, so where did that leave her with Peter?

"The news is not much." Victor was standing in front of her. Where in the world had he come from?

"Hi Victor."

"Hi Victor, is that all you have to say? No questions? Where did your mind wander off to this time, or shouldn't I ask?" She smiled a tired little smile, what could she say? Then she remembered.

"If you have no news then I have some for you. Ted called, he'll be here in two weeks time, won't that be great."

Although she appeared to be glad, he was sure that it wasn't what was going through her mind. He could almost bet that it had nothing to do with Laura either, but with a certain young doctor in Bad Reichenhall. His Autumn had flown the nest, she was in love. The painful tug in his chest reminded him of her sweet embrace just hours ago, but it was out of her need for comfort, nothing else. He had realized that some time ago, still, it wasn't easy to switch over.

"Are you still trying to figure out what's on my mind?"

"What do you mean by that."

"I can always tell when you're trying to solve riddles, you have that certain look on your face, like now. So, what did you find out about Laura?"

"Like I said," he broke off and asked: "What do you mean by, that certain look?"

She laughed: "Come on Victor, I want to hear about Laura?"

"Well, I finally got a hold of Harold and all he could tell me was, that she took a train to somewhere. No, don't look at me like that, it's what he said because that's all he knows himself. God only knows where she'll end up. Harold is pretty upset about it, he's worried about her condition."

"What condition? Laura was fine the last time I saw her. She looked a bit tired, but that's all."

Damn, that was a slip of the tongue. She didn't know. He'd better think of something fast, the news of Laura's pregnancy would not sit very well with her.

"That's just what Harold meant, she didn't look very well, sort of worn out or something. If you ask me, I think he cares for her a great deal, that's why he is so worried. Makes sense, doesn't it?" Autumn's look told him that she wasn't as convinced as he would have her be. After a slight pause she agreed.

"I guess. She'll be back, then we'll find out why she took the trip. I didn't tell her about going to Bad Reichenhall either, she's just trying to get back at me." This explanation seemed to satisfy her, so there was no reason to elaborate any further. He was relieved that she had answered her own question and the matter was dropped.

Two days later there was a knock on Harold's front door. When he opened it, a brightly smiling Laura stood in front of him.

"Have a minute for a weary traveler?" He stepped aside. She marched in, plopped herself on the sofa and asked for a glass of water. She gulped the cold liquid down all at once and asked for a refill. He still had not said a word and returned with another full glass, this time one for himself as well. The silence between them grew heavier by the minute. Neither was willing to make the first move. Then Laura's hand reached out and touched his.

"Can you forgive me?" The look in her eyes betrayed the tender spoken words. Those eyes were hard.

"What about the baby?"

"What baby?" Her laugh was a little bit too loud and too shrill.

"There was no baby, it was all a mistake. Anyway, I'm feeling great and I'm really sorry that I made up that stupid story. Forgive me?"

"Hell Laura, you are one crazy bitch. If I didn't love you so much I would kick your ass right out of here. When are you ever going to come to your senses?"

"Probably never, that's why you love me, isn't it? Let's just forget about those last weeks and start again. We're good for each other and I have forgiven you for all those rough times you gave me. So, what d'ya say, friends?"

Harold shook his head, he was angry, not so much with Laura as with himself. She was a devil woman and she knew how to play him. He couldn't give her up, regardless of what he had promised his highness. Hell, it was his life. With a swift motion he crushed her to him and planted a long wanting kiss on those inviting lips. This was his woman. He had treated her badly, but never again

.

News of Laura's return reached the big house. Victor felt haunted by unanswered questions and Autumn was more than ever convinced that her friend was just trying to get even. But too many other things needed her attention, like getting busy organizing a small party for her friend Ted. She went to the stables and asked Ruben to saddle Maharani. She noticed that he was unusually quiet. Once in the saddle she directed the horse toward the rose garden. The need to be close to her parents was very strong. There was so much to talk about. It would really help to get everything off her chest even if there were no answers. Kneeling by the graves her fingers gently traced the names engraved in gold. God how she missed them. Before leaving she placed a red rose on her father's grave and a silk bouquet of autumn leaves on her mother's. "I love you both," she whispered. Then she swung herself onto Rani's back and rode off toward the rushing water of a nearby brook. It was early evening and fairly warm, so she slipped off her shoes and stepped into the bubbly water. Her squeal echoed back from the mountains, the water felt like ice. Rani didn't seem to mind. Autumn splashed her with water and was rewarded with a healthy snort. It made her laugh.

CHAPTER FIFTEEN

Days went by. Autumn was busy planning for Ted's arrival while Victor occupied himself with his horses. Ruben was training the newest addition to the Schwarzenau stables, one of Victor's young mares. This horse would be even better than Red Devil. His hopes to enter it in the next race were very high.

His favorite horse however remained Maharani. He loved that horse. It was the most beautiful animal he had ever seen. But there was one person he loved better than anything else, Autumn. The thought of her dominated his every waking hour.

The day started like any other. Ruben checked on the horses and made a mental note that Maharani seemed a bit listless. He would look in on her again a little later. His thoughts went to the night before and Laura's unexpected visit. They had actually gotten along quite well. For the first time ever Laura's familiar sneer had been absent.

In the meantime the object of his thoughts was re-potting African violets. It was the last thing Laura wanted to do. She became increasingly restless as the day wore on.

Autumn Leaves

Finally she told her mother that she was going for a short walk. Selma nodded in agreement. She was glad to see her daughter look and feel better. Laura had been such a worry lately. She watched Laura walk down the pebble road toward the Schwarzenau Estate. Good, maybe she was going to visit with the princess. The closeness those two once shared seemed to have hit a snag, Laura hardly ever mentioned Autumn's name any more.

Selma decided to finish where her daughter had left off but stopped when a racking cough made her clutch her chest. She sat down gasping for breath. Then she thought about Laura. Yes, Laura's short trip seemed to have helped. She didn't regret one bit having given her all that money, her daughter's well being was the only thing that mattered. It would have been nice if Laura had told her why she needed such a large amount of money. Well, large in her way of thinking. Actually she had planned on using the money to get a thorough check up, but Laura's needs came first.

Laura was on her way to the big house when a station wagon sped past her at amazing speed. She recognized the car as belonging to Dr. Niemann, the Veterinarian. Her gaze followed the car as it was heading toward the stables. She just had to see what was going on but stopped when she spotted Victor's car parked in front of the barn. She turned on her heels and headed back home. Selma was surprised to see her daughter return so soon.

"My, you're back quick. I thought you might stay out longer, the weather is so nice." Even so the words were spoken casually, Laura sensed the question behind them.

"I never made it up there. Something's going on at the stables, I saw the vet's car speed down the road. I might just sit out here for a while. Anybody call while I was gone?"

"As a matter of fact, yes, somebody called, but I don't know who it was. When I said you weren't here they hung up." Selma didn't notice that her daughter had turned a shade lighter.

"Can I bring you something cool to drink?" Laura just nodded. Her mind was racing. Who in blazes could have called her? She didn't even ask whether it was a male or female. Her mother had said 'they hung up', probably just a slip up, only one person can talk at a time. Why in hell did she give her number to that creep who had arranged the abortion? That whole episode had been a nightmare and still was. Would he try to get more money from her? She didn't have any. Her head began to hurt in a bad way. She could never tell anybody what she had done. If only those sharp pains in her lower stomach would go away. Selma came out holding two glasses of ice tea and sat down beside her daughter. They sat in silence, each having their own thoughts. The phone call was not mentioned any more.

It was chaos down at the stables. Autumn was kneeling on the straw gently stroking Maharani's head. The mare was down and hardly moving. Autumn whispered endearments, her gaze fixed on those huge brown eyes staring back at her. She had a hollow feeling in the pit of her stomach. Ruben sat beside her, tears streaming down his face, totally inconsolable. Dr. Niemann was silent. He could not imagine what was killing this healthy animal.

"Dr. Niemann, what do we do now?" Autumn looked up at the Vet hoping for a reassuring answer.

"Princess, all we can do is wait." His voice was husky and his hands were trembling. He knew that it was only a matter of minutes before it would be over, but he could not bring himself to say it. He didn't have to. A cry pierced the air.

"Rani, don't go, don't leave me!" Autumn's head sank down and came to rest on the mare's head while her tears left dark spots on its cheeks. Autumn's lips whispered words nobody could understand, her hand stroking the bridge of the mare's nose. Suddenly, a gray film covered Rani's eyes, the shine was gone.

Autumn Leaves

Doctor Nieman shook his head, indicating it was over. Victor bent down and held out his hand to help Autumn up, she brushed it away, then rose and collapsed into his arms.

"No, no, no....I won't give her up!" She repeated those words over and over as he led her to his car, a grim expression on his face. Would it ever end?

Autumn retreated back into her shell, seemingly forgetting all about the impending visit from Ted. A week went by, nothing changed. Victor had heard from Doctor Niemann, the autopsy confirmed earlier suspicions, the mare had been poisoned, but who and why? He ruled Ruben out, the boy had been visibly shaken by the event and besides that, he was sure that Ruben's love for Autumn would not allow him to hurt her, not in such a way, involving one of his beloved horses. But on the other hand, there was the incident about the nail in Rani's foot? He shook his head. No, this was not Ruben's style, but somebody was responsible. He made up his mind to have a talk with Ruben.

A short while later he found him leaning on the empty stall that once housed Maharani. Victor called out to him and the boy visibly jumped.

"Sorry, I didn't hear you come in."

"That's all right Ruben, just wondering if you're doing OK." When he didn't get a reply he went on: "I was wondering if anything unusual happened the night before Rani took ill. Can you remember anything, even the smallest detail? I know we've been over this before but humor me and try again, please?"

"There is nothing else to tell. Laura was here for a short while and we talked, but that's all. I'm sure I mentioned it before."

"Laura? No, you didn't. When was that?"

"The night before Maharani got sick. She was in a good mood, even paid attention to the horse, which she seldom does. But that night she was OK and I was glad. We don't always see eye to eye." He looked embarrassed, as if he had said something he shouldn't have.

"Thank you Ruben, I won't bother you any longer. I just thought that maybe you remembered something new." With that Victor gave the young man a pad on the shoulder and left the stables. Interesting that Laura should have paid a visit to Ruben that evening, very interesting indeed.

Ruben was feeling uneasy. He was pacing back and forth in the halls of the stable. He recalled Laura's visit the evening before the horse got sick. They had been in the barn and she had shown unusual interest in Maharani, touching her, praising her, running her hand through her feeder right after he had put some oats in it. A chill ran down his spine. That is how he would remember it. At this moment he almost hated himself.

Tears of frustration formed in his eyes. He wished he had never set foot on the Schwarzenau property. His life was sheer hell ever since he got here when it should have been a dream come true... Well, perhaps not all the time. So Laura found out that he loved the princess, so what? It wasn't a crime to love Autumn, not then anyway, especially since she didn't even know about it. Why did it all have to turn so ugly? No more, he swore to himself, no more.

Autumn closed the book she was reading. It was a pretty day. Perhaps she should go for a swim. Too many days had gone by without any activity. She wanted to go riding, let the wind blow through her hair, go up to her favorite spot and touch the clouds, but her faithful companion was gone. The road was too treacherous to take another horse. She knew that she would never go up there again. She flung the book against the wall. A healthy anger welled up inside. She took another book off the shelve, throwing it in the same direction, only this time she missed the wall and it crashed through the window shattering it into a million pieces. The door flew open and Victor stood there, white as a ghost. He stared at Autumn with such a stupid look on his face it made her smile. Her casual remark, "Coming swimming?" really took him off guard.

"What?" He didn't understand.

"I thought we might go swimming. It's warm enough, don't you think?" He had heard her right.

"Swimming, right, that's a good idea." He left shaking his head nonstop. Sometimes he couldn't figure her out. She always took him by surprise.

They actually had fun racing back and forth in the pool. She was a good, strong swimmer. Could it be that she had accepted the loss of her horse, or was this another put on? This time he wasn't going to question it, she had grown up so fast lately. He decided that he would let her handle this at her own time schedule. Should he mention Ted's coming?

"By the way Victor, uncle Victor..." she smiled seeing him wince, "Ted should be here any day, have you heard anything?"

"You will see him at four thirty Thursday afternoon."

"Thursday? That's only two, no three days away?" She was sputtering water and for a moment he thought she might go under.

"The arrangements are made, Goldilocks, you made them, remember?" There was a moment of stunned silence, she swam to the edge of the pool and sat on the steps.

"Victor, how do you put up with me?"

"What do you mean?"

"I mean, how do you put up with me. I am never quite together, so how do you put up with me?" Her eyes were the brilliant blue he remembered from long ago, trusting and innocent.

"How do I put up with you? I love you and I want you to be happy, it's that simple. I promised your father to look out for you, that's what I am doing and that's why I put up with you, as you put it."

He joined her on the steps. Sitting side by side, she laid her head on his shoulder.

"I am so lucky to have you."

He got warm all over, his mind saying 'I am too.'

It was Thursday early afternoon. Autumn's arms were loaded down with towels when the phone started to ring. John came running, stopped short at seeing the princess so bogged down, but she motioned him away. He went on to answer the phone.

"It's for you, your highness,"

"Just take a message, I can't get to it now, can't you see that?"

"Yes, you're...." She walked through the big doublewide door leading to the pool. This was the first time she had ever been short with him, John decided that he did not like it. He picked up the receiver: "I'm sorry sir, may I take a message?"

"Just tell her that... no, no message." The phone went dead.

At the other end a young doctor led out a deep sigh, shrugged his shoulders and turned to hug his little girl, the sweetest young lady in his life.

At four thirty sharp a taxi pulled up at the Schwarzenau Estate. A young man jumped out, ran up the front steps and pushed the doorbell like there was no tomorrow. When John opened the door he ran right past him into the parlor. Autumn felt herself being lifted high up into the air and being twirled around.

"Hello Ted Warnham, welcome to Schwarzenau." Autumn gasped as he set her down, not too gently.

Autumn Leaves

"I can't believe I am here. You are so gorgeous, Autumn von Schwarzenau!" He looked at her for a long time. Victor had been right, she was even more beautiful. There was a new look in her face. She was more serious in a grown up kind of way.

The evening went by quickly. Victor opened a bottle of some old vintage for the occasion. They had fun talking about past events and making plans for the morrow. Autumn could no longer stifle her yawn, it had gotten late and the wine didn't help, so she bid them good night. Victor took his young friend out for a walk. Strolling through the garden, he could not help but notice the change in Ted's behavior. He had never seen him quite so vibrant one minute and so remote the next.

"What's up, sport?"

"She's even more beautiful than I had imagined. What happened, Victor?"

"What do you mean?"

"What made her so grown up? The little girl from yesterday is gone."

"Well, for one thing, her parents, as you well know. She's been through a lot, more than most young people experience, but she is surfacing, she's strong."

"But why does she have to be strong now? What can be more painful than losing your parents, and she's mastered that, so what else is there?" Ted's concern was real. He loved this girl, like a sister. Once, he thought he loved her for his own, but much had happened since.

Victor didn't know how to answer him. It was really up to Autumn to let him in on her personal life, if she wanted too. Did Ted really love her? Suddenly Victor had doubts.

"She's had her ups and downs, the worst lately was when her horse died."

"What do you mean? You're not talking about that gorgeous mare her parents had given her?"

"The same. She wasn't sick or anything, the Vet thinks it was poison, but the how is still one big question mark."

"Poor Autumn," was all Ted said. The two remained silent, each hanging on to their own thoughts. Then, out of the blue, Ted asked: "What else has been going on?"

Victor was taken back, the question was so blunt and sounded quite demanding.

"Ted, if you want to know about Autumn, I suggest you ask her yourself." That sounded kind of harsh, but he was a bit perturbed and he didn't mind if Ted knew it.

"Did I say something wrong? If so, I'm sorry. Some times I am real good at putting my foot into it." That crushed look on his boyish face was something nobody could resist, not even Victor. He realized that young people often spoke up with such candor, not meaning to offend in any way.

"Do you love Autumn?"

"Sure I do, I have from the beginning. I'd do anything for her. You know Vic, at first I thought that this was it, I mean I just knew that this was the love of my life. Then later on, when she didn't answer any of my letters, I realized that we had been nothing more than good friends, so I went on with my life. It wasn't as easy as it sounds. She really did get under my skin. Then along came this petite, black haired beauty from the ladies swim team who sort of helped me over it. I was going to bring her with me, she couldn't get away, but she said she may follow later, if that's all right with you?" There was a long pause. "Am I asking too much?"

Victor shook his head. He was trying to sort out this new development.

"No, of course not. I just didn't expect this. You never mentioned it to me on the phone. Does this mermaid have a name?"

"You bet, Dahlia is what her parents call her. Her mother is from India."

"Pretty name, it makes me think of a flower. Well, I think I'll let you tell Autumn all about it, she'll probably be delighted " silently adding - I hope. He shelved the thought of telling Ted about the letters. It didn't matter any more.

CHAPTER SIXTEEN

Even so she'd been dead tired, sleep would not come. If only she could shut off her mind. Her thoughts were running rampant between Peter and Ted. It was a mistake to think that Ted could make her forget about Peter, just the opposite seemed to have taken place. Sweet Ted, how in heavens name could she tell him that her feelings for him were those one had for a good friend, nothing more. There was no use trying to deny it, her heart belonged to Peter. It was impossible to sleep, so she decided to go and get a glass of milk. Her mother always said that this was the best remedy for a good night's sleep, a warm glass of milk. She preferred it cold. It was the very reason she could no longer drink the fresh milk they served up on the Alm, even if everyone insisted it was the best there was, coming straight from the beast to the table. Would Peter still approve of this old custom? As children they had often enjoyed a healthy chunk of cheese, freshly baked bread and a fresh glass of milk. Oh Peter...

It was almost midnight when she crept down the stairs, making her way toward the kitchen. She stole a glance in the direction where her fathers study lay. Even so the pain lasted only a second, it was long enough to make her eyes fill with water. The study was closed off to prying eyes, just like the blue parlor. God how she missed her daddy. She quickly turned and headed toward the kitchen.

She got startled; the overhead lights were on in the kitchen. Then she spotted John sitting at the table, a glass of milk in front of him and what looked like a mighty big chunk of pound cake. He jumped up when she entered.

"What a surprise, I didn't think anybody else would be up. Do sit down John, I didn't mean to startle you."

"Princess, I was just having a little snack, some times I have trouble sleeping."

"So do I. Where did you find that delicious looking cake?"

"Right beside the cooling box, no, not under the silver dome, the one next to it. Mary was busy baking earlier, for my birthday tomorrow." He glanced at the clock on the wall; "perhaps it's for today."

"So it is, John, that means we can start celebrating."

She rushed toward the old man and gave him such a tight hug that it brought tears to his eyes. Little princess, one minute she yelled at him and the next she loved on him, it was all right, he cherished her.

"Oh John, can you ever forgive me for being so mean to you?"

"Nothing to forgive, I've already forgotten about it." It did his heart good that she remembered.

Just as they sat down to enjoy the cake somebody else poked his head through the door, Victor.

"I thought I heard noise coming from the kitchen, what's going on?"

"We are ..." Autumn barely got out the words when another voice chimed in.

"Room for one more?" Now Ted was sticking his head through the door and everybody started to laugh.

"We're celebrating John's birthday, this is fun." Autumn's eyes sparkled and all traces of sleep had vanished. Soon everybody was enjoying Mary's cake.

"Somebody's missing." John looked from one to the other. Autumn knew exactly who, if Peter could be here the picture would be complete.

"Oops, not any more, there she is," Victor said as Mary's head peeked around the door. She didn't look all that happy. Autumn could feel the heat rising in her face. She felt as if her hand got caught in the cookie jar. Well, she couldn't help it if Peter just happened to be on her mind.

"Does anybody know what time it is?" Mary glanced from one face to the other, waiting for an answer. Suddenly she let out a shriek, pointing at the almost empty cake plate.

"My Frankfurter Kranz, where did it go?" All of them looked guilty; some with crumbs still clinging to their lips. Only Ted had a stupid look on his face. He couldn't figure out what in the world the old woman was yelling about. What in tarnation was a Frankfurter Kranz? The first one to recover was Autumn.

"Come on Mary, simmer down, we're just celebrating John's birthday. That was a wonderful cake, wasn't it?" Her head was nodding trying to make the others do the same.

"John's birthday is not 'til tomorrow and what you ate was going to be the most beautiful creation I've ever done, now it's gone." Was she actually going to cry?

Autumn got up and put her arms around the old woman's shoulders.

"There now, Mary, you can always bake another cake, you are so good at it, and John's birthday is already here. We're just a little bit early with our celebration, that's all."

Mary wiped her eyes with the sleeve of her robe and glanced at John, who sat there smiling right into her eyes. She walked over to him and kissed him smack on the lips.

"There, you old fool, and a happy birthday to you."

Autumn Leaves

"That's the spirit," Victor said as Mary took the seat beside John. He noticed her reaching for his hand and thought it rather sweet. They talked for a while but then the yawning started one by one.

"The Lord gave us the night for sleep, not to cackle around like a house full of chickens. How will we ever get anything done in the morning." Mary stood up and tugged on John's sleeve. They were so cute together, the first time anybody had ever seen them affectionately so openly. Victor also rose to say good night, leaving Ted and Autumn alone.

An awkward silence set in, then both spoke at once, stopped, looked at each other and busted out laughing. "OK, ladies first."

"If you insist, but what I have to say may not be to your liking." There was a serious tone in her voice.

"Why don't you let me be the judge of that, just tell me what's on your mind."

All at once she blurted out, " I'm in love with somebody else." Her face was red as a beet and her hands were twisting themselves into knots. She didn't dare look at him. After a moments silence, Ted cleared his throat.

"I am surprised at you, princess. Is that any way to treat a guest?" Now she was really getting upset. Once again she had put her foot in it, only this time it was much worse.

Ted enjoyed watching her squirm. It wasn't fair; he knew that, especially since she had taken the words right out of his mouth. He'd better hurry up and come to her rescue.

"Look at me, Autumn, it's OK, really it is. You see, I was going to tell you the same thing. I also met somebody else and could for the life of me not figure out how to tell you. We're a fine pair, don't you think? I am so relieved that you have somebody who loves you, you deserve it."

He took her face into his hands and for a moment she thought he was going to kiss her. Well, he did, but not on the lips, his mouth gently touched her forehead.

"Now we both can sleep better, right princess?"

"Right." How could she tell him that she was not happy? Somehow it hurt to have lost Ted, she only hoped it was to somebody very nice.

"Let's have that picnic in the park tomorrow, OK?" He nodded; it was time to go to sleep.

It turned out to be a brilliant day. A mouthwatering smell emitted from the picnic basket on the little table. Ted took hold of it and off they went. They chose a quiet spot near the lake. Laying on the blanket with hands folded under their heads they watched the white clouds sail by while each followed their own thoughts.

"Autumn, would you like to meet her?"

"Yes I would, when?" She knew right away who he was talking about.

"I phoned her this morning, she is coming Saturday. I thought I'd go and pick her up and bring her here, if that's OK with you." He was leaning on his elbow, looking down at her. When she agreed, he leaned over and kissed her lightly on the cheek.

The pair of eyes watching them only saw the kiss, the happy smiles, and drew their own conclusion. Those eyes turned dark with fury. The lone figure remained motionless, pressed against the fence.

That evening the discussion over dinner was not what Victor had expected. They were making plans as to the arrival of Dahlia, Ted's little mermaid. But when they decided to drive to Munich together, Victor insisted that the car should be checked over carefully. After all, it was quite a long drive. Ted volunteered to take it to the village garage the very next day.

Next morning, at breakfast, John announced an unexpected visitor, Laura. Autumn and Ted were alone on the verandah. Victor had already left to go down to the stables.

Autumn Leaves

Autumn motioned her in. "Come join us in a cup of coffee and meet Ted"

"Come on Autumn, you know we've met before, but it is good to see you again. You're still gorgeous." He had her full attention. Laura made no bones about admiring him. He only smiled and remained his polite self, offering her the chair beside him.

"Miss Laura, I must say, you have certainly become quite a lady." She had the decency to blush and took the chair offered, moving it just a bit closer. Autumn watched with amusement. By now she had caught on to Laura's tricks, knowing that the name of the game was to steal Autumn's man for herself. Her mind registered, good luck girl friend, he's not mine and won't be yours, so have fun trying.

"Have any plans for today?" The question was directed more toward Ted than Autumn, but Autumn chose to answer.

"No, nothing much. I have to take the car to the garage for a checkup, care to join me?"

Laura glanced toward Ted. "Are you going?"

"Autumn, I thought..."

"You really don't have to come if Laura is coming with me." Autumn winked at Ted hoping he would get the message, he did.

"Come on girlfriend." She nudged Laura out the door, grinning back at Ted. He liked this new Autumn, feisty and confident. Laura drudged behind Autumn, not really comprehending how things got turned around. Just as they were ready to climb into the car Autumn hightailed back to the house.

"Wait a minute, I forgot my purse." She heard Laura yell after her but didn't bother to stop. It sounded as if Laura said she wasn't going.

As soon as Autumn was out of sight, Laura reached into her pocket, pulled out a knife and began stabbing the right front tire. Then took off running toward her home like a cat out of hell, not once coming to a stop, sweat running down her body.

Autumn, in the meantime, informed Ted that miss Laura had made her excuses. They had a good laugh. Ted took the car keys from her and headed out the door.

"Be back as soon as I can. No need for you to come. Do you need anything from the village?"

"I don't think so, be careful."

Minute's later Victor returned from the stables. "Was that Ted in your car?"

"Yes, he's taking to the garage. Did you need him for anything?"

"No, except Ruben told me that you might need some new tires in the front. I guess the garage will figure that out. I'll call ahead and tell them about it, just in case."

"Thank you Vic, you always look out for me, don't you?"

"Have nothing better to do, little one." He gave her a pad on the rear and left to make the call. Their relationship had changed, it was more relaxed.

Almost an hour had passed. Autumn was changing into her bathing suit when she heard people talking downstairs. She recognized Victor's voice, but not the other. She was zipping her cover-up, coming down the stairs, and recognized the policeman from the village. He saw Autumn and notched Victor. Something was wrong. Victor's face was twisted, as if he were in terrible pain.

"Come on inside, Herman, so we can talk to the princess." Victor ushered both of them into the parlor. He went to pour brandy into two glasses, handing one to Autumn and one to the officer, then poured himself a stiff one. Autumn realized that the news had to be bad, Victor always gave her a drink when he had something terrible to tell her. Her chest started feeling awfully tight.

"Autumn, it's Ted. The car, it blew a front tire. He smashed into the big old oak at the bend." Silence...

Autumn Leaves

"Autumn, he didn't make it." It was as if time stood still. The glass she held slid out of her hand and fell to the floor, spilling it's contents all over the carpet. There was no scream. Those blue eyes looked up and the word "No" formed on her lips, but no sound came out. She lifted her shoulders, then let them fall in total resignation, got up and walked out the front door. The policeman wanted to stop her, but Victor held on to him.

"Let her go, she has to be alone. Too much has come down on those frail shoulders of late, she needs a moment to herself."

Had he known what would happen next, he would have stopped her. Instead he waited not knowing that she blindly ran toward the stables, grabbed the first horse in the stall, swung herself on it's back, no saddle, and rode off toward the woods. She had to get to her secret place.

Ruben heard a noise and when he looked up he saw Autumn vanish into the forest. Something didn't feel right, so he called the main house. John answered and assured him that the princess was in good spirits. He didn't know about the accident. Although Ruben was glad to hear that everything seemed to be fine, her had an uneasy feeling in the pit of his stomach. He checked the racks where the saddles hung and saw that all the saddles were there. Surely Autumn would not ride a strange horse bareback? He had to find Victor.

The policeman returned to the village after Victor assured him that he would come to the hospital as soon as the princess returned. He wanted to bring Ted's body home. It suddenly hit him; this could have been Autumn lying in the morgue. Shivers ran up and down his spine. He was standing on the front steps when Ruben came running. He was shouting.

"Something is wrong with the princess?"

"What do you mean?"

"She rode like the devil out of the stables into the forest, no saddle."

Victor's knees turned to rubber; he had to sit down.
"When was that?"
"Just now. I called and talked to Mr. John, but he said everything was all right, but when I noticed that she had no saddle, I got worried."
"And so you should. John doesn't know, she's in trouble Ruben, we have to find her." Ruben stared at him, not quite understanding, only that Autumn was in trouble.
"Find her" was what he understood and that was what he would do. There was still a lot of daylight left, they would find her. Perhaps she was already on her way back?

Only it was not so. She was on that narrow, winding road leading toward her secret place. The mare was on unfamiliar ground. Autumn constantly had to urge the animal on to keep moving. At times the reigns went slack as tears were blinding Autumn's sight, while her head was throbbing painfully from wanting to scream. Why Ted? Her agony was so great that without realizing, her foot hit into the mare's belly with full force, making the horse jump. She lost her grip, hit the rocks at the outer edge of the path and went sailing down into what seemed to be a bottomless pit. Her cry echoed back from the steep walls, then faded away. The now riderless horse turned and made its way back down the steep slope.

It was Ruben who spotted the animal emerging from the trees. He yelled for Victor frantically pointing to the horse. There was no sign of Autumn. An icy chill ran down Victor's spine. The horse trotted past him and on toward the stables. Victor's eyes followed every step it made, unable to move. Finally he shook his head and raised both arms in utter dismay. Autumn, where was Autumn? He slapped his head remembering her state of dress, a bathing suit with a throw over, that was all. They had to find her fast.
"Ruben, we have to find her, now!"

Autumn Leaves

It sounded like a command but it really was a plea.
"You go look after the horse first, then follow me."
With that, his heels pressed into his horse's belly making it pick up speed as he raced toward the wood. He called out Autumn's name, but there was no answer. There were so many paths she could have taken it was a nightmare. Which was the right one? Just a day or so ago things seemed to fall into place and life had begun to take on some form of normalcy, now this... Damn, everything was coming apart at the seams, again.

With horror he realized that there was somebody else he had to think about, Dahlia. She was supposed to arrive in two days. The dull pain in his head grew monstrous. This was way over his head. Right now there should be two of him, or three. It would have been so good to have Jane at his side. She would know what to do. He frowned and his mouth contorted as if he had just bitten into a sour apple. To this very day the thought of Jane left him with a bitter taste in his mouth. He was better off not to even remember her name. The sound of hoofs made him raise his head, Ruben was approaching.
"I think I know which way the princess may have gone, she went up the mountain, and there is only one path and it's not an easy one."
"How do you know that?"
"By the way the mare was sweating and all that dirt on her hoofs. Most other roads are easy traveling, nothing to make a horse sweat like that, besides, the pine needles cover all of the lower paths, very little dirt."
"Good God, she could be hurt up there." Their eyes met, both men thinking the worst but neither daring to utter a word.
They hurried to reach the path and began to urge their horses upward. They shouted her name, over and over, but the only sound echoing back was ... Autumn, Autumn, Autumn!

Anita Attwood

Nightfall set in, they had to get off the mountain and get help.

Autumn Leaves

CHAPTER SEVENTEEN

Ranger Marshall heard his phone ring once, twice ... Who in tarnation was interrupting his supper?

"If it's not urgent, call back in thirty minutes."

"It's urgent friend, this is Victor, our princess is missing, somewhere up on the east side of Big Eagle. You know this terrain, can I count on your help?"

"Did you say Big Eagle mountain? That's rugged and steep, nobody goes there."

"Believe me, that's where she went, only we can't find her. She's been gone a couple of hours, it's getting colder and she's not wearing a whole lot of clothes, we've got to find her."

Ranger Marshall could hear the panic in Victor's voice. Now why would the princess go up that treacherous mountain and why didn't she have clothes on, well he'd said not enough, whatever that meant. He scratched his head and gave his venison stew a sad look.

"All right, I'll be over there as fast as I can. Why in tarnation did you not call sooner?" There was no answer; Victor had already hung up.

He called his hounds, Bart and Bell, reached for his coat and stomped out the door. He had to convince the prince that there was no use trying to go up the mountain at night, it would have to wait 'until morning. God willing, the princess would be safe from harm until then, if she was still alive. This was tragic. The question came back, why hadn't they called on him earlier, but he would keep it to himself. Tragedy was haunting this house. The loss of her parents had been very hard on the young lass. He remembered the last time he was up on that mountain was when his son came to visit, that had been a few years back. Peter wanted to show him his favorite secret place. If memory served him right, he mentioned that the only other person that knew about it was his childhood friend, princess Autumn. He had to admit, on a sunny day it was a wondrous little piece of earth. Would she have still remembered the spot? Had she perhaps been up there since? Peter had said they used to touch the sky and pretend to be in heaven. A likely place to go for someone who wanted to be close to those they loved. It was possible that she had somehow managed to get up there. He silently prayed for her safety.

When he reached the chateau Victor met him on the front steps.

"I see you brought your hounds, that's good. Shall I get a piece of her clothing so they can get her scent?"

"Not now, we're not going to be able to do anything until it gets light. No sense in anybody else getting hurt. How do you know she's up on that side of the mountain?"

"Ruben figured it out, our jockey, he could tell by the horses condition and he also knows that Autumn often used to go in that direction. She called it her secret place, but nobody knows where it really is. There's got to be a way to get to her. If she is up there she's going to be mighty cold. It's already cooling off quite a bit and... what if she is badly hurt?" Victor almost shouted the last words.

"We'll just have to hope for the best. Let's be reasonable, there is nothing we can do in the dark. We'll start as early as possible. In the meantime I'll alert mountain rescue to meet us early in the morning. Try to get some rest, you will need all your strength in the morning."

"I wish I could but I'm on my way to go to the hospital. We lost a close friend today, a very dear young man." Victor's voice was not steady any more. The old ranger noticed tears in his eyes. So that's what this was all about, probably someone the princess was very close to. Life at times did not seem fair. Seems like the best of them were being dealt the hardest blows. Makes one wonder about the saying that God doesn't give us more than we can handle, he suddenly wasn't so sure about that any more. His heart felt heavy when he bid Victor good night, with a promise to be back before dawn. As he was making his way toward his home, he turned and glanced at the chateau, it was light up from one end to the other. He surveyed the rugged mountain terrain reaching toward the night sky, dark and sinister looking. His lips moved in a silent prayer for the young princess.

The big house was in turmoil. Sleep was the last thing anybody thought about. Victor took it upon himself to order the blue room to be opened and made ready to receive his young friend. He felt sure Autumn would want it that way. A short while later he left for the hospital, knowing that Mary and John would see to his wishes. He drove slower than usual, feeling the full impact of the day closing in on him.

At the hospital, Dr. Schwarz led him down the corridor toward the morgue.

"He didn't suffer, he probably never knew what hit him." The doctors statement should have made him feel better, but somehow it had an adverse effect.

"How would you know? Did you notice how young he was? Don't you think he saw the tree coming?" Dr. Schwarz placed his hand on Victor's shoulder. It was a good hand.

"I am deeply sorry about your young friend, but I do know for certain that he did not suffer. Just take a look at his face, he is at peace." Ted did look peaceful. He could almost see a smile on his lips. What a waste, he had so much to look forward too. The pain he felt looking at his young friends still face, even more handsome in death, almost knocked him down. He grabbed on to the gurney to steady himself, and touched Ted's hand. It was ice cold.

"Can I take him home?" His words were barely audible. He coughed to clear his throat, which had suddenly gone dry.

"I prefer to keep him here until tomorrow, a few minor details still need to be sorted out. Perhaps tomorrow afternoon would be better, if you don't mind?"

"I don't mind," and after a slight pause, "by then I hope to have found princess Autumn."

"What do you mean?"

"She is up in the mountains, we don't know where. She bolted after she heard the news about Ted. They had been very close. I just hope I don't have to bring another patient to you."

The old doctor did not answer. He thought about the young princess and his heart was sad. He was afraid of what tomorrow might bring. They walked slowly back down the corridor; each buried deep in thought. There really wasn't much anybody could say. The automatic door opened and a cool breeze engulfed them. Both seemed to take a deep breath before they parted with a solid handshake.

For Victor it would be a long night. He had no intention of quitting. He would go back to the forest and search for Autumn, but first he had to get a very strong light to guide his way. When he walked through the front door he noticed that the blue room was ready, an eerie resemblance of the past. He hesitated before walking in, the glow of the candles drawing bizarre shadows on the walls. Using his bare hands, he quickly extinguished the flames, then closed the doors on his way out. John came down the hallway and stopped when he saw Victor closing the doors to the parlor.

"He won't be coming home tonight, tomorrow afternoon. By then our princess will also be here, I promise."

"Yes, Mr. Victor, she will also be here, and she will be all right, won't she?" Victor noticed that the old man was trembling. His tried to give him a reassuring smile.

"Of course she'll be fine, we won't have it any other way. Maybe we better try to get some rest, tomorrow we'll need every ounce of strength, don't you think?" John nodded and shuffled toward his chamber, suddenly looking very old.

Victor watched until he was out of sight, his heart aching for the old man. He located the lamp and quietly left the house. The stables lay in darkness and he moved swiftly leading his horse outside, mounting and riding toward the black looking forest. He really had no idea where to begin looking and rode around aimlessly. He called out her name over and over but the only thing he accomplished was to disturb the animals. There was not a trace of Autumn. Although it was cold sweat was running down his back. A terrible fear gripped his heart. Being out here was useless, Ranger Marshall was right. If he wanted to go with the search party in the morning he would need a few hours rest. He didn't want to stop looking, but common sense told him to head back. It felt as if a huge rock was crushing his chest.

Hardly anybody at the chateau had gotten much sleep. Mary was in the kitchen brighten early making coffee, it was still pitch black outside. John and Victor were right behind her, dark circles under their eyes. Victor was anxious to be on his way, waiting for Ranger Marshall. He showed up only a few minutes later looking almost as bad as the rest of them. Sleep had evaded them all.

"I brought some powerful flashlights so we can start right away. Going in, the lower part won't be to bad, it's higher up where it gets rough. Hopefully by then it'll be getting light. Wouldn't mind a cup of that good smelling coffee so." Mary was already putting a steaming mug in front of him. Not many words were spoken. The task ahead was on everybody's mind. It was time to go. Victor noticed Mary reaching for John's hand just as he and the ranger walked out the door. "Gods speed," she whispered, still holding on to John. When they reached the bottom of the steps they heard Mary call out: "God's speed, bring her back safe!"

Ruben saw the two men approaching the stables. By the time they got there, three horses were saddled, ready to go. Ruben could not believe when Victor told him to stay behind, but Victor remained firm. Although he noticed Ruben's clenched fists, there was no time to go into any explanation; they had to move fast.

They entered the forest and soon reached the small trail leading up Big Eagle. In a clearing they tied the horses to proceed on foot. Neither had noticed the Rescue wagon parked in the meadow. The climb ahead would not be easy. Victor had one of Autumn's blouses tucked in his pocket, perhaps it would help Bart and Bell find her. The serious task ahead troubled his thoughts.

Thank God the moon was bright. It really helped to find the way among the dense pine trees. Now all they needed was one of those bright shiny stars leading them to Autumn, just like the three wise men had. Victor was not a very religious person, but at this moment he knew that they needed all the help they could get to find his little girl. That's what she had become again. He was breathing heavy and they were not even half way up. The much older Ranger seemed to be climbing upward, with the greatest of ease. Victor thought himself to be in top form, big mistake that was. Marshall stopped to wait for him. He had fallen way behind.

"Time to let Bart and Bell have a sniff at that blouse." A sharp whistle brought the dogs running. Victor, still puffing, held the garment under their noses. They sniffed and Bell nipped at it, but let go immediately. In a flash they were gone.

"Won't they run off?"

"Not hardly, they have a mission and they know it. If she's anywhere around here, they'll spot her and let us know." The ranger walked on but stopped again. It had gotten lighter. Up ahead he saw three men waiting. He raised his hand and waved.

"Mountain rescue is already ahead of us. Those guys are the best." Victor only nodded, he needed all his energy to breathe, but he did manage a weak smile. After a short greeting, the five men walked on in silence.

Victor was just about to suggest a short pause, when the sound of barking reached their ears, coming from still higher up.

"Yap, that's them, they found something." Marshall nodded his head in satisfaction. "Always can rely on them, have from day one."

Nobody said anything, they were eager to catch up with the dogs. Bart and Bell stood on the edge of the gorge, looking down.

"It's near the spot."

"Near what spot?"

Marshall finished, "the spot where Peter and the princess used to come too." Victor still did not understand.

Rescue had already begun to lower one of their men down into what seemed to be a bottomless pit.

"I can see her." The voice coming from below had a hollow sound, running shivers down their spine.

"Is she all right?" Victor shouted back, afraid to hear the answer.

"Don't know 'til I get there, no movement." Silence, more rope was needed, then it stopped. Did that mean he had reached her?

"She's alive!" The voice reached them and Victor sank to the ground, sapped of all his strength, big tears rolling down his cheeks. He didn't care who saw it, she was alive, that's all that mattered. Both dogs eased toward him and began to lick his face, he didn't mind. His arms went around them and he hugged them tight. Ranger Marshall smiled, he was proud of his hounds.

Finding her was one thing, but bringing her up was quite another. It took all their efforts to do so. A stretcher had to be lowered and a second medic went down to assist in placing her on the cloth, trying not to cause further injury. Autumn was unconscious. It took a long time heaving her up, one foot at a time, always mindful not to let the stretcher bounce against the rock wall. Finally they reached the summit and packed her immediately in blankets. She was pale with dark circles under her eyes, she felt cold to the touch and her breathing was shallow. It was essential to get her off the mountain as fast as possible. Victor tried to walk beside Autumn, but it was impossible.

"Hang in there, Goldilocks, hang in there." He gently squeezed her limp hand, then stepped behind the medics to allow them a speedy descent. The men from Rescue moved quick and precise on the narrow path.

Just as it had been when they came up, Victor and the ranger quietly walked down, each hanging on to their own thoughts. It was a difficult descent having to avoid many slippery spots. Finally, they reached the clearing and the waiting ambulance. Ranger Marshall offered to see to the horses while Victor jumped into the passenger seat of the ambulance letting the medics tend to Autumn. The ambulance took off and as soon as the village was in sight the siren was blaring. The emergency staff was already waiting. Everything happened so fast and before Victor could turn around, Autumn had been whisked away.

He ran after them, but the door to the emergency room slammed shut right before his nose and a stern looking orderly shook his head, indicating for him not to go any further. Luckily, a young nurse recognized Victor and came to his rescue.

"Please, your highness, come with me." He followed willingly, until he thought she was going to far away from the emergency room.

"I have to stay close to her, I need to know what her condition is."

"I know, we're already here. I thought you might want to wait in a quiet place. I'll bring some coffee, how do you like it?"

"Just black. But how will they know I'm here?"

"I'm going to tell them, please sit down and try to stay calm, she's in good hands, really." Her smile was pleasant and her voice soothing. A few minutes later, when she returned with a steaming cup of coffee, she found him with his head buried in his hands. She placed the coffee beside him and quietly left the room. Victor didn't hear her come or go, he smelled the coffee, that's how he knew she'd been there. The picture flashing before his eyes was always the same, Autumn falling into that black ravine, tumbling down into nothingness. It was like a bad dream from which he desperately wanted to wake up. But it wasn't a dream, she had been at the bottom of that gorge and he was here in the hospital waiting for some kind of report about her condition. How much longer would he have to wait? He jumped up, pacing back and forth. He couldn't wait another minute. He stormed out the door and was making his way to the emergency room, when a man in a white coat approached him.

"Victor von Schwarzenau?"

"Yes, do you have any news?" He had grabbed the doctor's sleeve, searching his face.

"Yes! The princess is a very lucky young lady, she is stable, but in serious condition. It's a wonder she is alive at all. I was told that was a very long fall. So far, we have determined that she has several broken ribs, a broken shoulder blade, a possible concussion and multiple bruises. We can't find anything wrong with her legs. What we are worried about is her head. Everything possible is being done. We will bring her through this. A thick blanket of leaves, that's what saved her, cushioned the fall. We think she might have hit something on the way down, a tree stump or rock. Most of her injuries are on the left side. You will be able to see her as soon as she comes back from the CAT scan, which will also give us better insight as to any brain injuries."

"Is she awake? How long will she have to be here? Does she remember anything?"

"Hold on, one question at a time. How long her recovery will take is hard to say. By the way, my name is doctor Kleinhaus. I can't answer all your questions just now; her attending physician will have to do that. I'm only here for a visit, from Munich."

Victor tried to digest everything the doctor told him. He never noticed the doctor's extended hand. What he mostly remembered was the fact that Autumn had a good chance of recovering, it really didn't matter how long that would take.

"You said you are from Munich, are you on staff at the Frauenklinic there?"

"How did you guess?" A bemused smile crossed the doctor's face. "I specialize in head injuries, among other things. I will be working very closely with the attending physician's. As I said before, all that can be done will be done. She's in excellent hands."

"Thank you doctor, may I see her now?"

"Mind you, she may still be unconscious, but come along, let's find out." They moved along the corridor.

Doctor Kleinhaus made some inquiries then led Victor into a small room, lined with glass covered cabinets holding all kinds of shiny instruments and other medical necessities. There was a huge lamp in the middle of the room, right over a narrow bed, where Autumn lay with her eyes closed, both shiny sidebars raised to assure her safety. Victor's breath caught in his throat. Was she breathing? There were several doctors and nurses around her, when suddenly one of them started giving orders, and everybody was rushing around in a frenzy. Somebody pushed Victor out of the room and ordered him to remain in the corridor. He thought he could hear a crunching sound, followed by an ear-piercing scream, then it was quiet. Did that scream come from Autumn? What the hell was going on? Not even ten horses would hold him now, he burst into the room and saw Autumn's right hand clutching the rail, her eyes wide open, tears streaming down. A nurse was gently wiping her forehead.

"I'm sorry princess, we had to do it, there was no time for anything else." Autumn just nodded her head, unable to speak. Now Victor noticed a tube dangling out from under the sheet near her upper body, red fluid draining down.

"Her lung collapsed, one of the ribs punctured it, we had to act fast." It was an explanation given by one of the attending white coats, but Victor could not accept the cruel treatment. His lips pressed firmly together, he shot an accusing look in the doctor's direction. His attention went to Autumn; she was awake, thank God for that. Doctor Kleinhaus stepped up to him.

"Some times we have to take drastic measures to save a life, I am sorry." Victor wondered if the good doctor had read his thoughts.

"The good news is that the concussion is not as severe as we first thought. We need to keep her quiet and awake for a while, and I'm afraid that she will be in some pain, but we can't give her too much to ease it, not just yet. Will you stay and talk to her, to help keep her awake for just a little bit longer?" Victor assured him that he would. He held on to Autumn's hand and gave her a crooked grin. She tried to smile back, but it looked more like a painful grimace. He knew that her body must be aching from head to toe. Had she heard what the doctor had said about keeping her awake? The pain shooting through her would most likely see to that.

"There doesn't seem to be any nausea, that is a very good sign, perhaps we can give her some additional pain killer." Now that's what he liked to hear.

A nurse came with a needle and Autumn closed her eyes. She was not fond of those things. When she opened them again the nurse was on her way out.

"Why didn't she give me the shot, Vic?" Her voice was barely above a whisper.

"She did sweetheart, she put it into the drip, no sense in giving you additional pain, is there?"

"I'm glad, I don't like those things." With that she closed her eyes and drifted off. Victor almost panicked. Just as he was going to try and wake her, somebody pulled on his sleeve.

"Let her sleep, the rest will do her good." It was the same nurse that had just given her the shot.

" You may stay with her as long as you wish. She will remain in intensive care over night, just to be sure. Can we bring you anything?"

He gratefully asked for some coffee, he did not want to go to sleep. Would she remember Ted's accident? He almost hoped that she wouldn't, not yet any way.

Then a thought shot through him like fire. Dear God, another task in front of him, taking Ted's body back to the chateau and calling Dahlia. He couldn't ask John to handle this; he would have to do it himself. What about Peter? Maybe his father had already notified him. Come to think of it, why should he, he probably didn't even know that Peter and Autumn ... Yes, what exactly was going on with those two? Whatever it was, Peter should know what happened.

Victor eased himself out of the chair and stepped closer to the bed. She seemed to be resting. He noticed a pained expression on her face, could it be that she was feeling pain even while sleeping? Poor little princess, life had not been her friend of late. He kissed her on the forehead, then let the nurse know that he would be at the phone down the hall.

"She should be asleep for quite a while, so take your time, we'll watch over her."

Why did people always use the word we, even when there was only one around? Just one of those things, he had probably done it himself hundreds of times. Strange that he should notice a thing like that now.

Making the call to Dahlia was not going to be easy. Then he remembered he didn't even have her number, now what? The only way to get it was by going through Ted's things. He shuddered at the thought. It would be a lot easier to call Peter first. Damit, that number was at the chateau. Frustration almost got the best of him. He was ready to punch a hole in the wall. Best thing to do at the moment was to go back to Autumn and think things out. He wished he could delegate his duties on to other people. Autumn's voice ripped him out of his stupor. She was calling his name. With a few long strides he was back at her side.

"I'm here, Goldilocks, I'm here."

"You left me, it hurts so bad, Victor, it hurts so bad." Those blue eyes had almost turned black, as pain after pain ripped through her fragile body. He felt utterly helpless, all he could do was hold her hand and reassure her, that it would get better. He took a cloth and wiped the sweat from her brows, then went to make it wet before laying it across her forehead, hoping it would help in some way. The nurse came in with more medication. Soon Autumn was resting again, the dark circles under her eyes standing out starkly in her white face.

"We are doing all we can." The nurse gave him an apologetic look, letting him know that all was done that could be done. Somehow he hoped she knew that his frustration was because his little girl was in pain. His little girl, that's what she had become again up at the mountain.

"Your grace, a phone call for you." He wondered who could be calling him here as he walked to the nurse's station. It was John.

"Yes John?"

"There was a call from a lady named Dahlia. She left a number to call her. She said that she had not heard from Mr. Warnham and I didn't want to say anything. Did I do right?"

"You did, John, you certainly did. If you have the number handy, please give it to me. I will call her right away."

It was a relief knowing that he didn't have to go through Ted's things. At this point any help, no matter how small, was welcome. Then he saw a figure walking toward him and everything within him turned cold, it was Laura. Of all the people in the world, she was the last person he wanted to see. Then he noticed her puffy looking eyes, telling him that she had been crying and his heart softened, but only a little bit. No harm in saying a few kind words to her.

"Ruben told me what happened, I am so sorry," the words gushed out of her as she grabbed on to Victor's shirtsleeve. He gently removed her hand and led her to a nearby chair. Whatever she wanted, he was not going to let her go into Autumn's room.

"What did Ruben tell you?"

"He said that Ted was dead and that Autumn had a terrible accident and might not live. Tell me it isn't so."

"He is right, Ted is gone, but Autumn will make it. She is hurt very badly, but the doctor's think that she is out of danger."

"My God, they could have both been killed, I didn't mean it."

Victor was dumbfounded. What in blazes was she babbling about? What had Ruben told her? A nurse came and offered to help. It was obvious that Laura was very upset, but he assured her that he could manage. His main thought was not to let Autumn hear anything; she didn't need the additional upset.

He was very concerned about Laura's state and gently managed to walk her down the hall, in the opposite direction of Autumn's room. Why in blazes would she think that both could have been killed? Did she think Autumn had been in the car with Ted? Had Ruben not told her about the mountain? What was going on?

They had reached the entrance and Victor held the door open.

"Laura, I need to go back, are you all right to go home?"

"Why would I want to go home? I want to see her, I want her to know that I didn't mean it, please Victor?"

"Laura, it wasn't your fault, there is nothing you can do right now. I really don't think you should be here, you need to go home, let me call Ruben..." At that very moment Harold walked in. He took one look at Laura and knew the state she was in.

"I'll take care of her, don't worry Mr. Victor, Ruben filled me in."

Victor's relief was only too obvious; he could have hugged the man. He had too many other things to attend to.

The first thing, before going back to Autumn's room, was to place a call to Peter. He got the number from the assistant at the front desk. He should have thought of that earlier. He dialed but the phone just rang and rang. Finally an answering machine picked up and he left a short message. Before he was through talking, Peter got on the line.

"Sorry about that, Victor, what was that about Autumn?" He sounded breathless.

"She's been in an accident, it's bad, but she'll be all right, in time."

"What do you mean, in time, come on man, what's wrong?" Victor could hear the frustration in Peter's voice. Did he really care for her?

"She's had a bad accident."

Peter interrupted him: "You already said that, how bad is bad?"

"Broken ribs, punctured lung, concussion, how much more do you want? She needs you."

"Oh God no, not Autumn!" Victor somehow felt that this man loved her, it was in his voice, the way he had cried out in frustration. Only a man in love would be this overwhelmed.

"Victor, I'll be on the next train out, don't tell her, please?" He assured him that he wouldn't say a word. He was glad that Peter was coming, maybe that's exactly what she needed. One thing was for certain, when the realization set in that Ted was gone; she would need all the help she could get.

He breathed a sigh of relief. The days ahead loomed before him dark and cold as a moonless winter night. He still had to call Dahlia and to top it off, there was Laura's strange behavior. My God, did she have a hand in Ted's death? No, it just wasn't possible, or was it? He shook his head; convinced he was going crazy. Not enough sleep, that's what it was. First things first. Dahlia, how could he tell her that her that her fiancee was gone, and what were the right words to use? Were there any right words? Once again his head started to throb, it was all too much.

He was dialing her number and almost got through, but hung up before dialing the last digit, he couldn't do it. A hand touched his shoulder. He looked up and saw the towns pastor giving him a worried look.

"Son, if I can be of help, say so. You look mighty worn down."

"I am father, but this is something nobody can do for me. Tell me, how does one tell a young lady that the man she loves is no more? How, father?"

"It's one of the hardest things one has to do, even for me. There is no easy way, just pray that this young lady knows the Lord Jesus and finds strength in him. The pain will be great, there is nothing you or I can do to ease the hurt. I will pray for her and all of you but it is all in God's hands now. I was just on my way to see the princess, would that be all right?"

"Oh yes, she would love that, that is, if she's awake." Victor's eyes followed him as he walked down the long corridor. He thought how good it would be to have him around when Autumn remembered why she went up the mountain in the first place. Also perhaps the pastor's prayers would help him to talk to Dahlia. Once again he started dialing.

"Hello!" Good God, she was there, what now? Little beats of sweat were forming on his forehead.

"May I speak to Dahlia?"

"This is she, who is calling?"

"You don't know me, my name is Victor von..." A delightful laugh could be heard.

"I know of you, you are the one Ted's always talking about. Are you two having a good time? I can't wait to meet you." Victor's heart sank, how could he tell her.

"Hello, are you still there?"

"Yes, of course. Dahlia, I need to tell you something, is someone there with you?" All was quiet. He could envision her going pale and knew instinctively that she was alone.

"Dahlia?" A tiny voice answered. "I am here, but where is Ted?"

"I'm so sorry, Dahlia, I'm so very sorry. There was an accident..."

"He's gone, isn't he?"

"Yes, I'm..."

"I know, you're sorry." Silence. Then her voice came back. "What am I going to do now?" Her heartrending sob left Victor all the more helpless.

"Dahlia, will you come over here anyway?" He really didn't expect an answer, so her immediate response took him back.

"I'll be there, I'll bring him home, I need to say good bye to him, don't I?" With that she hung up. Victor held the receiver in his hand for a long time, the steady humming of the dead phone line assaulting his eardrums. This conversation did not go as he had planned, he wanted to be of comfort to her, her wanted to bring the news to her in a gentle way, he wanted ... Hell, he didn't know what he wanted. He wanted out of this situation and back to normal, that's what he wanted.

He slammed the phone into the hook, angry at the world, angry at himself and angry with God. Nothing was fair any more. Exhausted, he leaned against the wall and closed his eyes. Sleep, that's what he needed, blessed sleep for days and days. Of course he couldn't afford to do that, there was much to be done, so very much to sort out. Where does one begin in all this mess? A big sigh escaped his lips, making a passer by look up in astonishment, his sympathetic eyes scanning him. Victor never noticed. When he opened his eyes the hall was empty. Each step was an effort as he made his way back to Autumn's room. He saw the minister standing there, looking down at a sleeping Autumn, a tear rolling down his cheek.

"This poor angel has had a lot to deal with lately, may God give her strength. Please call on me any time. The nurse said that she will be sleeping for some time, I will look in on her again. God bless you my son, I'll keep on praying for all of you." With that he walked out the door, his head hung low.

Victor let himself fall into the chair next to Autumn's bed, his mind reeling with Laura's words, not being able to make any sense out of them. Then his head fell back and he closed his eyes, fatigue claimed him. Soon he was in a deep sleep.

Harold, in the meantime, was guiding Laura out of the hospital toward his pickup truck. She followed without any resistance, sobbing all the way and muttering words he could not understand. She frightened him. Inside the truck he took her face into his hands and lifted it up.

"Now tell me what is going on." He meant to say it softly, but it came out harsh, his stomach tied in knots from fear of what she had done this time.

"I didn't mean to hurt anybody, I didn't mean to kill Ted."

Good God Almighty, had he heard right? A cold chill ran down his back and his first thought was to run away as fast and far away as was possible from this devil woman. He couldn't move nor talk; he just stared at her.

"Harold, you're scaring me! Say something?"

A shrill laugh pierced her ears. "Say something? Say something? What is there to say? You just said that you killed somebody, you killed Ted!" He laughed again, an ugly laugh. His face was contorted and his eyes were shooting forth daggers aiming straight for her heart. His hands let go of her face and he grabbed both her arms, shaking her furiously back and forth.

"How Laura? How in Gods name did you do it?"

"I didn't mean to hurt anybody, I didn't..."

"Shut up, you already told me that a thousand times! I want to know how?"

He pushed her away in total disgust and jumped out of the truck, afraid of what he might do to her. What now? His mind told him to go to the police. Yes, that's what he had to do.

He jumped back into the truck revving the engine.

"Where are we going?"

Was that timid little voice coming from Laura? Her face was white as a ghost. She had bitten her lips so hard blood trickled unto her chin. For just a split second he wanted to reach out and fold her into his arms, but he remembered her words. His voice was hard as steel: " We are going to the police and you better tell them everything."

The anticipated scream did not come. Nothing came out of her mouth. All he saw was a nod of her head, now resting low on her chest. Damn that woman, she tore at his heart and he hated her for it. Loving her had been the most wonderful thing he could ever have imagined, that was before it got ugly, but he still loved her, even now.

The truck rolled out of the hospital parking lot and on to main street, straight toward the police station. She remained silent. He parked the truck, walked around to her side and opened the door. She just sat there. So he reached in and lifted her out. Then he took her hand and began leading her up the few steps into the building. She walked beside him like a puppet, one foot in front of the other, her face expressionless.

"Harold, Miss Laura, what can I do for you?" The officer's voice from behind the desk was full of cheer, until he noticed their somber faces. "What happened?"

"Officer Tom, Laura has something to tell you," and turning to Laura "tell him what you did."

"I think..." she began to stutter, "I think ...I think I may be responsible for the accident." With that she flung her arms around Harold's neck and burst into loud, hard sobs that could have melted a stone. It did nothing to Harold, he knew her too well. True, she was probably scared stiff, and so she should be, having possibly taken the life of a young man. To think she would go this far out of sheer meanness gave him the strength not to soften. The officer's face showed concern for Laura but also confusion.

"Will someone tell me what is going on? What accident are we talking about?"

Harold pried Laura's arms loose and forcefully plopped her into one of the chairs lining the wall.

"I'll tell you what she is talking about, the accident that took Ted's life." Harold expressed doubt. "You do know about that accident?"

"Don't be insolent, of course I know about it, so does everybody else. It was an accident, plain and simple. What does Miss Laura have to do with it?" His eyes locked with hers.

"I only meant to frighten her, I didn't know that Ted would be driving, it was Autumn who was supposed to be driving, not Ted."

"Are you trying to say that you tried to kill the princess?"

"NO..." Her scream could be heard throughout the station house. Her eyes, wild with fear, were searching the officer's face.

"I didn't mean to kill anybody, I just, I just ... what's the use, he's dead." Resignation set in. Her head fell back. There was a sickening sound as it hit the wall, but she didn't cry out.

Officer Tom scratched his head. As far as he knew, the death of that young man had been an accident, caused by a blown out tire, nothing more. Maybe this needed some further checking. Maybe the tire didn't blow by chance?

"Harold, what is she trying to tell me?"

"Beats me, I don't know any details, I only know that she feels responsible."

"Miss Laura, talk to me. Why do you think that you caused the accident?"

"Because I did." It was a clear, simple statement. She was back in control.

"I took my knife and I stabbed the tire, over and over. That's what I did, that's why it blew and that's why Ted is dead. I did it."

She got up, stretched her arms towards officer Tom, waiting for him to slap the cuffs on her.

"Miss Laura, put your arms down. Have you talked to anybody about this?" She shook her head vehemently.

" Before you say another word let me make a phone call and get Sam, I mean Chief Rosenbaum, over here. Just sit down."

He motioned for both of them to sit down. As he reached for the phone to call his Chief, he noticed Laura reaching out to hold Harold's hand, only to have him push her away. Tom noticed anger in that young man's face. Strange, he would have expected pity, compassion, sorrow, but not anger.

Just out of curiosity he went ahead and pulled the file on the accident. It was exactly as he remembered the official report stated that the left front tire had blown, causing the car to spin out of control and hit the tree. So how did Laura's story fit into this picture? Nothing in the report indicated that the tire had been slashed. He would let the Chief handle this one. Just then Chief Rosenbaum entered the station giving Tom a quick salute and a friendly nod in Harold's direction. Then his gaze fixed on the young woman. He expected to see a hysterical female, but the girl sitting there seemed to be quite composed. Only those red eyes gave away to the previous crying spell. Even her voice was calm and matter of fact like. In her statement to Chief Rosenbaum she stated that she repeatedly stabbed the front tire. In her account of the incident, it was the right front tire she assaulted. Well, this would be easy to verify.

The garage confirmed Laura's statement. It was just as she had said she had indeed stabbed the right front tire, but the damage was not worth mentioning. She either had used little force or the knife had been a very small one. Any way, the damage resulting from her attack did not cause the accident since it was the left front tire that had blown. On the other hand, this woman had just admitted intend to do bodily harm. Could he go ahead and just dismiss it? Chief Rosenbaum did not have a good feeling about this at all.

"Miss Laura, your admission is a serious one. We need time to investigate further. Please don't leave this area. We will need to get more information from you. As for now, you are free to go."

He did not tell her about the tires, he needed more time to think about it. Something did not sit right, why would this girl want to hurt the princess? It just didn't add up. Had there not been several mishaps at the Schwarzenau Estate lately? Perhaps even some they didn't know about? He could think of only one person to shed some light on all of this, Victor.

The hand on his shoulder startled him out of his sleep. Victor looked up and saw Chief Rosenbaum standing beside him.

"How is the Princess doing?"

"Good God man, you gave me a fright. As for your question, she's resting peacefully, thank God. There is a good chance of a full recovery. It's good of you to stop by, only next time, don't sneak up one me, alright?"

The Chief displayed a hint of a smile. "It's not the only reason I'm here. I wonder if I might have a word with you, outside."

Victor rose after reassuring himself of Autumn's deep sleep and followed the Chief into the hall.

"Your High..." Victor raised his hand. "Please, not you too. We've known each other to long for that."

"As you wish, Victor then. I'm here to ask about a certain young lady named Laura." At the mention of Laura's name Victor's head jerked up. Chief Rosenbaum made a mental note of it.

"I gather you know her. She came to the precinct, or should I say a friend of hers brought her in, claiming to have killed this young fellow named Ted. She didn't, I mean her actions did not cause the crash or this young mans death, but she meant to hurt somebody. What can you tell me about her?"

Victor scratched his head and gave the Chief a long hard look. "Where do you want me to begin? The girl spells disaster and has from the time she was a little thing. She practically grew up with Autumn, supposedly being her best friend, worst enemy is what I call it."

"What do you mean?" Chief Rosenbaum's curiosity was definitely aroused.

"Well, when the girls were little, so many mishaps happened, always things to hurt Autumn. Mind you, these incidences were little things, nothing anybody could ever put their finger on, except that Laura was always in the middle of it. Now it is more serious. Take the incident with the broken saddle, causing Autumn to fall, then the poisoning of Maharani, the letters from Ted to Autumn which never arrived, want to hear more?"

There was a moment of silence.

"Was Laura ever connected with any of the incidents?"

"Well Chief, not really. I've had my suspicions for a very long time, but... wait a minute, the letters, it was her doing, of that I am sure. So tell me about Ted's accident. How is she involved in that?"

"Victor, I really can't say much right now. She didn't cause it, but she meant to hurt somebody. No, not that young man. Her anger was directed towards the princess. Can you tell me why?"

"Jealousy, plain and simple." When Victor said those words the Chief's expression changed into sheer disbelief. It's hard to imagine that somebody would go to such extremes out of jealousy, or is it? If there was any truth in what Victor just said, it would mean that they were dealing with a very unstable person. That's dangerous, any way you look at it. Had he done right by just letting her go? He really didn't have any other option. There was nothing for him to hold her on.

"I'm going to give everything you just told me some close scrutiny. Can't have some lunatic running free, can't we?" He didn't wait for an answer, tipped his hat and walked on. Victor suddenly experienced a feeling of satisfaction where Laura was concerned. Perhaps things were beginning to change. She'd need a good Attorney to get her out of this mess, but even if she had one, her own words had already convicted her, regardless. His lips twisted in a small grin.

Autumn Leaves

CHAPTER EIGHTEEN

Peter was dialing as fast as he could. The phone rang and rang. Finally a scruffy voice reached his ear. That could only mean that he had woken his father up.

"Pop, it's me, Peter. I just heard about Autumn, please tell me what's going on!"

"Not much to tell my boy. She's very badly hurt, fell down a deep ravine, still don't know how it happened. She's alive, that's the good news."

"But why did it happen? She's an excellent rider? Was the weather bad?"

"Peter, I don't have any answers for you. Who told you about it anyway?"

"Victor called, he didn't give me any details, just asked if I could come and see her. I don't know if I can get away so quickly. She does have her friend from the States there, unless Victor thought I could be of some medical assistance."

"Son, Victor didn't tell you?" There was a slight pause.

"The princess's friend got killed in a car crash. It was after she heard about it that she took off on that new horse, and didn't come back." Silence.

"Peter, are you still there?"

"My God, I didn't know, that changes everything. I'm knee deep in a few serious cases, but I'll see if I can arrange to get away as soon as possible. By the way Pop, there is a young lady here just dying to see her grandpa."

"I want to see her too. Bring her with you. I'm still able to look after a child, especially if it's my granddaughter. Give her a big hug and kiss from me and tell her I'm waiting. Tell her, Bambi is also waiting."

"Bambi who?"

A chuckle came through the line. "A real Bambi, I'm nursing it until I can release it back into the forest. Just come and bring my little helper, she'll love it."

Of that Peter was sure. Barbie loved animals as much as he did, still does for that matter. A baby deer, boy would that be a surprise for her.

Their good byes were always short, but both of them knew how deeply connected they were.

Peter was restless. He did not know what to do. Part of him wanted to rush to Autumn's side and comfort her, but his sense of duty wouldn't allow it. Had she not let him know that they could be nothing but friends? Then that call from Ted reassuring him that she did love him? He meant to call him back to find out more, now he was gone. It tore him apart just thinking about Autumn being in pain. He remembered the way she lay in his arms, the way she had answered his kisses, it seemed so real and then it had been over as quickly as it had begun. His head was spinning. At times he wondered if it all ever really happened or if had been just a beautiful dream. Why did Victor say that she needed him?

He didn't know it, but he was moaning with his head buried in his hands. He loved her with every fiber of his being, totally and completely. How in the world could he face her without giving himself away? His heart felt as if an iron fist was squeezing the life out of it. The mere thought of losing her forever was unimaginable.

Autumn Leaves

"If you tell me where it hurts I can kiss it and make it feel better. Momi always said that to me and you did too, daddy, remember?" Tiny fingers were prying his hands apart and he looked into those big brown eyes that were waiting for an answer.

"Momi was right. If you give me a big hug and an even bigger kiss I'm sure I will feel better instantly." With that he scooped his little daughter into his arms, making her squeal with delight.

Two days later they were on the train to Schwarzenau. Barbie lay snuggled on the seat, her head in his lap, sound asleep. All the excitement of seeing her grandfather and his four-legged surprise had finally gotten the best of her. God, did little girls have a mountain of questions. He had grown tired of answering, but didn't dare let Barbie know. Her trust in him was something he never wanted to jeopardize. Because of his work he had little time for her. The moments they did have together were used to it's fullest, he treasured them. She knew that she could count on him and come to him with everything, no matter how small or silly it seemed. Autumn would have loved her, but she never gave herself that chance. Maybe there was hope for them after all? His eyes grew heavy, the last two days had been cruel, and sleep finally claimed him. There was a hint of a smile on his face when his head fell back against the built in cushion. Father and daughter were blissfully asleep as the train thundered through the night. The eyes of many passer byes rested smiling on the two of them, especially those of the female gender. That darkly handsome man with that doll like little girl, resting so peacefully snuggled close together, a picture right out of an art gallery.

The train pulled into the small station in Schwarzenau and Peter spotted his father at once. He was a stout looking man, impressive in his ranger uniform. Barbie was still sleepy. He had to carry her off the train. Once she spotted her grandfather she wiggled right out of his arms and ran toward the big man whose arms were wide open to embrace this little whirlwind. Tears of joy were running down the old man's cheeks.

"You sure have grown a lot, Bambie."

She giggled and told him, "Grandfather, I'm not Bambie, you always call me that, I'm Barbie."

"So you are. I just like to call you that because you remind me of a little deer. But I guess from now on I have to call you by your real name, we don't want to have any mix-ups, now do we?"

Barbie looked at him with a big question in her eyes. He was not about to give his secret away, she would know soon enough.

Peter asked to be dropped off at the hospital. He had to find out what condition Autumn was in. Barbie was only too happy to go home with her grandfather.

At the hospital many eyes followed that handsome tall man as he strode down the hall.

He lightly knocked on Autumn's door and entered. It shook him to the core, looking down at her small, pale face. She was asleep. Now and then a soft moan escaped her lips and her hands would clench together in a tight fist. She was either dreaming or in pain, either way, it was not a restful sleep. Victor, who had been sitting in a chair next to the bed, got up and walked out of the room. Peter felt almost helpless. It was not fair that she should suffer so, he wanted to take her pain and make it his own. "I love you so much," he didn't know whether he had spoken the words out loud or just silently to himself. He saw her eyes flutter and slowly open, her full gaze upon him.

"Peter, you are here?"

"Yes Autumn, I am here."

His lips touched hers. "I love you" he whispered. He saw her smile and his heart skipped a beat.

"Did you come alone?"

Autumn Leaves

"Yes, no, I..." there was a flicker of pain across her face and she turned her head away.

"Thank you for coming, but I am very tired, please go." Her voice was only a whisper; he could barely understand her.

"But Autumn, I just got here and I thought ..." she raised her hand as if to silence him. He shook his head, not understanding what was going on, he walked out.

He saw Victor standing by the corridor window and walked up to him.

"She doesn't want to see me. Victor, she doesn't want to see me!" He had taken Victor by his shoulders as if to shake him, but his hands fell to his sides just as quickly as he had raised them.

"She sent me away," his voice was full of resignation.

"What did you say to her?"

"Nothing, I didn't have a chance. She seemed glad to see me at first, and then she asked if had come alone and then she asked me to leave. It doesn't make any sense, I shouldn't have come, I don't even know why you asked me to come, I just don't understand this." It was as if he was talking to himself. Victor could see the pain and disappointment in his face.

"She did call out for you, over and over. She was in a lot of pain and it was your name she said. I assumed that she wanted to see you, hell, I was sure that's what she wanted."

"Well, you assumed wrong. I'll be at my father's for a few days, please call me there and let me know of any changes. I care about her." With that he turned and walked away. Victor suddenly felt as if he had done something terribly wrong. A moment later Peter returned.

"I forgot to ask you about Ted, I mean what arrangements have been made?"

"We're waiting for his fiancée to get here. She's going to take him back. She asked me to wait until she got here before making any plans. He's still in the morgue. She'll be here by noon tomorrow."

"Need any help?" Victor's relief was obvious. There was a vigorous nod and a heartfelt "thank you". Perhaps he was mistaken but he could have sworn Victor's eyes looked kind of watery. That man carried a heavy burden. He would find a way to lighten it for him.

"Call me, you know where to find me." With that Peter walked out of the hospital.

Victor was back in Autumn's room. "Why was Peter here?"

"I asked him to come, I thought you wanted to see him."

He observed her tired smile; it was a smile of resignation? It was the same expression he had seen on Peter's face. The silence in the room was stifling, then he heard her say: "He didn't come alone, you know. You meant well and I'm glad I saw him. Thank you Victor."

What could he say, Autumn didn't make any sense. Peter did come alone; there was nobody with him. Perhaps she was still confused. By the time he was ready to respond her eyes were closed and she seemed to be asleep again. The only thing he could do was to continue watching over her.

Peter had no idea how long he had been walking. That strange encounter with Autumn had turned him upside down. He was convinced that she loved him too. It was all so confusing, so damn stupid. By the time he realized where he was his foot had set down on familiar ground. He had literally walked home to his father's house. A familiar thin line of blue smoke escaped the chimney, curling its way up toward the sky. He suddenly noticed how cold the air had gotten. His stride grew longer, he was anxious to reach the inside and the warmth of the fireplace. To hold his little daughter close to him, that's what he needed.

Autumn Leaves

Barbie was much too excited to be cuddled. She was talking a mile a minute all about a little deer named Bambi and how she had touched it and it had nibbled at her sleeve and how she tried to feed it with a bottle and on and on she went. Even so he felt totally worn out, he listened intently at what his daughter had to tell him which was obviously of major importance to her. God how he loved her. Although her chatter was intense, it could not remove the worry about Autumn from his mind.

He had no idea that his father was watching him, knowing that his son was deeply worried about something. Later on, when little Barbie was tucked into bed, they sat up and had a long heart to heart talk. The schnapps helped loosen their tongue and Peter confessed to his father how deeply he cared for Autumn, knowing all along that his father would not approve of it. But strangely enough, he did. More than that, he made it clear that he thought his son would be the most suitable choice for the princess. At that point, Peter knew that they both had been too deep into the elixir and called a halt to the evening.

When he woke up it was morning and he discovered that he had slept the whole night through. What surprised him even more was how good he felt. The expected hangover was not there. He made up his mind once and for all; he would confront Autumn one last time and let her know just how important she was to him. Having made the decision he couldn't wait to get back to the hospital. He was already outside when his father's voice called to him. Victor was asking him to hurry.

When he stepped through the hospital door a terrible fear gripped his chest. He made his way toward Autumn's room, tiny beads forming on his forehead. The tie around his neck seemed to choke him. He reached up and loosened it, almost ripping off the top button of his shirt. The door to Autumn's room opened and a nurse rushed out. His step automatically picked up speed. When he walked into her room his worst fears were confirmed. There were several doctors surrounding her bed, which could only mean that she was in trouble. She was battling a high fever and they had just decided to transfer her into ICU for closer observation. He could see her lips moving but there was no sound. Again, he felt so utterly helpless. For God's sake he was a doctor; he should be able to do something? The other doctors stepped back and he walked over to her. He gently took her hands into his and whispered: "I love you princess, with every beat of my heart. Please hang on, I need you, we need you."

For a moment she lay quiet. Had she heard him?

"Daddy?" She said, loud and clear. The thrashing about had stopped and it almost looked as if she were smiling. A deep sigh escaped her lips and now she seemed to drift away, her chest rising in an even rhythm of relaxed sleep. He noticed that the nurse watching the monitors was nodding in approval.

"Whatever you told her doctor, it did the trick."

"Thank you nurse, I just hope it lasts." For a long while he remained just holding her hand. Her face was so white; it almost matched the color of her pillows. He wanted to protect her. Why didn't she know that, why wouldn't she let him be there for her? What was it that made her turn away from him? Loving this girl was the greatest pain he had ever felt, even greater than when he lost his wife, Barbie's mother, and he felt ashamed for it. But Autumn had awakened a feeling in him so new, so deep and powerful, so urgent, and a wanting that would not be satisfied until she was his. They belonged together; even Ted had said so. He would fight for her, whatever it would take; he would not give up. The kiss he placed on her forehead was mingled with his tears and a promise to be there for all the time to come.

For the moment her move to ICU was canceled. He went to look for Victor and found him by the window at the end of the long hallway. He looked lost.

"She's sleeping peacefully."

Victor just nodded, a crooked grin on his face. Peter did not tell him that she had called him daddy, it didn't mean anything. He knew she was lost in the past with thoughts of her parents. She must miss them very much; there had not been enough time for her to start healing. It could be a reason for her sudden fever, the past had caught up with her all at once and her body rebelled. Poor little princess, if she only knew how many people where here to help her. A thought flashed through his mind.

What if Autumn was to come and spend a while at his clinic. After all, it was a place where people from all over the world came to recuperate and gather strength. Autumn needed to get away from this place where every stick and stone was a reminder of the tragedies she had experienced of late.

"Victor, Autumn needs is to get away from here." Victor turned and studied him, then his head nodded in approval. Peter continued: " Here, she is constantly faced with the past, making it almost impossible to come to grips with herself. Let her come to my clinic. It's a place of such tranquillity, beautiful gardens, a lake, an outdoor auditorium and so much more. So many people have found new joy in their life after spending some time there. She may even make new friends."

Peter had just put into words what Victor had been thinking about for quite a while. The daily reminders at Schwarzenau were pulling her down. She had been putting on such a good front. Ted's accident had pushed her over the edge. So perhaps Peter's suggestion was a Godsend. It was also the perfect solution for keeping Laura away from her. That vixen would have her day in court soon, he was sure of that.

"Peter, Ted's fiancée will be here in just under an hour. I was wondering, could you stay here while I'll go meet her at the train station? I'm going to bring her here, to see Ted, and I would really like for you to be with me when that happens."

"I'll be here."

Victor shot him a grateful glance and walked away. Peter watched until the door closed behind him. Now what? Going back to Autumn was out of the question. He would just have to wait out here, or, he could make arrangements for Autumn's stay at his Clinic. The wheels were set in motion.

Autumn Leaves

CHAPTER NINETEEN

It was a wonderful day. The sun was warm and the air was filled with the smell of lilacs, roses, gardenias and whatever else was blooming in this beautiful garden. Autumn was sitting under a tall birch tree. This was one of her favorite trees; it's shape reminding her of a huge umbrella. Although dense, it was letting the sun filter through just enough to warm her all over. She wasn't sure how long she had been here but she desperately wanted to come to grips with herself. She knew Peter was chief of staff in this place, but so far she had not seen him. Perhaps he had left, even gone to a new clinic? Funny that it hadn't bothered her until this moment? Perhaps it was a sign that she was starting to get better.

It would be nice to see him, she missed him. My God, she really did miss him. The realization send her heart a flutter. What if he was really gone, gone out of her life forever? She had lost him once, had she lost him again? Was it really such a surprise the way she had pushed him away? She loved him, truly loved him. There could never be anybody else, she was sure of that. Her hands began to tremble. She looked all around hoping to see him somewhere in the garden. Resignation started to settle in until her gaze settled on a young lady she had seen many times before. She always seemed to be writing something in a tablet, hardly ever looking up. She had never seen her smile. Autumn's heart went out to the stranger. If Laura had been here ..... Laura, she had almost forgotten about her. Laura was a chapter in her life that was closed, at least for now. Another chapter lost to her was Ted. He was gone, forever. All she knew was that Dahlia had come and taken his body back to America. She never even got the chance to say good bye to him. She said it quietly, here in the garden.

Autumn's thoughts got interrupted when something bounced off her knee. At her feet lay a blue foam rubber ball. Tiny hands were reaching for it and a pair of dark brown eyes focused on her face.

"Sorry lady, it won't happen again. Please don't tell, 'cause I'm not supposed to bother the patients." The little girl's eyes were big as saucers.

"Who would I tell and what would I tell? I don't see anybody bothering me, do you?"

"Thank you lady, I knew you were nice." With that she ran away, her dark curls flying in the wind, leaving a smiling Autumn behind. What a pretty little thing. To her amazement the little girls stopped in front of the young woman and gave her a hug before running off again, and Autumn could have sworn she saw a smile on the young woman's face.

The next day Autumn decided to approach that lonely lady. As it turned out, she did not have to; little brown eyes took care of it. She was leading her toward Autumn, well, pulling on her sleeve to be more accurate. "This is my friend Gabriella, she is very much alone and I don't have the time to play with her today, so would you please take care of her for me?"

Autumn glanced at Gabriella and noticed a shy smile, then she turned back to the little girl.

Autumn Leaves

"I would feel honored to take care of your friend, that is if she would want me too?"

"Oh, she will," was the positive answer. She nodded at her friend and said in a very persuasive tone: "Won't you Gabriella?"

Without waiting for a reply she pulled Gabriella's head down so she could whisper something into her ear. The response from the lady called Gabriella was a firm "Yes."

Just like before, the last glimpse Autumn had of the little girl was her hair flying in the breeze.

Autumn and Gabriella watched the tiny figure until she disappeared from sight. There was an awkward moment of silence, broken up when both began to talk at the same time, followed by a shy laugh. It marked the beginning of a beautiful friendship.

They soon discovered that they came from similar backgrounds, except that Gaby, as Autumn called her for short, had not only lost her parents but her home as well. With a name like Gabriella, Autumn concluded that her new friend might be from Italy, but she would wait until Gaby was ready to reveal her story.

What she did learn from Gaby was that the little girl's father was a doctor on staff here at the clinic and that everybody called her Barbie. Autumn was tempted to ask Gaby to tell her more about Barbie, but something held her back.

They didn't see the little girl for quite a while and their conversations hardly ever touched on the subject. It was obvious to Autumn that Gaby missed her little friend, although she never said so.

Then one day, they were sitting in the solarium quietly reading, when the sound of small feet, running as fast as they could, echoed through the hall. Then she stood before them, eyes shining, red cheeks and her little chest heaving from having run so fast. She just stood there, grinning from ear to ear, looking at them. She was way too much out of breath to utter a single word. All the joy of being here sparkled from her eyes and when Gaby and Autumn held their arms out, she just flung herself between them trying to hold them both at the same time. It was such an impact and the three of them tumbled to the ground. There they lay, hugging and kissing each other. The sound of happy laughter rang through the solarium. In the midst of this happy reunion a sharp cough demanded their attention. One of the nurses stood over them, glaring down.

"Ladies, do we have to make such a spectacle of ourselves?" That's all she said with a face red as a tomato. Then she turned on her heels and stalked away.

They realized at once that she had not seen Barbie between them and the realization of what she must have thought made them giggle even harder. Miss Sourpuss sure had a dirty mind. Barbie only noticed the smiles and giggles and was overjoyed at seeing her friends in such a happy mood.

"I wish you would laugh all the time, you are both so pretty." She looked from one to the other. "I'll tell my daddy and he will be happy to."

Gabriella's head spun around; "But your daddy is still away, isn't he?"

Barbie's laugh sounded like a silver bell. "No, he came back. Why do you think I couldn't come and see you?" She didn't wait for an answer. "I was with my daddy and we had the best fun in the world."

Autumn observed the two and came to the conclusion that there was more to the relationship between Barbie and Gaby. It made her think of Peter again. He still had not come to see her. Victor had told her that Peter was away a lot. She would call Victor and ask him to come for a visit. She missed him. But to be truthful, it was Peter her heart was reaching for.

Autumn Leaves

A few days later, Autumn was waiting at the front gate for Victor's arrival, when she heard Barbie's voice and a man's voice. Her heart almost stopped, she knew that voice. It was Peter. He came strolling down the gravel road, Barbie on one side and ... Gabriella on the other. Autumn could feel her hands turn cold as ice. So this was the young lady in his life. She tried to hide herself behind some of the bushes. She felt totally embarrassed. Had he not told her that he loved her, and had he not kissed her passionately and had he not .... Oh Peter! Her vision became blurred, tears were streaming down her face as they passed by chatting away merrily, they didn't see her.

A silver Mercedes swooshed by. Autumn knew it was Victor. She ran into the road and waved frantically. Victor saw her in the rear view mirror and brought his car to a screeching halt, pebbles flying. In no time Autumn was at his side. She hugged him so tight, he could barely breathe.

"That's the kind of welcome I like, I've missed you golden girl." They hugged again and Autumn placed a light kiss right on his lips. He didn't quite know how to react. He parked the car and they walked to her living quarters in silence. The view from the verandah was beautiful.

"It's nice here." Victor glanced in all directions and noticed a small lake very close by. "Can one swim in those waters?"

Autumn smiled. "Not likely, it's more of a pond for the ducks and swans. We swim in a pool. They have two, one indoor and one out of doors. I haven't been in either one."

Silence. Victor wondered why it was so hard to talk to her today. He had to ask her: "Autumn, you look well, except that I noticed the traces of tears on your cheeks. Did you miss me that much?"

He meant it as a joke and was surprised to see her eyes get all watery again. She must have noticed the question in his eyes for he didn't have to wait long.

"Remember when you told me that Peter was in love with me? Well, you were wrong. He had told me that there was a young lady in his life he wanted me to meet. I will never understand why he said that. He made it sound so... I met her today. That is, I saw them today. It's the young lady I wrote to you about and ... she's my friend. Can you believe that? ... Victor, I don't know what to do."

His first thought was ' I don't either', he was baffled. As far as he knew there was nobody in Peter's life. Peter had assured him that it was Autumn he loved. This didn't make any sense. Autumn must be mistaken.

"Have you spoken to him?"

She shook her head. "No, not since I got here, but I saw him today. He was walking with Gabriella and Barbie, that's the little girl I mentioned. They didn't see me, but I sure saw them, boy did I ever." She suddenly slapped her hand to her forehead. "I must be a real dingbat. Laura always told me to wise up and I hate to say this, but she was right. Why could I not see through his lies?"

Victor felt the heat rise under his collar. The mere mention of Laura's name set him on fire. If Autumn only knew the evil this woman had conjured up, she would never utter her name again. As for Peter, he would find out for himself what was going on. Right now he had to do something to distract Autumn from all of this, so he suggested they should go sightseeing and Autumn agreed. He wanted to tell her about Laura's trial, but thought better of it. This was not the time to bring that up.

They had a great time exploring the town and when they returned to the clinic Autumn was relaxed and happy; until she spotted Gabriella sitting on the steps. Victor took one look at the young beauty, long golden reddish hair and slender legs, and loved what he saw. Gabriella jumped up. Victor noticed her eyes surveying him. He could almost understand Peter falling for this beauty, if this was the young lady in question.

"Autumn, I have been looking for you. Sorry, I didn't know you had company." At the last sentence her eyes once again rested on Victor and she added: "Did you have a good time?" He grinned and nodded. Autumn had regained her composure.

"Thank you Gaby, we did. Hopefully you enjoyed yourself as well. Let me introduce you to ... to my father's younger brother, Prince Victor." With that she made a slight bow and stepped back. Victor was dumbfounded. He had never seen Autumn act this way. He would have liked it better if she had left that prince stuff out. It seemed that Gabriella was also slightly confused. Oh hell, he would just have to save the day. He took a hold of Gabriella's hand.

"If I am not mistaken, you are the fairy princess from another continent. I am so glad to finally meet you. I am Victor, plain and simple. Princess Autumn, if you don't mind, let's just leave all that title stuff behind."

"That suits me fine." Although she said it with a smile, Victor knew it didn't come easy. But, her good manners prevailed and in a matter of minutes she seemed to be her old self again. Gabriella never noticed the slight friction and the three of them went to sit on the terrace to enjoy a nice cool drink of ice coffee. For a while they chatted on about meaningless things. Finally, Autumn could not contain herself any longer.

"Gaby, did you do anything special today?" Victor shot a warning glance in her direction. She pretended not to notice and smiled back at him. Gabriella thought for a moment, then her face lit up like a Christmas tree.

"How could I forget. He is back, Barbie's daddy!"

"Gaby, I know that! Barbie told us that herself, don't you remember?"

"Yes, of course I do. What I'm really trying to say is, that I didn't see him until today. We spend the whole morning together, walking through the park, and Barbie's little mouth was going like a waterfall. She loves her daddy so much. I am just glad that I can be a friend to her, she doesn't have a mommy any more."

Victor noticed the stunned look on Autumn's face and he had to admit, he was quite taken back himself. He could not figure out what Gabriella was trying to tell them. Autumn obviously had the same problem. Had Autumn not told him that she saw her friend with Peter? But Peter did not have a daughter. Once again he would take the bull by its horns and try to clarify things.

"Gabriella, did you say you spend the day with Barbie's father?" He held his breath, hoping the answer would not be .....

"Well yes. I met the little girl shortly after I got here and also her father. We became friends, mostly with Barbie, but her father was grateful for my looking out for his daughter." Then she added: "Specially since Dr. Marshall has to be gone so much." Victor's sigh of relief was so overwhelming that it startled both girls. Autumn's mind was spinning, she was afraid that she had misunderstood. If Barbie was Peter's daughter, then ... Instead she said: "Are you all right Victor?" Well, his answer didn't make much sense to either one of them when he exclaimed with a sheepish grin on his face: "Now I am!"

Then he did something totally unexpected. He reached out and took one of Gabriella's hands in his, his eyes searching her face. For one brief moment Autumn was forgotten as their eyes locked. Victor knew right then and there that this was not Peter's woman. It made him very glad.

The exchange did not go unnoticed. Autumn was aware of the attraction between those two. How could that be? Things just got more confusing by the minute. Then the sound of an all too familiar voice shattered the silence. Autumn's heart was beating so fast she was sure it would jump right out of her chest. Peter had come out of nowhere. She looked up and thought the fire in his eyes would consume her. With one big step he was beside her, holding her face in both hands. She was mesmerized. She knew he would kiss her, she did not have the strength to push him away, so she just closed her eyes. The feel of his lips sent shivers down her spine, followed by a rush of heat spreading to every part of her body. She totally forgot about Victor and Gaby, all she knew was that he was here, kissing her. Was it minutes, seconds or what? Time had stopped. Finally he let her go but the way he smiled right into her eyes told her everything. Oh how she loved him.

"My beautiful Autumn, how I've missed you." Could it really be true that he felt the same way? At this moment the only thing that mattered was that he was here, right by her side. She was happy, really happy.

Victor and Gabriella watched them, wide-eyed, and they were not the only ones. The little girl's tiny face was one big question mark.

"Daddy, why are you kissing Lady Autumn on the mouth and not on the cheek like you do with Gabriella?" Good question. All eyes turned to Peter.

He motioned his little daughter to come closer. "This, young lady, is the princess I have told you so much about. Do you remember when I first told you that you would meet a real princess?"

"Yeah, but she never came and then you got all sad."

"Well, she is here now." He had placed one protective arm around Autumn's shoulder while his other hand motioned Barbie to come closer. She grabbed his hand with both of hers and looked up to him.

"Then where is her crown and her robe?"

"It's a bit too warm for that, don't you think? I left it at the castle, so I guess you'll have to come and visit me if you want to see it." Autumn's soft voice spoke straight to little Barbie's heart. She let go of her father's hand and moved to stand right in front of Autumn.

"Can I? Can I really come and see you in your castle?" The little girl's excitement was so great that she danced from one foot onto the other. Then she stood still and her voice was quite serious.

"You know what? I even liked you when you were just a Lady." Leave it to the young to be blunt. "So because you are a princess my daddy can kiss you on the mouth, right?" Her little head nodded in answer to her own question.

Peter grinned from ear to ear. "Give me a break, young lady, will you? Daddy kissed the princess on the lips because he loves her. I hope that you can love her too."

"So I can also kiss her on the m... on her lips?" Peter just grinned.

Autumn stretched her arms toward Barbie. "Come here you little angel, sit on my lap. Of course you can kiss me, I think I would really like that, but we can do it on the cheek if you like."

"No, I just as soon kiss you on the lips. 'Cause that means that I love you too, right?" Smack, there was the kiss before Autumn could even blink.

It turned out to be a very memorable afternoon. Even so the four adults had much to talk about Barbie still remained the main attraction. Suddenly they realized that her idle chatter had dwindled away and Victor spotted her curled up on one of the lawn chairs, sound asleep. At that moment the little girl reminded him of Autumn, when she was that age. Children grew up so fast, Peter would have to watch out so he won't miss those precious years. And Autumn, how did she feel about having a ready-made family? But he was jumping the gun, nobody had mentioned a wedding yet.

The day had just flown by and none of them were willing to let it end. Victor should have been on his way back hours ago, but he could not tear himself away from Gabriella. He hoped that she would feel the same way. When he asked if he could see her again she nodded and the sparkle in her eyes told him all he needed to know. For the first time in ages he felt truly happy. Could he dare steal a kiss from her? Better not. So he kissed her on the cheek instead and took with him a lingering fragrance of lavender. It was intoxicating. He did not notice the disappointment in Gabriella's face.

On the drive back to Schwarzenau he felt his spirits soaring. He had the urge to yodel; and that's just what he did. Not bad, not bad at all.

Anita Attwood

CHAPTER TWENTY

There was so much to plan. Chateau Schwarzenau hummed like a huge beehive. Old Mary was wringing her hands at the slowness of some of these young servants. At this rate they'd be lucky to be ready by Christmas. Even so the floors were shining so bright that one could see ones face in it and the windows had turned nearly invisible in their clarity, Mary would still find something wrong at every turn of her matronly frame. There was already a chill in the air, indicating that fall was not that far away. The servants were glad of the cooler temperature for Mary proved to be a real slave driver.

There was a wedding to be gotten ready for. Autumn and Peter had announced their engagement and their wish to have an autumn wedding. Some thought it a bit hasty, but those who knew the couple were delighted at their decision. Old Mary would have preferred a spring wedding. In her eyes, it was so much more romantic. Victor, on the other hand, knew exactly why Autumn had chosen that time of the year. Fall gave her a strong connection to her mother and her childhood. Also, had it not been the autumn leaves that saved her life not too long ago? Now it would signify the beginning of a brand new era.

Autumn Leaves

The young lovers walked arm in arm through the rose garden. Now and then they stopped and kissed, then giggled like teenagers. They would glance all around, making sure nobody had seen them. Although they were engaged, it still made them feel as if those were stolen kisses. For Peter, those times alone with Autumn were heaven and hell all wrapped in one. He was having a hard time controlling his need, with Autumn constantly wanting to cuddle close and caress him. Didn't she have any idea what she was doing to him? The wedding was still five weeks away, might as well be five years.

Peter felt none of the cool breeze on this sunny late morning stroll. They had kissed and were holding hands, except that he wanted more than this, much more. He made a sudden stop and took her into his arms. She did not reject him, even when his hand lightly brushed over her breast. He saw her catch her breath, her eyes were closed. Slowly he reached over and began to unbutton her blouse, watching her closely. He promised himself to stop at the slightest sign of objection, but all he noticed was her breathing becoming more rapid. His mouth claimed hers with increasing urgency, his hand slid into her bodice, caressing the satin swell while searching for the nipple. She leaned into him so that their bodies were as one, his hardness pressing into her, his thumb caressing her breast. Her little moans encouraged him to seek further. Now her tongue invaded his mouth, locking them together and the fire of their passion seemed to consume them. Time stood still.

When he gently lowered her to the ground there was a sudden outcry. For a minute he didn't know what had happened. Autumn had pushed him away and was glaring at him, her eyes dark with fury. She was shaking from head to toe, unable to speak. He knew right away that he had gone too far. But hell, what was a man to do? Seeing her in such a state made him want to kick himself. Her trembling fingers were fumbling with the buttons on her blouse while tears streamed down her face. Had he spoiled it once again?

"Autumn ...." She didn't let him continue. Instead she placed her fingers on his lips to silence him. "Don't say anything, it wasn't your fault. I want you just as much as you want me, I love you Peter, but we must not give in, not yet."

He heard the words, but he could not understand her reasoning. They were about to get married, they were in love, why on earth was it so wrong to let their passion take over and carry them away?

She must have seen the frustration in his face, for she took his face in her hands and her voice was very gentle. "Peter, I promised my parents that I would save myself for the man who would be my greatest love. I can not break my promise. I want to come to you on our wedding night unspoiled. Please understand, I can't do it any other way."

The words were spoken with such depth and conviction; they penetrated deep into his heart. The woman before him was beautiful and gentle. She loved him and she wanted him. Her strength and inner will almost made him feel ashamed. At this moment he wondered if he even deserved her.

The episode in the garden did not go unnoticed. Peter and Autumn were unaware of a figure crouching in the bushes barely able to contain the fury within. With clenched fists, mouth pressed firmly together, eyes almost black with fury it kept watching, ready to explode. This could not go on any longer, something had to be done to stop them.

This time, when Peter reached the clinic, he felt totally washed up, as if he had been on a strenuous mountain climbing expedition. Just the mere thought of her brought forth a stirring in his loins. His cold showers were taking longer and longer. Lucky his little daughter was not around to see him act like a lovesick fool.

He thought it amazing how quickly Barbie and Autumn had bonded. Through a terrible misunderstanding they had lost precious time. Well, they were together now. He felt just a tiny jab of jealousy when he remembered how happy Barbie was to be able to stay at the Chateau with Autumn instead of returning with him to the clinic. She could at least have shown just as the smallest sign of regret at seeing him leave, instead she gave him a hurried kiss and off she was to whatever had her in a tither at the time. Another good thing was that she would be able to see her Grandpa more often. It brought a smile to his face, knowing his little daughter was in good hands and that she was happy. Soon they would be together as a family, forever.

Barbie was planting some flowers in the garden. At first that gardener Harold didn't seem to like her very much just because she had dug up some ugly plants to make room for the flowers she had picked in the park. He said that the ugly plants were something that was needed in the kitchen. But then he gave her a little spot all her own and now she could do whatever she wanted. He even gave her some flowers with dirt on the bottom, saying they would grow better than what she had picked. He had stuck her small bouquet in a tin with water so they would last longer.

She also loved the park, the big house and especially her big bed with the ceiling covered with loads of stars. She knew that only princesses had a bed like that so maybe some day she was going to be a princess too. The bed was so high that she needed steps to climb into it. Getting out was the best part. She just let herself slide down onto the thick carpet. It was so much fun that she would do it several times every morning. She was so glad that her daddy had found his princess again. Now he was almost always happy, except some times when he let out those big breaths, just like he did when he had a lot of trouble at the clinic. Since there was no trouble anywhere around here, it had to be his work he was thinking about.

Little Barbie was taking her new life in, one day at a time.

The weekend was near and Peter was finishing up with his last patient. Autumn had called earlier to make sure he would be there for the evening meal. There was something in her voice that alarmed him, but he would wait until he got there to find out. Or should he call back and make sure everything was all right? No, better get on the road as soon as possible. If traffic wasn't too bad he would be there even earlier than she expected. That grin on his face spoke volumes. There was never enough time when it came to being with Autumn.

As usual, his housekeeper had everything ready. She was a jewel. What would he have done without her all these years.

Just as he hoped, the traffic was light and he let his sportster zoom down the highway, enjoying the speed. In only a short while he reached the winding road going through the mountains. Deep in thought he didn't see the sign signifying an upcoming curve. His car was going way to fast. Hitting the brakes would have spun him out of control. He did the only thing he could think off, grip the steering wheel with both hands while letting off the gas pedal, praying hard that God would allow him to make it. The drop on his right was hundreds of feet down a rugged cliff with only a small barrier. Not enough to hold back a speeding vehicle. As he flew into the curve a mental picture of Autumn and Barbie flashed before him. He heard the crunching sound of metal on metal as his right side hit the rail and large beads of sweat formed on his forehead. In his mind he was already spiraling down into the endless depth. Then he realized that the car had slowed down and the tires had a firm grip on the road again.

Autumn Leaves

Luckily he was going uphill, which helped to slow him down. Realizing his luck, it was all he could do to hang on to the steering wheel, his whole body was shaking. He pulled into the first pullover spot and just sat there, resting his head on his arms that were slung over the steering wheel. He realized just how close he had come to loosing his life. Fear and anger took a hold of him and he cried like a baby. How stupid could one get, how utterly stupid. He vowed never to let his mind give into daydreaming again, not while he was driving. He sat there for a long time.

Someone tapped him on the shoulder and the worried face of a forester looked down on him. He assured the elderly man that he was all right. When offered a swig of the brandy bottle he politely refused but gladly accepted the hot coffee from the flat round thermos hanging on the old timers belt. For a brief moment he thought about his dad, he had one of those bottles. It brought him back to reality. After a hearty 'thank you' he pulled back into the road. He didn't check the damage done to his car, he just wanted to hold his two ladies in his arms and never let them go.

It was getting dark when he finally pulled through the gate. He saw two shapes on the front steps, huddled together, one taller than the other. They jumped up as he rolled to a stop at the bottom of the stairs. The smaller version flew down the stairs while the other remained standing. Peter had just enough time to close the car door before Barbie flew into his arms. He hugged her so tight that she cried out, giving him an accusing look. He didn't care; it was good to hold his little daughter. Then he rushed to greet Autumn and noticed that her eyes were glued to the car. The two lanterns at the bottom of the steps illuminated a deep dent and scratches. The shiny burgundy color was marked with ugly gray streaks. From the rear door a wide gash gaped at them. He didn't realize that it would be that bad, it happened too fast.

Autumn's face was pale, her eyes waiting for an explanation. "I'm all right, Darling. See .." he stretched out his arms and turned around, "not a scratch on me." He placed his arms around her and kissed her very gently. She felt stiff in his arms.

Inside Victor and Gabriella were waiting with supper. It was a quiet meal, not at all what they had planned. Autumn barely touched her food; she had yet to say anything. Barbie was the only one chatting along, and then even she gave up. Peter gave account of what had happened. Not in much detail since he did not want to frighten his daughter, but enough for the others to realize that it could have turned out very bad. Thank God it hadn't. Gaby offered to tuck Barbie into bed and Victor volunteered his help. Autumn was glad for their help and the three of them clattered up the stairs but not before Barbie lavished big fat kisses and hugs on Peter and Autumn.

Alone, Autumn turned to Peter, obviously in a state of panic, and shouted. "I can't lose you Peter, I could not go on living if anything ever happened to you. Please don't leave me, I need you! Promise not to leave me?"

"I promise. I am so sorry about today, it should never have happened. All I can say is that my mind was on other things, mainly on you. It will not happen again. I love you my darling and I want to spend the rest of my life with you. You, Barbie and our babies." He noticed a faint blush spreading over her still pale face. He could not help himself, he had to kiss her. This time she kissed him back. They held each other tight and slowly their breathing became labored as the heat of their bodies signaled the need to be together. Peter nuzzled her ear, whispering: "We could start on those babies right now."

She didn't pull away, but she stopped those roaming fingers from pulling her deeper into a state where she would be unable to stop him. It made him happy to see her struggle with her own need, it was a sign of how much she was part of him. Soon, very soon they would consummate their love and it would be heaven.

Autumn Leaves

He picked up a glass with ice water and rolled it gently across her forehead, mindful of not spilling it on her dress. He knew it made her feel good for she closed her eyes and purred like a kitten. Her next move took him totally off guard. She snatched the glass out of his hand and poured the contents over his head. Ice-cubes were flying everywhere. Peter looked aghast. He would have never thought that she could be so devilish.

"That should cool you off a bit, my hot blooded racetrack driver." Not likely, he thought, perhaps just the opposite. He was not through with her. He took hold of an ice-cube and with a fluid motion let it slide down in between her breasts. At first she let out a scream, then the coldness began to feel good, very good. It created a new feeling within her, making her ache deep down below. God, what was wrong with her. She felt like a wanton woman.

Lucky for both, Victor and Gaby returned just in time to let them know that Barbie was well on her way into dreamland. The two flushed faces spoke volumes. Gaby and Victor knew at once that those two needed more time alone. So they excused themselves to find their own garden of Eden.

.

Anita Attwood

CHAPTER TWENTY ONE

Autumn looked into the mirror and hardly recognized herself. The image looking back, was that really she? She sat very straight, afraid to move. Gabriella was putting the finishing touches to her hair. It was piled high on her head with soft curls cascading down either side of her face. Attached to a slender tiara was a snow white veil, made of the finest lace, spilling down her back to rest in a pile on the floor. The white damask gown hugged her slender figure, then billowed out into soft folds with the back ending in a four-foot train. It was magnificent. She truly looked like a fairy tale princess.

Autumn was almost afraid to breathe. This was the day she had been waiting for. Now, that it was here, she wished she could move it farther back. Suddenly she knew that she was not ready for this to happen, she needed more time. She told Gaby to stop fussing over her hairdo. Gaby looked bewildered. She noticed the change in Autumn's face but before she could say anything Autumn asked her to leave. She saw tears forming in Autumn's eyes and quietly walked out the door. Whatever the problem was would have to be dealt with by Autumn herself. Gaby decided to wait in the hall.

Autumn was not herself. Her hands trembled as she uttered the words: "Mommy, please help me, am I doing the right thing?" There was no answer, only silence. She let her hands drop in resignation realizing that her parents would not be here to guide her on this journey. She wanted to marry Peter; she loved him with all her heart. So why was she suddenly so afraid?

Last night had been magical. It made them both wish that this day had already passed so they could succumb to the feelings of wanting to be one. It was Peter who had been the strong one and she loved him all the more for it. She didn't hear the door open and it took her by surprise when a tiny hand snugged into hers.

"Are you my mommy now 'cause you're a bride?" Barbie's eyes held so much hope; it warmed Autumn's heart. This was her answer. She hugged her tightly and whispered: "Almost, we're almost there."

Gabriella tried to stop Barbie from entering, but when she looked in she was mighty glad she hadn't.

Victor's head appeared above Gabriella's. "Can a guy have a few moments alone with the woman he is about to give away?"

Barbie was ushered toward Gabriella. The door closed on their way out. Victor stopped, taking in the sight of his lovely ward. She turned toward him and placed her hands on his shoulders. They looked at each other for a long moment, and then he gently embraced her and placed a lingering kiss on her forehead.

"A while back I would have never thought I could let you go." He said it quietly.

"A while back I would not have wanted you to let me go," was her answer.

They smiled at each other and they knew that everything was just as it should be. He was happy that Peter was the man she had given her heart too, he was a fine, caring person and most of all, they were so completely in love.

"Time to go princess." He took her arm and led her down the stairs to the front door where a carriage was waiting to take them to the old village church.

Hundreds of people were waiting to witness the marriage of their beloved princess. When they entered the Chapel all went quiet. Heads turned to behold the bride walking down the aisle on the arm of her uncle who was dressed in full uniform looking very regal indeed. There was not a single dry eye at the sight of the little girl sprinkling her rose pedals before the stunning pair moving toward the altar.

Holding on to Victor's arm, Autumn could not take her eyes off Peter. Standing to the right of the altar he looked so handsome in his silver grey tuxedo, his best man at his side. If Autumn was taken in by his appearance, Peter's heart almost stopped when he looked at his bride. He was so mesmerized that he almost forgot to breathe.

Hundreds of candles illuminated the church and after the vows were exchanged and the pastor declared Autumn and Peter to be man and wife, everybody started clapping, except one. It seemed that their kiss would never end. Barbie put a stop to that by demanding that she be included in those mushy kisses. She declared with much authority: "I'm glad we finally got married," which drew laughter from everyone within reach of her voice.

As they were leaving the church nobody paid any attention to the lone figure slipping down the stairway, vanishing around the corner in a great hurry.

The procession toward the Chateau was indeed a long one. The whole village was invited to the festivities. The young couple stood at the portal to welcome their guests. For a split second another moment flashed before Autumn's eyes as she looked out over the crowd streaming by. It was on a blustery day and the crowd that had gathered in the rose garden had also been very large. Only on that day there was no laughter and no cheerful music, only tears and sobs and the song...

A slight chill run through her but she willed those dark thoughts away. When Peter gave her a worried look she answered with her brightest smile. After all, it was their wedding day.

It was a great feast that would long be remembered, including the finale when hundreds of balloons were released, filling the sky with colorful bubbles as far as the eye could see. Just as always, some just burst with a loud pop while the rest floated away. Tomorrow the children would have fun trying to gather those that had gotten caught in the trees and bushes.

For the young couple the world had just begun. Barbie had gone to stay with her grandpa and Gabriella offered to help Victor look after things at the chateau. Peter took his bride to their honeymoon suite. They would leave in the morning to spend a few days in a secret hideaway, but for now, this was all they needed.

There was champagne in a cooler and a fresh fruit tray with assorted cheese bits on the table. The bed was turned down and a fire crackled in the fireplace.

Peter took Autumn's hands in his; they felt like ice. He knew by the look in her eyes that she was uneasy, it tugged at his heart. His beautiful bride was a virgin and he would have to use all his skill to help her become his wife without hurting her too much. The previous nights had shown him how much she wanted to be close to him, but did she really know what it would take?

He poured two glasses of champagne. "Let's just sit in front of the fire and enjoy the flames for a while. I love you Autumn, my precious wife."

Her glowing look told him that he had done the right thing. "Peter, thank you for wanting me and loving me. I still can't believe that we are husband and wife, I love you to."

With that she bent forward and kissed him gently at first, but then her tongue caressed his lips and probed deeper to explore the inside of his mouth. Peter let out a moan. Soon they were entangled, hands roaming, pulling and fumbling at their clothes. The struggle proved to be too much and they had to come up for a breath of air.

"There is an easier way, my darling, let me show you." Peter stood up and pulled Autumn to her feet. He slowly turned her around and began to unbutton her dress when her hands flew up holding on to the front before it could drop to the floor. Oh God, he thought, this is going to be harder than I thought. Then he heard a giggle.

"It's not fair that I should be the first to be naked with you standing there totally dressed." She had already taken hold of his shirt and one by one it came undone while her dress billowed around her ankles. What a lovely sight. There she was standing in her frilly undergarments while struggling to get his shirt off. Peter wouldn't have believed it. This virgin, this innocent wife of his, was actually taking the initiative in seducing him? When had things turned around? There was no doubt that he was enjoying this. Shy little Autumn, turning into a vixen, he was in heaven. Autumn had removed his shirt and was actually trying to undo his trousers, when things got in the way. Well, what can one expect? "Oh..."

For a moment she stood rigid. Then she put her arms around his neck and kissed him hard on the mouth. He took this to be his cue.

Their eyes locked and he slowly unhooked her bra. He almost forgot to breathe, she looked magnificent. His gently kissed each nipple. Then he swung her into his arms and lowered her unto the bed. His gaze never left her face as he pulled down one petticoat, then another, then another and still another. Finally she lay before him with only a tiny garterbelt holding up her silky white stockings and white lace panties, leaving nothing to the imagination. God she was gorgeous, much more beautiful than he had ever imagined, and she was his. He noticed that her eyes were now tightly

Autumn Leaves

shut, so he shed the rest of his clothes and lay down beside her, placing one hand on her flat belly. She turned her head to look at him, her eyes dark with desire. He began to stroke her breasts while his lips caressed her neck, then moved lower and lower until they reached one mound. Slowly his tongue circled the hardening nipple and she arched toward him, her hands pulling his head even closer. He reached down to stroke the soft flesh of her belly. His fingers traced lower until he could feel the moisture as he gently touched the tender folds and found the core. He could hear her moaning softly. At times it looked as if her breathing had stopped but then her body would writhe in sweet agony. Would he dare go further?

Yes, her body was crying out for him. She had turned into a seductive woman over night. It was more than he had bargained for.

"Darling, are you sure you want me to go on?" Her look was that of a bewildered child. He felt stupid. She wanted him and he was ready. He broke out in a sweat, beads rolling down his forehead. He didn't want to hurt her, he wanted to be gentle, but her body gyrating under his did not help matters.

"Peter, please love me."

Well, that did it. He removed the rest of her clothing and lowered himself on top of her. He suddenly gasped when her hand touched him and was actually guiding him. Her whole body arched toward him, inviting the intrusion. He could hold back no longer. There was a short cry followed by a moment of stillness. Then the clouds swirled around them and they went higher and higher into oblivion. It was a fulfillment so unlike anything either of them had ever experienced. It left them spent; lying in each other's arms until sleep claimed them. The rest of the champagne went flat and the cheese and fruit dried up.

CHAPTER TWENTY TWO

Saint Michael's. Laura's hands clutched the iron bars covering her tiny window that exposed part of the magnificent mountain terrain. The place looked like a fortress, it was quiet up here. She was desperately trying to find peace. Perhaps Saint Michael's would give her that. It had broken her mother's heart, hearing from her own daughter's mouth, how cruel she had been to Autumn. But when she said she had never harmed Autumn's horse or had anything to do with the broken saddle, only her mother believed her. It was also proven that her foolish attempt at cutting the tires on Autumn's car had nothing to do with Ted's death, except the intent to hurt Autumn had been there. Her admission to feeling sorry for her actions meant little to anyone. Outside her mother nobody believed her to be innocent. She had come to accept that. After the hearing she had been given a choice, either go to a mental hospital or into the convent. She had chosen the latter.

Not that it really mattered; she had lost Harold's trust as well. Ruben had little to say to her, which could only mean that he also thought her guilty of tampering with the horse. He of all people should've known that it was not so. She also

Autumn Leaves

realized that Autumn was forever lost to her. It was her own damned fault, so why did it hurt so much?

It was Harold who had driven her up to the Monastery. Their parting moments had been painful, for both of them, especially after he told her that he would always love her. She had long realized that she really did love him too, alas, it was to late.

Here, in her small cell, she had all the time in the world to recall her messed up past. She asked God daily for forgiveness. Would he hear her through these thick, old walls? Would he even want to listen to her?

What she really needed was Autumn's forgiveness. This morning the nuns had brought her a paper showing pictures of a wedding, Autumn and Peter's. Hot tears spilled over her cheeks and fell unto the paper. She was not sure if they were tears of joy, regret or both. She was glad that for her very best friend the times of pain and agony were over. Very best friend indeed. Not any more, not after what she had put her through.

Would Autumn ever believe her to be innocent of Maharani's death? For some reason that question haunted her day and night. On the other hand, it really did not matter any more; she would never leave the convent anyhow. But Autumn's happiness made her very glad. It was good of the nuns to let her know this.

In the Schwarzenau stables Ruben's thoughts were with his cousin. Brother, did he let her down. It really began to gnaw on him. How did things get so fouled up? As much as he loved working with these horses he knew his time had run out. Laura had been send to the convent and Autumn had gotten married. Come to think of it, the man she chose wasn't her equal either, so why couldn't it have been him instead? He had only one choice, get as far away from here as possible. No way would he let himself be implicated in anything.

Although he knew that Laura's mom needed help, with her health dwindling fast, he would not be the one to give it. The other day he noticed Harold over at the nursery. Maybe Harold was taking over that place as well. It would be an excellent choice. For a second he wondered what Laura would say about that. She had been pretty thick with that guy. Then he wondered if Laura even knew the shape her mother was in. He himself had never been close to Selma, so it didn't face him a whole lot that she might die soon, but Laura would be devastated. Perhaps he should stop by the convent before heading out; he owed her that much.

The day Pauli found a letter behind one of the feeders would prove to be a turning point in the lives of many.
Pauli was one of Victor's stable hands. He had transferred the boy to the Schwarzenau stables when Ruben so mysteriously disappeared.
The boy didn't know what to make of the letter, there was nothing written on the envelope and it was obvious that it had been there a while. Curiosity got the better of him and he opened it. When he began to read, he realized that this was something of great importance. Pauli walked back and forth in the barn, not knowing what to do with this letter. Instinct told him that he should bring it to the big house at once, or maybe he should just put it back where he found it. After what seemed a very long time he found himself walking up the road toward the Chateau. He didn't get very far; Victor had been on his way to the stables. Pauli never said a word; he just handed the letter to Victor, turned and ran back to the stables.
It took Victor quite a while to comprehend the content of this writing. He read it over and over to get a clear picture. Ruben! It was he, who cut the saddle, put the nail in Maharani's foot and finally killed her. He said he did it out of love for the princess. What a warped mind. My God, how

could he have been so wrong as to credit Laura with all these wrong doings? Ruben, it had been him all along. Worse yet, he was out there, somewhere.

Victor remembered at Laura's hearing that nobody believed her when she said that she was innocent of the crimes dealing with the horse. He remembered her finally giving up on defending herself and quietly accepting the verdict. Even Harold didn't believe her, only her mother stood firm.

The letter burned in his hands. He had to get it to the authorities as fast as possible. Ruben needed to be found and dealt with, without delay. This would help Laura, not that she was squeaky clean, on the contrary, but she stood accused of things she didn't do.

Victor didn't waste any time rushing to town. The wheels were set into motion to get Laura back into the real world. Harold would be interested in this new development, Victor was sure of that. He found him in the park pruning hedges. Harold listened intently at what Victor had to say but in the end shook his head and told Victor that it would never work for him and Laura any more. Harold had aged. As Victor walked away he heard him blow his nose in a most noisy way. That man still loved her.

Victor wondered if he should tell Autumn about the letter but thought better of it. She didn't even know about Laura's hearing or that she was in Saint Michael's. Why disrupt her happy little world which she had fought so hard to reach. His main concern was finding Ruben and making sure Autumn was safe.

CHAPTER TWENTY THREE

In Bad Reichenhall, they were happy. Barbie got the best of both worlds. Her daddy was around so much more and she had a full time mommy. When Peter had to go away on business Autumn and Barbie would stay in Schwarzenau. Barbie's grandfather was able to see her a lot more, making their bond even tighter. Barbie reminded Autumn of Peter, when he was young. She was very good with animals of all sorts, specially the ones that got hurt. A little Veterinarian in the making.

It was on one of those visits that the call came. Autumn had just gotten back from taking the little girl over to her grandfather's. She didn't recognize the voice or the name on the other end.

"Are you sure you have the right number?"

"Quite sure. That is, if I'm speaking to princess Autumn?"

"You are. Am I supposed to know you?"

"Not personally; I am...I mean I was Ted's fiancé, Dahlia. Surely you have heard of me."

Autumn paused for a moment, and then recognition set in.

"Yes of course I remember, how nice of you to call. What can I do for you?"

"I had actually hoped that I might be allowed to come and see you. There are a few things I'd like to talk over. Mostly I want to apologize for my rude behavior after Ted's death."

Autunn learned that Dahlia was already in the village and they decided that they would get together that very afternoon. It would be good to meet the woman Ted had fallen in love with. She didn't expect Victor back until late afternoon and Barbie was spending the night at her grandfather's, so this was perfect. Just as she was leaving for the kitchen the phone rang again. This time it was Peter and her heart skipped a beat. She told him about Dahlia's visit and he was delighted. He told her that the conference had gone so well, they were finishing up early and he could be home as early as seven this evening. Perhaps he could meet Dahlia. When he told her that he planned on staying several days to make up for lost time Autumn's eyes began to shine. Once again she headed toward the kitchen to tell Mary about Dahlia and of course about Peter's early arrival. She could hardly wait to see him. She had some wonderful news to tell him.

Dahlia arrived at three thirty. There was an awkward moment when they first looked at each other, but the spell was quickly broken with big smiles and a hardy handshake. Autumn was pleasantly surprised how petite and slender Dahlia was. Ted would have towered over her by at least a foot. Black long hair framed her fine china doll like features. Her laughter surprised Autumn; it was strong, and not at all what one would expect from such a tiny person. Her handshake had been so powerful that Autumn had to make sure all her fingers were still intact. Autumn silently vowed to avoid another handshake.

Their conversation was mostly about Dahlia's adventures with Ted. Now and then Autumn noticed a crack in Dahlia's voice, especially when she recalled the tender moments with him. She could tell that the great love Dahlia had felt for Ted was still there. It made her sad knowing that their time had been cut so short. They both fell silent.

When it became obvious that gloom seemed to take over Dahlia let out one of her powerful laughs compelling Autumn to chime in. They decided to take a bottle of wine and go out to the pool. Might as well make use of the sunshine and go for a swim. John followed the girls with glasses and some refreshments.

"Autumn, is he always so attentive?"

"John? Yes, always. He is pure gold. He's been with us as long as I can remember." After a slight pause: "I'd like to show you the rose garden, that's where my parents are resting."

"Thank you Autumn, I'd like that." Then she added casually: " Ted is resting in the ocean, I scattered his ashes."

Autumn was taken aback. She didn't know how to respond to that. Dahlia had a far away look on her face and was obviously not expecting an answer.

After a few minutes, just like before, Dahlia suddenly laughed out loud. She certainly was a person of quick mood changes. Soon after that the girls were swimming and splashing each other, seemingly having a wonderful time. John came out to see if they needed anything but went back into the house, deciding to check back later, seeing how much fun they were having.

Dahlia had kept an eye on John and was pleased to see him returning to the house. Now was the time to act. Autumn was in the middle of the pool, doing her breaststroke, slow and easy, Dahlia was at the deep end. She propelled herself away from the edge. Like an arrow she dove down and came up right under Autumn, punching hard into her stomach.

Autumn gasped and lost control. As she went under there was another punch, this time into her side. She fought to get to the top, but she couldn't. Something was holding her under. Her head started swimming, she knew she did not have the strength to fight whatever it was that had a hold on her. Suddenly she realized that it was Dahlia who was pulling her down. "Why" her mind was screaming. At the same time things around her got fuzzy and blurred. She knew that she was in trouble, she didn't have the strength to fight back. She was floating, floating ...

Peter walked toward the pool expecting to see the girls frolicking in the water, when he saw somebody rushing out of the pool and run toward the back of the garden. Where was Autumn? A sudden fear gripped his heart. Then he saw it, a shape at the bottom of the pool; it was Autumn. Without any further thought he dove in and took hold of her lifeless form. When he brought her to the surface he was gasping for air but still managed to yell for help. Autumn's face was white as a ghost. He gently laid her down and immediately applied CPR. Nothing! He pounded her chest and cried out her name, again and again. No response. My God, why wasn't she responding? Then he noticed a red stain on the cement, blood. His outcry was so wild it sounded inhuman. He pulled her up and crushed her to him in a fierce embrace. "No, no, no ..."

There was a gurgling sound, her body convulsed and water began to gush out of her mouth. Peter held her, calling her name again and again until she finally opened her eyes. Those beautiful eyes were dull, but she was alive. He could hear the faint sound of a siren; help was on the way. Mary came running. Her arms were loaded down with blankets. John was right behind her. Neither of them spoke a word; it was dejavu all over again.

The ambulance arrived. No doubt it was John who had acted so quickly. Autumn was loaded into the ambulance and Peter jumped in after. The blood, why was she hemorrhaging? A chill ran through him when realization set in.

It was confirmed that Autumn had miscarried. The doctor concluded it was most likely through a severe blow to her abdomen. The bruises were proof of that. Thank God she was out of danger. Peter worried about additional internal injuries. He hadn't known about the baby and desperately hoped she hadn't been aware of it either, although it was highly unlikely. She would need to remain at the hospital where she could be closely monitored. He was glad that Barbie was at her Grandfather's house. His dad wouldn't mind keeping her for another day or two so he could be at Autumn's side until he could bring her home.

It was the following day when Autumn asked Peter why Dahlia had attacked her. He had no answer but vowed to find out. As far as he was concerned there was no excuse acceptable for hurting his beloved wife, none whatsoever.

After two more days he was able to bring her home. Victor was waiting for them. Once Autumn was tucked onto the sofa, Victor came out with some startling news.

His face drawn into a grim expression, "Dahlia is already apprehended. She confessed to the assault. You won't believe this but she claimed that she was seeking revenge for Ted's death. In her mind it was you, Autumn, who caused his death."

Autumn visibly shrank into herself but her voice was firm when she said: "Well, she's wrong. I'll talk to her when I feel stronger. I want her to tell me to my face why she thinks I'm responsible." She shook her head in disbelief. How had Dahlia come to such a foolish conclusion? Peter must have had the same thoughts. "That's utterly ridiculous!" His words were underlined by a hard slap against the sofa cushion. His lips were pressed into a thin line. He was angry.

Autumn Leaves

Dahlia was under house arrest. She was being held at the inn right next to the police station, the White Swan. Her voluntary confession kept her out of jail until she was officially charged. Nobody knew that it was Victor's gentle persuasion, as he called it, that prompted the confession. A smile crossed his face just thinking about it. For a short time he had that bitch shaking in her boots. He would do anything for Autumn and Peter.

Autumn appeared to be strong about the loss of her baby, except when she was at her parent's graveside. In those quiet surroundings she would shed bitter tears. She desperately to clung to the hope that there would be a time when she and Peter would have another child.

One day, while visiting her parents resting place, she knew that her dreams would come true. A sense of calm engulfed her whole being.

It was time to confront Dahlia. She went to the White Swan and was greeted with a smirky remark: "Glad you're still breathing, princess."

Autumn was taken back but chose to ignore Dahlia's sarcasm. What she saw made her pity the other woman. Dark rings circled her eyes and her complexion was pale. Her hands were moving constantly with her fingers entwining and releasing. Something must have shown in Autumn's face for Dahlia turned beet red and spat in her direction. Autumn ducked and Dahlia missed her target. Totally infuriated she shrieked: "You think you are so high and mighty. Well, let me tell you missy, your so-called friends have done a number on you and you are to stupid to realize it. Do you know who I'm talking about?" Autumn just shook her head.

"Let me enlighten you, princess. You do know a little fellow named Ruben, don't you?" Her laugh was shrill and she went on to say, "little Ruben is a real gem. He even used his own cousin to cover up his evil deeds. Yeah, he fooled all of you, isn't that a scream?"

Autumn's face went pale; she didn't want to hear any more. This woman was crazy. She took a deep breath. "Dahlia, I don't know why you say all these things, but I came here to tell you something important. Please listen to me."

"Please listen to me…" Dahlia mimicked Autumn's voice while racing back and forth. It made Autumn almost dizzy watching her. When Dahlia finally took a pause Autumn quickly yelled as loud as she could, "Ted's death was an accident. It was nobody's fault. He loved you and if you don't know that than there is nothing else I have to say to you. You need help. I will not excuse your attack on me. You caused me to lose my baby and that I can not forget. I'm sorry you're hurting, but so am I. I won't listen to any more of your wild talk and I don't ever want to see you again. Go home Dahlia, go back home." With that Autumn ran out the door hearing Dahlia's screaming voice bouncing off the walls. She covered her ears with both hands while trying to get as far away from that place as possible. Dahlia's screaming could be heard long after she had left the hotel.

That short meeting with Dahlia left Autumn in a state of confusion. For the first time in ages her thoughts went to Laura. Dahlia had made some pretty wild accusations. Could any of it be true? Had she let her old friend down?

She shared her concerns with Peter and together they decided to consult Victor. .

The wheels of justice were rolling. Victor had no intention of letting Dahlia get off scott free and Peter supported him. At first Autumn did not want to press charges and when she did, she asked for leniency. Peter and Victor did not approve, but Autumn remained firm. Nothing would bring her baby back and Dahlia was a disturbed woman. Deportation was all she wanted, but Dahlia was also

Autumn Leaves

forbidden to return for the next twenty years. She was told that in case of a violation she would be charged in the death of Autumn's unborn child. Victor watched as the police escorted her to the plane and noticed a small figure of a man running toward them and hug Dahlia, but the police pulled him away and he vanished as quickly as he had appeared. Now Dahlia was inside the plane. The two policemen emerged and the door was firmly shut. Only after the plane was well up in the air did he return to his car.

CHAPTER TWENTY FOUR

The past few months had not been easy for Victor. Gabriella had gone back to Italy and Jane was trying to stop the divorce since she found out he had a title. The mere thought of it made him want to smash a hole into a wall. What made matters worse was the fact that it still hurt to think about her. He had really loved that woman.

Now there was Gaby. He had actually been thinking of a future with her. Well, she had left on short notice. Family matters, that's what she had told him, something about saving her inheritance. That was three weeks ago, three weeks of silence. Maybe he had read too much into their relationship. He would wait, just a little longer.

Anyhow, the matter Dahlia had brought up about Ruben kept his mind busy. It just confirmed what he had read in the letter, not one finger pointing in Laura's direction. She was still at the convent and he began to wonder if she had any idea how ill her mother was.

Another thought crossed his mind, would she know how to get in touch with Ruben? That weasel had disappeared into thin air. Then it occurred to him. The guy at the airport, hugging Dahlia, it had been him.

He was so deeply buried in thought that he didn't hear the phone and jumped when John handed him the receiver. The voice on the other end sounded strange, then he recognized it as belonging to Harold.

"Victor, I'm calling about Selma. She died half an hour ago. What should I do now?"

At first he didn't comprehend, then his head cleared. Good God, that poor woman. He had meant to visit her but never got around to it. He never thought her time would be so short. Now he felt ashamed.

"Just sit tight, Harold, I'm on my way."

The two men were sitting in Selma's living room, trying to figure out what to do next. Their biggest concern was Laura. Harold asked Victor to bring her the news. He just couldn't trust himself around her. One look into those dark eyes and his resolve would melt in a heartbeat, but that was his secret. Victor drew the wrong conclusion. So he reminded Harold about the latest developments concerning Laura, that there was a real chance that she was not guilty of all those things she was accused off. He was hoping this would soften Harold's heart. Harold didn't comment. Victor wondered if he had been listening to anything he had said.

After a short pause they decided it would be best to let the Mother Superior tell Laura about her mother's death. Victor realized that now was the time to tell Autumn all the new developments in regards to Laura and Ruben. Selma's death had changed everything.

The search for Ruben had begun; it was done very discreetly. It was important not to scare him away. The truth would come out, Victor was sure of that, especially since Chief Rosenbaum was just as eager to set the record straight. Victor remembered a few moments, at Laura's hearing, when he'd felt a little bit uneasy but he could never put his finger on it. Now it made sense. That scoundrel had to be found, and soon.

At Saint Michael's Mother Superior approached Laura's cell with a heavy heart. She had grown very fond of this quiet, dark haired girl.

Laura took the news well. There were no outbursts of anger or pain, just silent tears rolling down her cheeks. The next day, however, when she didn't show up for early morning mass, they found her lying in a pool of blood. She had somehow managed to cut her wrists; there was so much blood. Her face looked like that of an angel, peaceful and so very white.
The nuns crowded into the tiny room when one of the sisters cried out: " We have a pulse!" Some were rushing to gather the necessary bandages and alert their medical team, while others gathered in the chapel to pray. Nothing like this had ever happened at Saint Michael's.

The news about Laura's attempted suicide stunned everybody, especially Harold. He was convinced that this wouldn't have happened had he been man enough to bring the sad news to her himself. How utterly alone she must have felt. He could have told her that she could count on him. He realized that his stupid pride had nearly destroyed her and it made him sick to his stomach. Would she allow him to see her now?

The infirmary was not very big, only six beds stood side by side with small white nightstands between them. The place seemed like a narrow hallway, but the windows were much bigger than those in the nun's cells. Sunlight was beaming in making the room seem bright and cheerful. Only one bed was occupied. Laura lay sleeping; her arms stretched on either side with her palms turned up. Thick bandages were wrapped around each wrist. Autumn and Peter stood at the foot of the bed, watching her. Poor Laura, she had been through some hard times and now it was time for those old wounds to heal. Autumn was silently praying for a quick recovery and just as she placed a small bouquet of daisies on the nightstand, Laura's eyelids began to flutter. Their eyes held for a long time.

"Autumn...?"

How strange to hear this small voice coming from Laura. Laura, who had always been strong, loud and boisterous.

"How's it going girlfriend?" Autumn smiled, choking down the tears that threatened to spill over. Laura managed a crooked smile; then her eyes got all watery and both girls cried. Autumn bent down and placed a kiss on Laura's cheek. Peter turned away, seemingly studying the garden.

Words were not needed, they knew that the past was behind them. This day would mark the beginning of a much stronger friendship. Peter checked Laura's pulse and found it strong. She seemed to perk up quite a bit. But when they asked if she would allow Harold to come in, her eyes clouded over.

"Why would he want to see me? I've hurt him so much."

"Just say yes, Laura. He really would like to see you." Laura could not deny Autumn's request and agreed with a nod. Peter was already at the door, motioning Harold to come in. He had been patiently waiting in the hallway, wondering if she would allow him to see her. His heart was pounding as he slowly made his way toward Laura's bed, a single red rose in his hands. He laid it across Laura's chest and whispered: "A rose for my rose, I love you."

She was speechless. Her eyes began to shine and her lips parted in a wonderful smile. That's when he couldn't help himself and he kissed her. Autumn and Peter left quietly; there was no need for them to stay any longer. As they walked down the long corridor, their arms wound tight around each other, the nuns smiled at the passing young couple. Once outside Autumn turned to her husband. "I hope Laura and Harold will find happiness the same way we have. They deserve it, don't you think?" Peter just smiled, he was proud of the way his little wife was handling things.

A few days later a small group of people gathered in the village cemetery, among them a very large man who cried unashamedly. Nobody thought it strange; they all knew him to be a gentle giant. Laura sat in a wheelchair clutching a bouquet of colorful carnations. Autumn's hand was resting on her shoulder, which gave her lot of comfort, and Harold and Peter were standing beside them. Having her friends close by made the pain of losing her mother a bit easier. She hardly understood a word the preacher said, her heart cried out to hold her mom. She was still ghostly white. But when Victor recalled how proud and unselfish her mother had been, how hard she had worked to make a life for her little girl and herself, Laura broke down completely. Harold knelt beside her chair and held her tight.

Having friends who cared and a man who loved her was all she needed. She would always miss her mother; she was the only one who had believed in her. At this moment she knew the pain Autumn must have felt at the loss of her parents, hers had been a double tragedy, but her friend made it through and so would she.

When Laura looked at the few people standing quietly around the casket, one face was missing, Ruben. She had not heard from him since the hearing and not a soul had mentioned his name, how strange.

Little did she know how quickly that would change.

Next days Newspaper had a bold headline – Local man arrested! Ruben Hauser had been apprehended and the charge against him was grave; assault with intent to cause great bodily harm. His biggest downfall however was, that he was willing to let someone else suffer for his crime, namely his cousin Laura. His arrest affected quite a few people, among them Autumn.

Victor had a lot of explaining to do. He should have mentioned things earlier to Autumn or allow Peter to do so. Now she was furious, with both of them. But when she announced that she was going to see Ruben, they tried hard to stop her. He would be just as cruel as Dahlia had been, they were sure about that. It was Ruben who had planted the seed into Dahlia's head that Autumn was responsible for Ted's death. In a way he was also responsible for the loss of Autumn and Peter's baby. She should not have to go through any more traumas.

It took Victor most of the morning to explain the whole scenario. He was exhausted and just about to give up when Autumn turned to him.

"Victor, I do understand why you acted the way you did. Now you need to understand this, I am a woman; there is no reason to shield me from anything in the future. Promise me, both of you, no more holding back." Her look underlined how serious she was.

"Now I will go and see Ruben and don't try to stop me. I need closure, no, we need closure, all of us!" She got up and walked out.

The two men didn't quite know what to do next, until the phone rang.

Both ran, jumped into Peter's sports car, leaving a cloud of dust behind. They had to overtake Autumn before she got to the jail. Ruben had hung himself.

Harold offered to talk to Laura and explain how things had gone from bad to worse. It was such an unbelievable story with another tragic ending. This was the day he was to bring her home; perhaps he would let her spend a few extra days in the care of the nuns. Their gentle ways had a great healing power, more than he could give her now.

Anita Attwood

Beside the preacher, this time only five people stood beside the grave, Laura, Harold, Autumn, Peter and Victor. The preacher's words were kind, as they should be. Yes, there were tears. Tears for a misguided young man who had such great potential. Laura clung to Harold; he was all she had left in the world.

Harold moved into the house at the nursery. There wasn't any reason to wait, he and Laura knew they belonged together. In a quiet ceremony they vowed to love and cherish one another for the rest of their lives. It felt right.

Harold took on the added responsibility running the nursery and hired a young man from the village as helper. Laura blossomed in her duty as housewife. The things she had learned from her mother about keeping the nursery in good shape were a major fact why everything continued to go so smoothly.

Still, it took a while for everyone to come to grips with all that had happened. Some shadows would always linger, but life must go on.

Autumn Leaves

CHAPTER TWENTY FIVE

They were back in Bad Reichenhall. Peter spent long hours at the Clinic while Autumn and Barbie did their best to run the house, trying not to miss him too much. Autumn loved their villa with its wide-open space and splendid surroundings. She spent more and more time here and the trips to Schwarzenau grew less frequent. She knew that she was missed at the Chateau, but her place was at Peter's side and he couldn't afford to be away from his clinic so much.

Barbie missed seeing her grandfather. She still did not understand why grown-ups had to work so much. Lucky for her that her new mommy had lots of time for her.

A decision was reached by Autumn. She was going to ask Victor to take over Schwarzenau for good. She felt that it was his home even more than hers. After her parent's death it should have gone to him right away, he was the rightful heir to the Estate. He had been running it ever since their death and he was kind and fair. Peter was glad about Autumn's decision. He would have never complained about the many journeys back and forth, but it had become increasingly difficult for him.

On the next visit to Schwarzenau Autumn confronted Victor with her decision. They argued back and forth, each determined to win.

"No, Autumn, this is your home and always will be!"

"Don't give me a hard time about this, please Victor?" She put her hands together imploring him to agree. He kept shaking his head. Frustration was slowly taking the upper hand.

"Look at it this way" she finally said, " I'm not a Schwarzenau any more, I am Mrs. Marshall, Doctor Peter Marshall's wife and my place is with my husband and our little daughter. This place needs you Victor. You can always keep one wing reserved for our visits, but you must make this your home. Most of your horses are already in our stables and you live here, so what's the problem?"

He opened his mouth but thought better of it. There was no use arguing any further. He knew Autumn's mind was made up and it would be nearly impossible to change it. Her triumphant smile did get under his skin and his grunt was an indication that he was not pleased. Since when did females run his life anyway? Without another word he walked away. He had to cool off and get his thoughts together. Autumn was right in many ways, but this was her home left to her by her parents. It just didn't feel right to take over and act as if he owned it all? He would find a way that would make it right for all concerned.

Two weeks later, Victor was in the middle of breakfast, when Jane strolled in. He almost choked on his coffee. Old John hurried after Jane who obviously had gotten by him. With his face totally flustered he just shrugged his shoulders. Victor motioned him to go and he trotted away obviously not pleased with himself.

Jane had stopped in the middle of the verandah, waiting for Victor to make the next move. They just looked at

Autumn Leaves

each other, neither knowing what to say. Finally Jane uttered the first words. "I don't want a divorce."

Her intense look made him feel somewhat uneasy. She was even more beautiful than he remembered. She looked frail, but very elegant. Her voice was soft and he could have sworn there were tears in her eyes. Still, he remained silent.

"Victor, I made a mistake. It's been long over. I'm on my own and I've made a lot of money. I guess that really doesn't matter. What I am trying to say is that I've missed you and I want it to be like it was before. That is ... if you still want me."

Yes, at this very moment he wanted her, but he kept himself in check. How dare she'd just come waltzing in here thinking everything would be just as before. His silence spoke louder than words. He noticed her shoulders slump ever so slightly. A whispered "I'm sorry" reached him as she turned and fled through the parlor and out the front door. Victor didn't react until he heard the motor start and rushed to stop her. To late, all he saw was the taillights disappearing through the gate.

He hated to admit it, but Jane still had his heart. So she made a mistake? Many people make mistakes, including him, and go on living. Why was this different? Well, for one thing, she had abandoned him at the most critical moment in his life and that he could never forgive. Never?

Jane in the meantime clutched the steering wheel with both hands to keep the car on the road while tears were streaming down her face, making it hard to see. She had to come and see for herself if there was still a chance for them. Well she got her answer; it was over. Now tell that to her heart which was hurting like hell. Knowing that it was all her doing didn't ease the pain, just the opposite. Through a veil of tears she noticed a huge object looming in front of her and she hit the brakes. Too late. Her body propelled forward and she felt a splitting pain racing through her head, before darkness engulfed her.

She was hearing voices. "That tree is coming down, the village council agreed unanimously. There will not be another life put into harms way. That young man of yours was not the first victim, but he will be the last. Your young lady friend will recover, thank God for that."

Jane had no idea who was talking to whom, but she realized that she would be all right. Someone pushed the door to her room open. She had to blink twice to make sure her eyes were not deceiving her. Victor walked toward her bed, so tall and handsome. Was that a worried look on his face? When she realized that he was indeed worried about her it made her feel good. He stood at the foot of the bed and just looked at her. That wonderful feeling she had a minute ago was dwindling fast. Why didn't he say anything? He must have noticed the fear in her face because all of a sudden he broke into a big grin, then walked around the bed to take her hand.

"I'm so glad you're alright. You gave me quite a fright, young lady." All she could think was 'please don't let go of my hand' and he didn't. Not for a while anyway. Then he said the sweetest words. "When you get out of here, let's sit down and talk."

After much thought he had come to the conclusion that he still had a lot of feelings for Jane. He had hoped for a future with Gabriella, but she had left him and it was like an omen, having Jane return at this very moment. Their divorce was so close at hand, now he would put a stop to it. He convinced himself that this was what he should do even so there was this little voice in his head doubting his wisdom. Jane needed him; it was that simple. Then why did Gabriella's face appear in front of his eyes every time he thought of Jane? He didn't like the conflict within him and decided to call Autumn and let her know about Jane. Somehow Autumn didn't react the way he had hoped she would. Was it because she had become so close to Gaby? But Gaby had left him out of her own free will and never once contacted him in all this time. Love does not act this way. Two people in love want to be as close as possible, not run away from each other. When Jane had left him it was to be with another man, Gabriella left him, for what? Gabriella, such a rare beauty, tender and loving ... However, it was Jane who had returned.

Autumn hung up the phone and glanced toward the verandah where Gabriella stood, hugging herself. There was a slight chill in the air. How could she tell her friend what Victor had revealed. In her heart Autumn knew that Gaby loved him. She had explained the mystery of her disappearance and Victor would have understood. That was before Jane's sudden appearance. Of course now he was drawn back to Jane, if for no other reason but pity after she got hurt. He was that kind of a guy. Autumn had learned much about human emotions since the loss of her parents. She realized that Victor could not act in any other way but to be on Jane's side, whether it turned out good or bad.

These thoughts did not help her with bringing the news to Gaby. On her way out she fetched a sweater and placed it around Gaby's shoulders. She thanked her with a smile and asked: "I heard the phone ring, was it good or bad news?" Autumn shrugged her shoulders.

"I guess a little of both." There was a moment of silence.

"Do you think I could call Victor and let him know that I'm back?"

"No, don't!" It shot out so fast that Gaby raised her eyebrows. The look she gave Autumn was one big question mark. It left Autumn no choice, she had to tell her.

As Gaby listened her head fell forward, red curls covering her face. She made not a sound. Long afterward her tearstained face raised up. "I love him so much, I must go away. This place is not big enough for both of us."

"You just got here, please stay," Autumn pleaded, but all she got was a shaking of the head. Autumn didn't want to let her go, she was somehow hoping for a miracle.

"I want to share a secret with you, ok?" No response.

"Gaby, I think I might be pregnant and I would like to ask you to be the godmother to our baby." Finally a faint smile played on Gaby's lips.

"I would be honored."

The girls remained on the verandah for a long time, taking in the majestic mountain range and the brilliant display of colorful leaves in the lower regions. Yes, autumn had definitely arrived; one could feel it in the air.

The pain was written all over Gaby's face. Autumn reached out and covered her hand. "I'll always be here for you, remember that, please?"

Her voice choked with tears she softly answered: "I will remember you and I will be godmother to your child. But Autumn, for now, I must leave. I can't bear to be so close to him and not be with him. I thought we would … never mind, it doesn't matter any more. He will always be part of me, I think about him day and night. I was forbidden to contact him and now it's too late. Perhaps it was never meant to be. Please don't tell him that I was here, I don't want to spoil his newfound happiness. I'll miss him and …" Her voice trailed off as she slowly edged away toward the living room. She dropped the sweater, took hold of her coat and handbag, blew a kiss in Autumn's direction and rushed out the front door.

Autumn was to stunned to react quickly. She tried to rush after but the phone started ringing.

"Hello"

"She's dead!" It was Victor. He repeated himself. "She's dead. Jane is dead!"

"My God, what happened?"

"An aneurysm in the brain." After a moment of silence he blurted out. "I wish Gaby was here!" At that moment the sound of a car leaving faded away.

Autumn Leaves

Autumn's heart began to beat faster. What could she say? Should she tell him? No, not now, perhaps later.

How twisted life can be. Laura, her long time best friend, had found happiness with Harold. Her own life was a wonderful dream, with Peter, little Barbie and a new life growing inside her. Her beloved uncle's life was in shambles and so was Gabriella's. There must be a way to bring those two back together again.

Just then she heard a car drive up and rushed to the front door hoping Gaby had returned, but it was Peter. She ran down the stairs to greet him and slipped, but he caught her just in time. She clung to him, sobbing, as if her heart would break. Words spilled out and nothing made much sense to him, except that he would be a daddy in the near future. Then the wind came up and a red leaf tumbled down landing in Autumn's hair. Peter held it in his hand while Autumn silently said, 'hi Gaby.'

That night they held each other for a long time, vowing to treat each day as if it was their last. With a love like that how could anything go wrong?

Although their future looked bright, who knows what is lurking around the bend?

Gabriella von Hohenstolzen, where are you?

ISBN 1412013763